MW01129130

Shiloh Ranch

Book Four

The Blackout Series

A novel by

Bobby Akart

Copyright Information

Thank you for purchasing
Shiloh Ranch by Bobby Akart

For free advance reading copies, updates on new releases,
special offers, and bonus content,
Sign Up at BobbyAkart.com:

eepurl.com/bYqq3L

or visit us online at

BobbyAkart.com

Other Works by Bestselling Author Bobby Akart

The Blackout Series
36 Hours
Zero Hour
Turning Point
Shiloh Ranch
Hornet's Nest
Devil's Homecoming

The Boston Brahmin Series
The Loyal Nine
Cyber Attack
Martial Law
False Flag
The Mechanics
Choose Freedom!
Seeds of Liberty (Companion Guide)

The Prepping for Tomorrow Series
Cyber Warfare
EMP: Electromagnetic Pulse
Economic Collapse

DEDICATIONS

To the love of my life, thank you for making the sacrifices necessary
so I may pursue this dream.

To the *Princesses of the Palace*, my little marauders in training, you have
no idea how much happiness you bring to your mommy and me.

To my fellow preppers—never be ashamed of adopting
a preparedness lifestyle.

ACKNOWLEDGEMENTS

Writing a book that is both informative and entertaining requires a tremendous team effort. Writing is the easy part. For their efforts in making The Blackout Series a reality, I would like to thank Hristo Argirov Kovatliev for his incredible cover art, Pauline Nolet for making my important work reader-friendly, Stef Mcdaid for making this manuscript decipherable on so many formats, and The Team— whose advice, friendship and attention to detail is priceless.

The Blackout Series could not have been written without the tireless counsel and direction from those individuals who shall remain nameless at the Space Weather Prediction Center in Boulder, Colorado and at the Atacama Large Millimeter Array (ALMA) in Chile. Thank you for providing me a portal into your observations and data.

Lastly, a huge thank you to Dr. Tamitha Skov, a friend and social media icon, who is a research scientist at The Aerospace Corporation in Southern California. With her PHD in Geophysics and Space Plasma Physics, she has become a vital resource for amateur astronomers and aurora watchers around the world. Without her insight, The Blackout Series could not have been written. Visit her website at www.SpaceWeatherWoman.com.

Thank you!

ABOUT THE AUTHOR

Bobby Akart

Bestselling author Bobby Akart has been ranked by Amazon as the #3 Bestselling Religion & Spirituality Author, the #5 Bestselling Science Fiction Author, and the #7 Bestselling Historical Fiction Author. He is the author of nine international bestsellers, in thirty-three different fiction and non-fiction genres, including the critically acclaimed Boston Brahmin series and his highly cited Prepping for Tomorrow series, which includes three books on Amazon's Bestseller lists since they were released.

Bobby Akart has provided his readers a diverse range of topics that are both informative and entertaining. His attention to detail and impeccable research has allowed him to capture the imaginations of his readers through his fictional works, and bring them valuable knowledge through his non-fiction books.

SIGN UP for email updates here:

eepurl.com/bYqq3L

and receive free advance reading copies, updates on new releases, special offers, and bonus content. You can contact Bobby directly by email (BobbyAkart@gmail.com) or through his website:

BobbyAkart.com

ABOUT THE BLACKOUT SERIES

WHAT WOULD YOU DO
if a voice was screaming in your head – *GET READY* –
for a catastrophic event of epic proportions
with no idea where to start
or how, or when?

This is a true story, it just hasn't happened yet.

The Blackout Series is a new dystopian, post-apocalyptic fiction series from nine-time best-selling author Bobby Akart (The Blackout series, The Boston Brahmin series and the Prepping for Tomorrow series).

The characters depicted in The Blackout Series are fictional. The events, however, are based upon fact.

This is not the story of preppers with stockpiles of food, weapons, and a hidden bunker. This is the story of Colton Ryman, his stay-at-home wife, Madison, and their teenage daughter, Alex. In 36 Hours, the Ryman family and the rest of the world will be thrust into the darkness of a post-apocalyptic world.

A catastrophic solar flare, an EMP—a threat from above to America's soft underbelly below—is hurtling toward our planet.

The Rymans have never heard of preppers and have no concept of what prepping entails. But they're learning, while they run out of time. Their faith will be tested, their freedom will be threatened, but their family will survive.

An EMP, naturally generated from our sun in the form of a solar flare, has happened before, and it will happen again, in only 36 Hours.

This is a story about how our sun, the planet's source of life, can also devastate our modern world. It's a story about panic, chaos, and the final straws that shattered an already thin veneer of civility. It is a warning to us all —

never underestimate the depravity of man.

What would you do when the clock strikes zero?
Midnight is forever.

Note: This book does not contain strong language. It is intended to entertain and inform audiences of all ages, including teen and young adults. Although some scenes depict the realistic threat our nation faces from a devastating solar flare, and the societal collapse which will result in the aftermath, it does not contain graphic scenes typical of other books in the post-apocalyptic genre.

PREVIOUSLY IN THE BLACKOUT SERIES

The Characters

The Rymans:

Colton – Colton Ryman is in his late thirties. Born and raised in Texas, he is a direct descendant of the Ryman family which built the infamous Ryman Auditorium music hall in downtown Nashville. His family migrated to Texas from Tennessee with Davy Crockett in the 1800's. The Ryman's became prominent in the oil and cattle business and as a result, Colton inherited his skill for negotiating. After college, he landed a position with United Talent, the top agency for the country-western music industry. He eventually became managing partner of the Nashville office. He is married to Madison and they have one child, Alex.

Madison – Madison, in her mid-thirties, is a devout Christian born and raised in Nashville. She grew up a debutante but quickly set her sights on a career in filmmaking. But one fateful day, she was introduced to Colton Ryman and the two fell in love. They had their only child, Alex, which prompted Madison to give up her career in favor of a life raising their daughter and loving her husband—two full time jobs.

Alex – Fifteen-year old Alex, the only child of Colton and Madison Ryman, was a sophomore at Davidson Academy. Despite inheriting her mother's beauty, Alex was not interested in the normal pursuits of teenaged girls which included becoming the prey of teenaged boys. Her interests were golf and science. It was during her favorite class, Astronomy, in which the teacher encouraged his students to become *solar sleuths* that Alex learned of the potential damage the sun could cause.

Supporting Characters of Importance:

Dr. Andrea Stanford – Director of the Joint Alma Observatory (JAO) Science Team at the Atacama Large Millimeter Array (ALMA) in the high-mountain desert of Peru. She is a graduate of the Harvard-Smithsonian Center for Astrophysics in Cambridge, Massachusetts. Her long-time assistant is Jose Cortez.

Members of the Harding Place Association (HPA) – In 36 Hours, book one of The Blackout Series, Shane Wren and his wife Christie Wren make their first appearance. They have two daughters and live just to the north of the Rymans. Shane Wren is the President of the HPA. In Zero Hour, two other members of the HPA are important players in the saga. Gene Andrews, a former director of compliance with the Internal Revenue Service, and Adam Holder, a former banker, make their appearance. Jimmy Holder, Adam's stepson, is a key player in the story as well.

Betty Jean Durham – In Turning Point, we are gradually introduced to Betty Jean Durham, the only child of the infamous former sheriff of McNairy County, Tennessee, Buford Pusser. Betty Jean had a tragic childhood that shaped her into a hardened woman—Ma Durham. Following the murder of her husband which resulted in her banishment from the sparsely populated southwest Tennessee county, Betty Jean and her two young sons relocated across the Tennessee River to Savannah in adjacent Hardin County. She rose to political power the old fashioned way, via luck and trickery, and became the iron-fisted Mayor of Savannah. The solar storm wreaked havoc on the world, and ruined the ambitions of many a politician, but nobody stops Betty Jean Durham. No sirree.

Leroy Durham Jr. – But his friends call him Junior, all five of them. Junior is the youngest son of the now deceased Leroy Durham, and Betty Jean Durham. Likened to Deputy Barney Fife, Junior was elected to become sheriff of Hardin County, Tennessee at the age of twenty-seven, just like his grandfather—Buford Pusser. Junior missed out on the Pusser genes somewhere in the process. While his grandfather was nicknamed Bufurd the Bull, during his short-lived wrestling career, Junior stood five-foot-eight and weighed one-hundred-fifty pounds soakin' wet. Now, Junior didn't have a big stick like his grandfather, but he wielded power nonetheless, with the aid of his Ma, who was very encouraging. Like all great antagonists, Junior always thinks he's right.

Coach Joe Carey – Unless you've lived in Smalltown, U.S.A., it's hard to appreciate the importance and grip high school football has on a community. While some may look up to their political leaders for inspiration, most will see the coach of the local high school football team as their guide to the Promised Land. In Turning Point, we are introduced to Joe Carey, former Head Coach of the Hardin County Tigers who has taken on a far more important role—leader of an underground resistance comprised of the brave young men and women of Hardin County High who stand opposed to the tyrannical actions of Ma Durham and her son Sheriff Junior Durham. The Tiger Resistance will play a big role in the Blackout Series.

Beau Carey – son of Coach Joe Carey and QB1, captain of the Hardin County Tigers football team. He is also the undisputed leader of the *disdants*, as Junior Durham calls 'em, those members of the Savannah community that fight back against the tyrant Mayor—Ma Durham. By the way, Beau is sweet on Alex, but then, what high school boy wouldn't be.

The Bennett Brothers, Jimbo and Clay – twin adopted sons of Coach Carey and therefore the brothers of Beau. Jimbo and Clay's parents passed away in a tragic accident and as Beau puts it, "they were left to us in their parent's will". Now the twin starting linebackers of the Hardin County Tigers join with the Carey's as an active thorn in the side of the Durhams.

Russ Hilton and family – Retired country crooner who found his way to the tiny town of Saltillo, Tennessee located on the west side of the Tennessee River in upper Hardin County. Hilton was of Colton's first clients and the two were surprised to run into each other toward the end of the Ryman's journey to Shiloh Ranch. Saltillo immediately accepted Hilton as their adopted son so he rewarded the community with its own honky-tonk, The Hillbilly Hilton.

The Tennessee River – Wait, hey Bobby, shouldn't this be under the next section titled Primary Scene Locations? Not in my book. You see, throughout history, bodies of water have played major roles in the development of mankind. They are the sources of life, providing hydration and food to all species on the planet. Bodies of water are also significant geographic boundaries, or barriers, to the movement of man. Before there were boats, planes and rocket ships, the vast oceans blocked man's migration. Then the new world was discovered, but for those without the ability to sail her waters, the rivers and lakes separated whole communities of people. The Tennessee River is one such body of water, dividing Hardin County in half both geographically, and politically.

As The Blackout Series continues, and pay attention my friends because this is important, you'll find that life is like a river. It's always easier to flow with the current. To turn against the current takes effort and fortitude.

Sometimes, going against the flow was necessary.

Introducing in Shiloh Ranch

Jake Allen and family — Jake Allen is a country music star who began his career like so many others, in a honky-tonk on Printer's Alley in Nashville. Like Russ Hilton, Jake hired Colton to be his agent and the men remained close friends for years. The Allens live halfway between Springfield and Branson, Missouri where Jake performs in his newly created music venue. Emily Allen went to nursing school before marrying Jake and becoming a full time mom to their son, Chase. Chase is in his late teens and has a bit of a wild streak, as most boys his age have.

Stubby Crump and his wife, Bessie — The Crump family has resided on the west side of the Tennessee River for many years. The small town of Crump was founded by Stubby's grandfather and the family ran a farming operation for many years. Following high school, Stubby embarked on a two year stint in the St. Louis Cardinals baseball organization during which time he married the love of his life, Bessie. He realized baseball wasn't for him and like so many other young men in the Hardin County community, he enlisted in the military. Stubby's military career as an Army Ranger found him in the jungles of Cambodia, an experience which deeply affected him. Now in his late sixties, Stubby has converted a lifetime of experiences into making Shiloh Ranch a prepper haven.

Primary Scene Locations

Ryman Residence – located on Harding Place in Nashville. It is located approximately two miles east of historic Belle Meade Country Club and just to the west of Lynnwood Boulevard. It is a two-story brick home similar to the one depicted on the cover of Zero Hour.

Harding Place Neighborhood – The portion of the Harding Place Neighborhood depicted in The Blackout Series is bordered by Belle

Meade Boulevard to the west, Abbot-Martin Road to the north, Hillsboro Pike to the east, and Tyne Boulevard to the south. Generally, this area is southwest of downtown Nashville in an area known for its historic homes—Belle Meade.

ALMA - the largest telescope on the planet—the Atacama Large Millimeter Array, or ALMA. It's located at an altitude of over sixteen thousand feet in Atacama, Chile.

The Natchez Trace – Well, this scenic route developed in the mid twentieth century was ordinarily a leisurely trek from Nashville to the Mississippi River. In Turning Point, it became the proverbial highway to hell. In our pre-apocalyptic world, don't let the experiences of the Rymans during their bug-out influence your decision to enjoy a long drive on this four-hundred-forty mile stretch of southern hospitality. But know this, you never what lies around the bend.

Savannah, Tennessee – the county seat of Hardin County, Tennessee, population six thousand (pre-collapse) and lies on the east banks of the Tennessee River. It is a beautiful southern town with gorgeous antebellum homes and lots of friendly faces. Historically, Savannah has played a role in the Civil Way. Fictionally, Savannah represents a microcosm of the small towns across America which chooses a path after TEOTWAWKI to be feared by every prepper. Beauty is only skin deep, but evil cuts clean to the bone.

Saltillo, Tennessee – the perfect prepper hideout. Sitting on the west side of the Tennessee River in the uppermost corner of Hardin County, Saltillo still maintains its local charm from two hundred years of sleepy isolation. Larger than life country music star Russ Hilton moves there with his beautiful family and now Saltillo has a claim to fame. Russ built his own music venue, the *Hillbilly Hilton*, and the town enjoys a close knit relationship centered around country music, southern comfort food, and the Tennessee River. Prepper Utopia.

Shiloh Ranch, Tennessee – the Ryman's bug-out destination. That's all you get for now my friends. You must read on.

Previously in The Blackout Series

Book One: 36 HOURS

The Blackout Series begins thirty-six hours before a devastating coronal mass ejection strikes the Earth. Dr. Andrea Stanford and her team at ALMA identified the largest solar flare on record—an X-58—hurtling toward the Earth.

This solar flare was many times larger than the Carrington Event of 1859, widely considered the strongest solar event of modern times. Alarm bells were rung by Dr. Stanford and soon eyes at NASA and the Space Weather Prediction Center, SWPC, in Boulder, Colorado, were maintaining a close eye on Active Region 3222—AR3222.

AR3222 was a huge dark coronal hole which has formed on the solar disk. It had grown to encompass the entire northern hemisphere of the sun. As the story begins, AR3222 had only fired off a few minor solar flares, but as the hole in the sun rotated out of view, Dr. Stanford knew it would be back.

That same evening, Colton Ryman was in Dallas, Texas on business. One of his country music clients was being considered for a spot on the upcoming Super Bowl halftime show. Colton participated in a dog-and-pony show hosted by Jerry Jones, owner of the Dallas Cowboys which included tours of the Cowboy's stadium and a concert in downtown Dallas.

Via news reports and text message conversations with Madison, Colton became aware of the unusual solar activity. At first, he brushed off the threat, but as time passed he became more and more convinced.

Madison and Alex were in Nashville going about their normal routine. Alex was the first to ring the alarm that the threat they faced from a major solar storm was real. She tried to raise the level of awareness in her mother, but Madison initially brushed it off as the overactive imagination of a teenage girl.

By noon the next day, all of the Rymans were beginning to see the signs of a potential catastrophic event. While the rest of the country went about its normal routine, Colton, Madison, and Alex made their decision—*Get Ready!*

The initial reports of the solar event were widely downplayed by the media. Even the President refused to raise the alarms for fear of frightening the public unnecessarily. But the Rymans were convinced the threat of a catastrophic solar flare was real, and the three sprang into action.

Colton, unable to catch a flight back to Nashville from Dallas, rented a Corvette and began to race home. Madison, using a valuable resource in the form of a book titled EMP: Electromagnetic Pulse, studied the prepper's checklist which enabled her to apply a common sense approach to getting prepared in a hurry.

Madison pulled Alex out of school and they immediately hit the Kroger grocery store for food and supplies. It was during this shopping expedition that news of the solar flare broke. Society began to collapse rapidly.

After forcing her way out of the grocery store parking lot using her Suburban's bumper to shove a KIA out of the way, Madison and Alex made their way to an ATM. The lines were long, but Madison waited until she could withdraw the cash. However, she let down her guard and was assaulted by a man who tried to steal her money. While the rest of the bank customer's stood by and watched, Alex sprang into action with her trusty sand wedge. She beat the man repeatedly until he crawled away—saving her Mom, and the cash.

Meanwhile, Colton's race home—doing over one hundred miles an hour in the rented Corvette—was almost red flagged when he was stopped by an Arkansas State Trooper. While he was waiting for the trooper's deliberation of what to do with Colton, a gunfight ensued between two vehicles in the southbound lane of the interstate. Having bigger fish to fry, the state trooper left Colton alone, who promptly hauled his cookies toward Memphis.

Madison, despite being battered and bruised, elected to make another *run* with Alex. They added to their newly acquired preps but encountered a group of three thugs on the way home. Frightened for their safety, Madison once again used her trusty Suburban bumper to pin one of the attackers against the car in front of her. This brought an abrupt end to the assault.

As Colton drove home, he listened to the scientific experts on the radio broadcasts talking about the potential impact an EMP would have on electronics and vehicles. He learned pre-1970 model cars were more likely to survive the massive pulse of energy associated with an EMP. This knowledge served him well when he stopped at a gas station in eastern Arkansas.

Colton was confronted by three men who took a liking to the shiny red Corvette. Not wanting any trouble, Colton made the deal of a lifetime. He traded the new 'vette for a 1969 Jeep Wagoneer. The good ole boys thought they'd gotten the better of the city slicker, but it was they who were hoodooed. Colton took off with his new, old truck and sufficient gas to make it to the house.

Madison and Alex's exciting day was not over. After dark, a knocking on the door startled them both. It was their friendly neighbors, Shane and Christie Wren. Madison attempted to keep her conversation with them brief, and her newly acquired preps hidden, but the simple mistake of turning on a light revealed her bruised face to the Wrens. The couple immediately suspected Colton of being a wife abuser despite Madison's explanation to the contrary.

After Madison sent the nosy Wrens on their way, she and Alex settled in to watch CNN's coverage of Times Square and the Countdown to Impact Clock. Thousands of people had gathered in New York to witness the apocalypse's arrival. The drama was high as the scene in Times Square was reminiscent of a New Year's Eve countdown without the revelry and deprivation.

The girls anxiously waited as they were unsure of Colton's whereabouts. Then they heard the kitchen door unlock, and Colton entered—reuniting the family. They began to move into the living room when Alex exclaimed, "Hey, look! The clock stopped at zero and nothing happened."

The CNN cameras panned the mass of humanity as a spontaneous eruption of joy and relief filled the packed crowd. The trio of news anchors couldn't contain themselves as they exchanged hugs and handshakes. Jubilation accompanied pandemonium in Times Square, the so-called Center of the Universe, as the bright neon lights from the McDonald's logo to the Bank of America sign continued their dazzling display. Then—

CRACKLE! SIZZLE! SNAP—SNAP—SNAP!

Darkness. Blackout. It was — *Zero Hour.*

Book Two: ZERO HOUR

The central theme of The Blackout Series is to provide the reader a glimpse into a post-apocalyptic world. Book One, 36 Hours took a non-prepping family through a fast-paced learning curve. In the period of a day, they had to accept the reality that a catastrophic event was headed their way and accept the threat as real. Once the decision to *GET READY* was made, then the Ryman's scrambled around to prepare the best they could with limited time and resources.

Book two, Zero Hour, focuses on the post-apocalyptic world in the immediate hours and days following the collapse event.

Zero Hour picks up the Ryman's plight immediate after the collapse of the nation's power grid and critical infrastructure. First, they accept the challenges which lie ahead and then they apply common sense to establishing a plan.

First order of business was security. Colton recalls a story from his grandfather who reminds him to never underestimate the *depravity of man*. While they accept their fate, and attempt to set up a routine, there are neighbors who have other ideas about what's best for the Rymans.

Under the pretense of banding together to help the neighbors survive, the self-appointed leaders run a survival operation of their own. Using the intel willingly provided by unsuspecting residents, the three leaders of the Harding Place Association loot empty, unguarded homes and keep the contents for themselves.

When a rift forms between the Rymans and some of their neighbors, things turn ugly. There are confrontations and arguments. One of the leaders attempts a raid on the Ryman home at night with plans to steal the generator and some supplies. A gunfight ensues which wounds several of the attacking marauders. One of the three HPA leaders later dies due to lack of sufficient medical care.

There are also undercover operations including one involving Alex and a teenage boy. Alex recognizes the family's weakness in not having sufficient weapons to defend themselves and this boy's stepfather has an arsenal ripe for the pickins. Alex befriends the boy, procures weapons and ammunition, and everything is going smoothly until she finds the stepfather abusing her teenage friend. In self-defense, Alex shoots and kills the man, who happened to be one of the HPA leaders.

The death of the other two leaders has a noticeable effect on Shane Wren, the ringleader of the HPA who is the cause of the rift between the Rymans and the other neighbors. We're left in the dark as to whether the death of his cohorts resulted in the turnaround, or simply the knowledge that the Rymans are capable of defending themselves with deadly force, if necessary.

As a new threat emerges, the HPA and the Rymans come together to repel the vicious group of looters as they make their way deeper into the neighborhood. It was, however, too little too late for the majority of the neighbors in the HPA. Many, because they were out of food, and scared, opted to leave their homes and walk to one of the many FEMA camps and shelters established in the area.

The Rymans debated and considered their options. Madison stepped up and set the tone for the next part of their journey by making a large meal and announcing that it was time to go. The family gathered their most valued belongings to help them survive. It was time to go.

Here are the final paragraphs from ZERO HOUR:

Madison shed several tears as she closed the kitchen door behind them. Colton opened the garage door, revealing the trophy received for the most cleverly negotiated deal in his career—the Jeep Wagoneer. This old truck was their lifeline now. It was their means to a new life far away from the post-apocalyptic madness of the big city.

Colton eased the truck out of the garage and worked his way down the driveway until he had to veer through the front yard to avoid the Suburban. As he wheeled his way around the landscaping, all three of them looked toward the west where fire danced above the tall oak trees. Reminiscent of a scene from *Gone with the Wind*, the magnificent antebellum homes of Belle Meade were in flames.

Madison began to sob now. "Will we ever be able to return?"

"What about our things?" asked Alex.

"Having somewhere to live is home. Having someone to love is family. All we need is right here in this front seat—our family." With that, Colton drove onto the road and led the Ryman family on a new adventure and to a new home.

They'd reached their turning point—a point of no return.

Book Three: TURNING POINT

If you've come this far, you know The Blackout Series is designed to provide an imaginative journey into life after a major collapse event. Not everyone is a prepper, and the Rymans certainly fell into the non-prepper category. However, they're learning—the hard way.

At the end of book two, Zero Hour, they'd reached a consensus as a family that Nashville and the areas surrounding their home were unfit. The unknown destination of Shiloh Ranch seemed less dangerous than the known perils threatening them on Harding Place. So they bugged-out.

The perils of bugging-out are on full display in Turning Point—especially if (a) you wait to long and (b) you don't plan for all unforeseen contingencies. My goal in writing Turning Point was to provide the reader many of the realistic scenarios one might face as they're forced to leave their home.

In our busy lives, we scurry to and fro, using the highways and the byways to move from Point A to Point B. We take this freedom of movement for granted. In a post-apocalyptic world, everything changes, especially freedom of movement.

You see, in a grid down scenario like the one experienced by our characters in The Blackout Series, your world gets much smaller. The center of your universe starts with where you live, and can only expand as far as your means of transportation will carry you—feet, horse, bicycle, old car, canoe, etc.

The Rymans, thanks to some forethought and the art of negotiation on the part of Colton, were fortunate to have a pre-1970 vehicle which was immune to the massive blast of electrical energy released by the solar storm. The old Jeep Wagoneer served them well throughout the truck, showing its ability to get shot at with both bullets and arrows.

During their bug-out expedition, the Rymans faced a number of obstacles. There were the marauders who manned overpasses, underpasses, bridges, and town boundaries. They experienced natural roadblocks including fallen trees, horrendous storms and an important factor in this saga—The Tennessee River.

Above all, they experienced the depravity of man, and child. Children will grow up fast in the post-apocalyptic world but they will still need the guidance of an adult. The boy scouts at the Devil's Backbone were led down the wrong path of survival by their scoutmaster, who paid the ultimate price at the hands of Madison, who notched a couple of kills in Turning Point. Alex has grown into a woman with nerves of steel and an eye for trouble. She has an intuition that has developed throughout her post-apocalyptic experience. She also has learned that her fellow teens are prepared to step up as well.

The quaint town of Savannah has a problem—Ma Durham and her offspring, Sheriff Junior Durham. Like every tyrant before her, she takes over everything for the *greater good* and the *protection of Savannah's citizens*. However, it's not Savannah's citizens who benefit. There are those who are prepared to resist Ma Durham's tyranny.

Enter the *disdants*, as the dissidents are referred to by Junior

Durham. Led by beloved football coach Joe Carey of the Hardin County High School Tigers, local students and athletes went into hiding for the sole purpose of fighting back against Ma Durham, and surviving. A few of these young men play an instrumental role in saving Colton from discovery and assisting the Rymans in escaping the grasp of Junior and his Ma.

But, despite their successes and evasion of imprisonment, or worse, the Rymans still have a major obstacle to overcome—the Tennessee River. The route through Savannah was out of the question. The Pickwick Dam to their south was closed and blocked by the National Guard. The bridges farther north were either blocked by locals or manned by ransom-seekers.

As luck would have it, there was another option, one that hadn't been used regularly in decades. Old Man Percy, an elderly black gentlemen pushin' a hundred years old, owns the dormant Saltillo Ferry. He agrees to fire up the old vessel and tote the Rymans to Saltillo, a small town of three-hundred-three inhabitants.

And one very dear friend, one of Colton's earliest clients, Russ Hilton. Hilton and his family moved to the tiny town to make a home for themselves as his country music career faded. They constructed the Hillbilly Hilton as a hangout for their neighbors and friends. The Rymans enjoyed a night of their southern hospitality, which included a song by Colton and Russ, and a respite from the travails of the road.

Invigorated by their fun, relaxing evening in Saltillo, the Ryman's head south for the final thirty miles to Shiloh Ranch. It was intended to be an easy trip until a brutal thunderstorm collided with their progress.

The Rymans had lost their windshield wipers on day one of this bug-out when a marauding woman attempted to bash in their windshield with a tire iron. Madison, who was the family expert in using a vehicle as a weapon, shook the woman who was holding onto the windshield wipers for dear life, back and forth. Finally, utilizing the age-old technique of punching the gas and abruptly stopping, Madison threw the woman, and the windshield wipers, to the asphalt pavement. The wipers were ruined, as was the skull of the marauder.

In any event, wiper less, the Rymans elected to ride out the storm after a bolt of lightning brought a tree down right in front of them. In Colton's attempt to hide the truck, he got it stuck.

So they decided to hoof it—a fifteen mile hike to the Promised Land—Shiloh Ranch.

From Turning Point …

They made their way onto Federal Road and once again took in the smells emanating from the Tennessee River. The sounds of overflowing, rain-swollen creeks became deafening as they entered the canopy of trees which enclosed the quickly narrowing road that ended at Shiloh Ranch.

Excited, yet nervous, Colton could sense Madison and Alex picking up the pace. Madison giggled a little as she broke out into a slight jog. Alex laughed as she began to run and pass her mother.

Not wanting to be left behind, Colton joined them and grabbed his girls' hands as they rounded the bend to the entrance of Shiloh Ranch, giddy with excitement—until they stared down the barrels of half a dozen rifles.

The saga continues in — SHILOH RANCH

Epigraph

The hand of the aggressor is stayed by strength – and strength alone.
~ Dwight D. Eisenhower
*****

Tyranny and anarchy are never far apart.
~ Jeremy Bentham
*****

Hogs get fat, pigs get slaughtered.
~ Molly Ivins
*****

Saw a man build a bomb shelter in his garden today;
As we stood there idly chatting, he said,
"No, no. I don't think war will come."
Yet still, he carried on digging.
~ Billy Bragg
*****

Sometimes, going against the flow was necessary.
~ Ma Durham

PROLOGUE

Early Morning Hours
April 6, 1862
Headquarters of Confederate General Albert Sidney Johnston
Shiloh, Tennessee

During the latter part of 1861 and into early 1862, the Civil War reached levels of violence that shocked the North and South alike. For months, the Union Army had worked its way up the Tennessee and Cumberland rivers. By February 1862, Kentucky was firmly in Union hands and the fight came to Nashville, Tennessee's capital. Major General William Harvey Lamb Wallace, an Illinois attorney, commanded the second brigade against the confederate stronghold of Fort Donelson. The southerners attacked Wallace's brigade with a vengeance, killing over five hundred Union soldiers. Wallace prevailed nonetheless, but the battle had a profound effect upon him.

A collision was coming between the mighty armies of Major General Ulysses S. Grant and the confederate forces led by Generals Albert Johnston and Pierre Beauregard. On the morning of April 6, 1862, General Grant was having coffee at the home of William and Annie Cherry — Cherry Mansion, located on the east bank of the Tennessee River in Savannah. Grant was joined by General Wallace and General Prentiss, as well as Mr. and Mrs. Cherry.

Mrs. Cherry, a southern sympathizer, had been irritated with her husband, a pro-Union partisan, for allowing the Union generals to occupy their home. Cherry had assured her that the stay was temporary while they awaited their troops in Nashville to join them.

Nonetheless, this was an opportunity for her to voice her displeasure to her guests about the war between the states.

"My family has never owned slaves," said Mrs. Cherry. "This is only one aspect of why this confrontation with the government was

1

necessary. Every state, north and south alike, was granted the power to govern its people by the Constitution. As Washington continues to force it's will upon us, our hand was forced."

"Madame, I am a guest in your home and as such, I will respect your opinion," started General Grant. "But I must remind you that it was the Confederacy which fired the first shot upon our Nation at Fort Sumter almost one year ago. President Lincoln did not wish to pursue a war, he merely wants to preserve our Union."

Mrs. Cherry persisted. "But is it not true that President Lincoln is using slavery as an excuse to spread his brand of federalism across the South. In fact, the issue of slavery is a means to an end. He wishes to force our state governments to stop exercising our sovereign powers."

Mr. Cherry stepped in. "Now, Annie, please. General Grant is a guest in our home. He is not here for political discussions nor will he change his plans based upon ..."

The pounding on the front door startled the group and a soldier abruptly entered the foyer.

"General, a courier has arrived sir," announced Grant's aide-de-camp.

"Read the message," said General Grant.

"Sir, from the south, elements of the armies of the Confederacy, *Crew's Battalion*, have advanced across Pittsburg Landing. A larger advance has been observed from the armies of Generals Johnston and Beauregard."

Grant stood and slammed his coffee onto the table. This development complicated his strategy of awaiting General Don Carlos Buell, Commander of the Army of Ohio to march to Savannah along the Natchez Trace from Nashville. One the two armies were merged, Grant intended to engage the forty-four thousand troops of the Confederacy gathered at Corinth, Mississippi. His goal was to cut off their supply lines by destroying the Confederate railroad center there.

"As surprise attack, sir?" asked General Wallace.

"Indeed, William," replied Grant. "This is Johnston's doing. He's the finest general in the south and he deserves our respect. We have to move quickly to slow his advance until General Buell arrives."

Grant pulled out a map of the area which identified Shiloh, Pittsburg Landing, and Savannah along the Tennessee river. He began to trace his fingers across the map.

"Johnston will move along the banks of the river, using the landing at Pittsburg to resupply," he began. "That places the strength of their forces within two miles of our main army. They've got to be slowed until General Buell arrives."

General Wallace joined his side. "General, I learned at Fort Donelson that these southerners have a will to fight like no other. There passionate about their cause as opposed to being hired soldiers like the majority of our troops. From my experience, they will fight night and day to advance through our foothold."

"If we don't stop the advance, they'll drive my army into the Tennessee River."

Wallace made a suggestion. "General, allow me to reinforce our lines here, at the church located at Shiloh — meaning *place of peace*. My men know the enemy. They have gained the fighting spirit from their opponents. We will do our duty for you General, and the Union. We will fight fire with fire."

General Wallace's troops quickly advanced to the white-washed Shiloh Church where the Union's resistance stiffened. For nearly eight hours, Wallace's men fought in a thick area of woods near the church. General Wallace himself led the defense of a sunken road which ran past Shiloh Church. They held their position for hours until they were overrun late in the afternoon.

They valiantly sacrificed their lives to buy precious time to allow General Buell's Army of reinforcements to arrive. They ultimately perished but the exhausted Confederates chose to wait until the break of dawn on April 7th to continue the Battle of Shiloh.

As the lines broke, Wallace was wounded by a piece of fragmented shell which struck him in the head. He lay there as the battle raged around him, unable to move or communicate. He watched his men die and the Confederate soldiers advance.

Throughout the night, he waited. He listened. The war quieted and the aura surrounding Shiloh Church settled in. The sun rose and the battle ensued. He began to see the uniforms of the Army of the Ohio — dark blue jackets with shoulder straps, adorned with nine brass buttons down the front.

General Buell had arrived in the night!

General William Wallace was removed to Cherry Mansion where he died with his wife by his side. He was hailed as a hero for turning the tide on the bloodiest battle between north and south of the time. This small area of woods at the Shiloh Church where Wallace's men took a stand became known as the *Hornet's Nest*, and is considered one of the major turning points in the Civil War.

Chapter 1

12:12 a.m., September 28
Front Gate
Shiloh Ranch

Colton tried to shield his eyes from the blinding light. A low-lying fog began to settle in, causing the ground to disappear within an eerie, dramatic glow. His mind raced, but not toward a solution.

He thought of his daughter, Alex, as a newborn. She was lying in her crib—crying. He couldn't discern whether the grating sound of her cries were on some level from a distant memory or in the present.

His memories shifted to the moment when she was born—the moment his beloved wife, Madison, gathered the strength for one last push. He remembered Alex's head appearing. *I saw her first!*

We all know about life's forks in the road—those seminal events that create a turning point on our respective journeys. One door closes, and then another door opens. Each of us has cycles like the changes in seasons. But the moment his child was born, the moment was beyond surreal. He'd transformed from a free-wheeling, high-flying talent agent to a dad charged with the responsibility of keeping this tiny baby alive.

Everything became different for Colton when Alex was born. His world was gone, but a new one had opened up. It was much smaller, shrunk down to the dimensions of a six-and-a-half-pound squallin' mass of baby girl. In that moment, he promised God, and his newborn's mother, that he'd always protect their daughter.

Now, as threatening guns held by faceless men behind blinding spotlights placed the Rymans in danger, he felt utterly helpless and trapped with no way out.

Clippity-clop. Clippity-clop. Clippity-clop.

A familiar sound, yet he couldn't place it. The fog consumed his brain and the surroundings.

A horse—approaching at a steady pace.

"Whoa!" shouted the rider. "What do we have here, boys?" The creaking sound of metal accompanied the rider as the gates to Shiloh Ranch opened. Boots crunched onto gravel as the horse whinnied.

Colton tried to speak, but couldn't. He was back in the present but still frozen in time.

"*Un hombre, dos mujeres,*" replied a Hispanic voice. *One man, two women.*

The silhouette of a large man approached, causing Colton to instinctively step between the approaching figure and the Ryman women.

"Daddy," whispered Alex, "what do we—"

"Lower your arms so I can see your faces," instructed the man.

The reflection of light upon a nickel-plated sidearm caught Colton's attention as it was pulled from the man's holster. Colton hesitated and then lowered his arms slowly. He contemplated pulling his own weapon to defend his family but knew it would result in certain death.

The man laughed, deep-throated and genuine. "Well, slap my head and call me silly!" he roared. "If it ain't Colton Ryman. Why you little cotton-picker! What the heck are you folks doin' out here in the middle of the night?"

"Jake, is that you?" asked Colton, exhaling a sigh of relief so big that it could've knocked down the doors of all three little pigs' homes at once.

Jake Allen holstered his weapon and stepped into the light, all six feet six inches of him. He was grinning ear to ear.

"Of course it's me, Colton!"

Colton stepped forward to shake hands and bro-hug his old friend. "Sorry to show up unannounced. We tried to call but got your voicemail. Then my email server was having trouble and, well, you know."

"Verizon, right?" Jake laughed. The men shared an embrace of two old friends who were both dang glad to see each other. "Ladies? Madison and Alex?"

"Hey, Jake," replied Madison, still trembling as she received a bear hug of her own. Tears of joy and relief began to stream down her face.

"Now, c'mon, darlin'," started Jake. "Why the tears? Did Chevy stop makin' trucks?"

The jokes spurred the Rymans and the onlookers into laughter. It eased the tension of the earlier standoff and allowed everyone to relax. Colton said a quick prayer to God, thanking Him for restraining nervous trigger fingers on this night.

"Listen up, boys," yelled Jake. "These folks are the Rymans from Nashville. They are pert near family. A couple of y'all grab their things and take them up to the main house." Three of the ranch hands immediately shouldered their rifles and hopped the four-rail fencing that surrounded the Allens' property.

"I'll keep this, thanks," said Alex politely as one of the men offered to take her AR-15. Colton touched his daughter on the shoulders, attempting to reassure her.

"Honey, we're safe now."

"I'm not giving up the rifle, Daddy."

Colton put his arm around his daughter, who had grown up a lot in the last four weeks. "Jake, you remember Alex, don't you?"

"Well, look at you!" exclaimed Jake. "You're all grown up and pretty as a peach. Taller than your momma already!"

"Hey, Mr. Allen," said Alex as she gave him a hug. Alex seemed reserved, anxious about the whole situation. Colton hoped she could find a way to relax.

"Are y'all up for a short walk?" asked Jake. "From the looks of those backpacks, it appears you've been hoofin' it for a ways at least. I can have the boys run to the stables and rustle up a wagon if you'd like?"

Colton looked to the girls and then responded, "I think we can walk another half mile, if my memory serves me correctly."

"It does," said Jake. "This fog has been settling in along the Tennessee River for the last several days as the nights have gotten cooler. Tomorrow, we'll walk around the place after it burns off in the morning. We've added some things since y'all were here last. Plus, it's a little more crowded around Shiloh Ranch, you know, under the circumstances."

Madison spoke up. "I hope we're not imposing."

"Oh no, Madison. I didn't mean it that way. It's just that we've added quite a few ranch hands. Life is a lot different now and more dangerous."

Colton laughed. "That's an understatement."

It took the group about ten minutes to reach the main house, where candlelit lanterns swayed slightly on the ropes that held them to the wraparound porch. They talked about the last time the Rymans had visited and a little bit about the extraordinary event that led them to the front steps of the Allens' magnificent log home.

"These solar flares happen all the time," started Jake. "But I had no idea they could knock out all the power."

"I did," said Alex. "I learned about it in school and then I was able to convince Mom that the threat was real."

"It's hard to imagine the power of the sun until you've experienced it firsthand," said Jake. "I told Emily it was kinda like a gas buildup in your belly. If it's just a little gas, you might politely let out a little toot."

Madison and Alex giggled. Colton simply shook his head. He could only imagine where the rest of *Professor Jake Allen's science lesson* was headed.

Unfortunately, he was about to find out as Jake continued. "But let's say you've got a lot of gas. You know, after eating a plate of burritos or something. This gas, you see, has to escape your belly. So it does, but still isn't massive, right?"

The girls were in stitches. Madison was pleading for Jake to stop. "No more, Jake," she said with tears of laughter streaming down her face.

Jake was relentless. "But, back in the day, when we were kids, sometimes you'd like to really drop one on your friends. You know, let it build up and time it just right so as to blast them real good. So you let it build up and set your internal stopwatch."

Colton joined in the laughter. "Jake, *no mas! No mas!*"

"When the time is right," Jake continued, ignoring the pleas for mercy. "You drop your F-bomb. Boom! The room is cleared out, or in the case of this solar flare—boom-boom, out go the lights!"

Now, all three of the Rymans were bent over in laughter, holding their knees. Jake hopped up the steps and opened the front door. He turned to them and proudly announced, "Welcome back to Shiloh Ranch, my friends. *Mi casa, su casa!*"

CHAPTER 2

8:00 a.m., September 28
Main House
Shiloh Ranch

Colton sopped up the red-eye gravy with a biscuit. He and Madison had woken up at sunrise in the guest bedroom facing the east. They were exhausted the night before and had forgotten to draw the curtains, creating a natural alarm clock. Not that it mattered, however, as the main house was bustling with activity before dawn.

A plate of ham and grits coupled with what was commonly referred to as poor man's gravy made for a filling country breakfast. The Allens had a smokehouse filled with cured country ham, and when it was pan-fried over their wood-burning stove, the drippings made for a tasty sauce to add to the meal.

"The smokehouse is one of the things we've added since y'all were here a few years ago," said Jake. "We built it old-school, if you know what I mean. There are no windows and only a single entrance. We've got a fire pit in the center, where we burn hardwoods to dry the meat. First we cure the meat with a salt rub, then we smoke it."

"That explains it," said Alex as she took another sip of water. "I've never tasted anything so salty."

"The smokehouse was Stubby's idea," interjected Emily Allen, Jake's wife. At thirty-nine, Emily was slightly younger than her husband of twenty years. They'd married when he was still a country crooner on Printer's Alley in Nashville. The two had been through some trying times in their marriage, as Jake had enjoyed his fame, and alcohol, a little too much. But the bond they shared over their son, Chase, and Jake's subsequent maturation kept the family together.

"Where is Stubby?" asked Madison. "I haven't seen Bessie either."

"Oh, they get a real early start." Emily chuckled. "They get goin' way before the crack of dawn. They feed the hands and then the livestock. Jake and I try to stay out of the way during this process."

"The hands?" queried Alex.

"Yeah, the farmhands," replied Jake. "We have eight now, plus our gardener and landscaper. You'll meet them all later. Trust me, we're one big extended family now."

Colton removed Madison's plate and took it to the sink, where Emily was scrubbing the dishes with a soapy sponge. His mind replayed breakfast at the Hiltons' just a couple of days prior. He wondered if Russ and Jake knew each other.

"Do you know Russ Hilton?" asked Colton, leaning against the kitchen cabinets. Jake finished up his plate and pushed away from the table.

"We've met. He played a few weeks in Branson just before I opened up my place. Good man. He had a great career."

"Like you, Russ was one of my first clients," said Colton. "You guys are practically neighbors."

"You're kiddin'?"

"Nope. They bought a place up north of here in Saltillo. Russ built his own honky-tonk in the middle of town called the Hillbilly Hilton."

"Wow, who knew?" quipped Jake. "We'll have to check it out. By the way, are you still pickin'?"

"Great, here we go," groaned Alex.

Colton ignored his daughter's protestations and answered, "Yeah, now and again. Russ and I belted out a couple of tunes while we stayed the night with them. I remember our nights around the campfire from our last visit. I suppose we could pick up where we left off."

"Heck yeah!" said Jake. "I've actually got a couple of new songs rollin' around in my head. When we find the time, I'll run 'em by ya."

Suddenly, the door flung open and in walked Stubby Crump, who at five feet eight inches tall and nearly two hundred pounds was the textbook definition of a man built like a fireplug. In his late sixties, a lifetime of athletic endeavors maintained a muscular build with thick arms and legs and a neck that wasn't readily visible.

Born as Darren Wayne Crump, Stubby's family had owned all of the land on the west side of the Tennessee River near the original Milo Lemert Bridge, which crossed into Savannah. The bridge was taken down by explosives in 1980 and replaced with a more stable one. During the expansion efforts, the Crump family was paid handsomely by the government for their property and ultimately sold off their remaining acreage located south of the bridge to several Hardin County ranchers and farmers. This two-hundred-acre tract was purchased by Jake and Emily fifteen years ago and the Crumps, despite having enough wealth of their own, chose to work for the Allens as caretakers of the place. Money didn't mean much to the Crumps. They gauged their worth and success by a good day's work.

"Well, lookie here what the cat's drug in." Stubby laughed. He was followed into the large open living space by his wife of nearly fifty years, Bessie.

Alex sprang out of her chair to greet them. She'd taken a liking to Bessie in the past when they spent a lot of time in the kitchen, whipping up Southern delicacies designed to harden the arteries of any human being.

"Hi, Bessie!" she exclaimed as she ran to give the older woman a hug. They say old married couples begin to look alike and the Crumps were no exception. Bessie was as round as she was tall but a perfect match for her stocky husband.

Bessie gave Alex a hug and then stood back to survey the budding young woman. "Aren't you somethin', Alex. And so tall, too! You Ryman women got all the good genes up in the big city."

Alex gave her another hug and then hugged Stubby as well. Colton noticed the transformation in her demeanor. He must've missed the connection that his daughter had made with the Crumps before, but he was glad to see the relationship rekindled.

Colton and Madison exchanged pleasantries with the Crumps as the group moved into the living area to recap the events of the last month. Jake relayed the string of coincidences that had led to their unexpected stay at the ranch.

On the Sunday before the solar flare hit, a drunk driver had careened out of control in his pickup and crashed into the gas pumps at a local convenience store in Branson. The truck burst into flames and instantly ignited the fuel, which spread across the parking lot and into the adjacent fireworks store.

"It was straight out of a Stephen King novel," explained Jake. "The local fire department quickly became overwhelmed, and the whole block began to burn."

"Did your place catch on fire too?" asked Colton. "I don't remember seeing anything about that in the news."

"No, we were okay, but the extent of the damage caused the buildings to crumble, and the street where many of the venues were located was closed. The local officials announced that it would be unsafe to operate any large-scale music events for a week or so until the cleanup could be completed and the fire department could get back on its feet."

Colton leaned back on the leather couch and contemplated the ramifications of shutting down Branson for a week. Millions of dollars were lost by the merchants, hotels, and the performance halls.

"That sounds drastic," Colton added.

"Yeah, we thought so as well, but you can't fight city hall," said Jake. "Stubby had just finished another project, and we needed a quick vacation. We loaded up and headed down. It worked out, obviously."

Alex edged up in her seat. "I feel terrible, but I haven't asked you about Chase. Did he not come with you?"

"Oh no, he's around," replied Emily. "He went huntin' with the Wyatt boy from the adjacent farm. They love to explore and look for food. I really think it's because he gets bored around here."

"He wouldn't get bored if he'd pitch in with the chores, right, Stubby?" asked Jake.

Stubby shifted uneasily from one leg to another and didn't respond. Colton surmised the older teen was not interested in the day-to-day activities of running a ranch and would prefer to play in the woods.

The awkward moment lingered, so Colton decided to change the subject. "Last night you said something about a grand tour. I'd love to see what you and Stubby have done with the place."

"Let's do it," declared Stubby, also appearing anxious to move on from the subject of Chase's contributions. "Bessie, you wanna bring Madison and Alex up to speed on what you've got goin' on?"

"Yes, sir, I do. C'mon, ladies. We'll tidy up the kitchen and I'll show you what keeps this place hummin' along."

"Okay, Colton, time for the nickel tour," said Jake as he led the men out into the bright morning sun.

CHAPTER 3

10:00 a.m., September 28
The Grounds
Shiloh Ranch

"We're up to a hundred Holsteins now," said Stubby as Jake and Colton followed along. "When I convinced Jake to add the dairy operation to the ranch, his first question was who's gonna milk 'em?" Stubby paused the tour as one of the Mexican farmhands ran up to him with a bottle of warm milk. He took a sip and smiled.

He offered the bottle to Colton, who hesitated.

"It's safe," said Stubby. "A lot of folks think that drinking milk straight from the cow isn't healthy because of *E. coli*. That may be true on those big corporate farms, but we take care of our dairy operation and the cows. They're all grass fed and monitored for sickness."

"Well, I hadn't thought about that," started Colton apologetically. "It's just that I've never drunk warm milk before, especially straight out of the cow." Colton took a sip and then another.

"Whadya think?" asked Jake.

"Not bad. Does it come in chocolate?"

Stubby laughed. "Give me that!" He took the bottle and finished it off before handing it back to the young man.

"I was hesitant when Stubby recommended the dairy cows," said Jake. "The Wyatts offered to set us up with their beef cattle, but Stubby had an overall plan."

Stubby motioned them toward the barn. "I felt like the Wyatts had enough beef cattle, so I decided to go in a different direction. The Holsteins are one of the best milk producers in the country. Most of the dairy farms are located in Middle and East Tennessee. That set us apart."

"So you started this as a commercial operation?" asked Colton.

"In part, with other possibilities in mind," replied Stubby. "The average Holstein cow produces about nine gallons of milk per day when they're lactating."

"That's a ton of milk!" exclaimed Colton.

"Well, more like ten tons over the course of a year," added Jake. "They lactate for around three hundred days."

"You can't possibly drink that much," said Colton.

The men approached a pair of the doe-eyed black and white dairy cows and rubbed their soft muzzles.

"That's true, but we have a lot of uses for the milk produced," said Stubby. "We lop off the cream, which is great for desserts and fruit. Bessie has a number of yogurt recipes, and Maria, whom you haven't met yet, is an expert cheese maker."

"I'm impressed, guys," said Colton.

Stubby pulled a block of cheese wrapped in red wax out of his pocket. He handed it to Colton. "Try this later," he said. "After they make the cheese, it's dipped in hot wax to seal it. Some is stored in the root cellar around fifty degrees. It'll last for nearly twenty years that way. We leave some at room temperature, which accelerates the aging process and creates sharper flavors. That's what you have there."

"How much do you have?" asked Colton.

"A day's milk production of roughly nine gallons will produce a one-pound block of cheese. Since the power went out, we've accumulated several hundred pounds."

"Good grief," said Colton. "Now I see why you have all the help."

The three men walked through the barn, where a couple of cows were isolated in pens. Stubby stopped to check on them.

"They're ready to calve," said Stubby.

"How do you know?" asked Colton. "They look just as fat as the others."

"Without getting too technical with a description of cow parts, you can first tell by their behavior," replied Stubby. "Initially, they separate themselves from the herd during calving season. But once they're really ready to calve, they'll pace a lot and paw at the turf. They become restless, constantly getting up and down. That's when I bring them in here."

"Are you nervous about birthing a calf without a vet around?" asked Colton.

"Yeah, a little," replied Stubby. "The Wyatts offered to help. Emily went to nursing school and trained in an emergency room, so we told them we'd trade her doctorin' for their vet experience courtesy of Lucinda Wyatt, who grew up on a cattle farm."

Jake led the group from the barn and turned to Colton. "The world has gone to crap, Colton. I don't think I need to tell you that. We all have to rely upon each other to survive. Stubby had some excellent foresight and led me into a direction of self-sustainability without me knowing it."

Stubby protested. "Now listen up, Jake. There wasn't any trickery here. Everything had a valid business purpose too."

"Oh, don't get your hackles up, old man, or I'll whoop ya." Jake, who towered over Stubby by a foot, laughed. "The decisions you made the last couple of years will save all of our lives. All I'm sayin' is if you'd come to me two years ago and said we need a hundred dairy cows in case the world comes to an end, I would have probably run ya off!"

"But Bessie could stay, right?" asked Colton, laughing.

"You betcha!" replied Jake. "Her cookin' skills allow for being opinionated."

Two men rode by on horses at a pretty quick pace. They were headed out towards the northern part of Shiloh Ranch, where the cows grazed.

"Do you think everything is okay?" asked Colton.

Jake led them to three cut tree stumps where they could sit and talk some more. "I'm sure it is. I would've been told if there was a problem."

"This was a pretty big operation before the grid collapsed," said

Stubby. "Now, we have our regular chores in addition to securing two hundred acres. Jake and I've been very concerned about people wandering onto the ranch by accident, or intentionally. I want to believe the best in our fellow man, but you never know."

Colton uttered a nervous laugh and then shook his head. He spent the next twenty minutes recapping the trip to Shiloh Ranch in detail. It was the kind of frank discussion men had without unnecessarily frightening everyone.

"Memphis has the largest population of any city in the state, and it has the highest crime rate," said Jake. "It's a matter of time before refugees spill out of Shelby County in our direction."

"Or tribes will form," interjected Stubby.

"What do you mean by that?" asked Jake.

"Well, look at it from our point of view first," replied Stubby. "Around Shiloh, Pittsburg Landing and throughout West Hardin County, landowners are binding together to protect their farms, exchange services, and trade goods. The same type of arrangement will be taking place in the cities."

"We came together in our neighborhood eventually," added Colton. "Then everyone got scared or weary of the effort and turned to the FEMA camps for protection."

Stubby walked over to the barn and grabbed a rake. He began to push the dirt and rocks around and created several piles. He continued to doodle in the dirt while he spoke. "It won't take long for the city dwellers to realize there's strength in numbers. Tribes will be formed for the purposes of looting, murder, and creating criminal gangs to survive. As is the case here, like-minded people will flock to one another, which is where things will become incredibly dangerous."

Stubby began to drag a pile of rocks away from the other piles to the edge of some fescue grass. He continued. "The smart looters will parlay their early successes in the first couple of days into employing junior mercenaries or pirates to expand their operations. Career criminals will turn into career post-collapse pirates, pouncing on the weak and taking their supplies. It's just a matter of time before they take their show on the road, leading them right to our neck of the woods."

Stubby caused the rake to scatter the pebbles into the tall grass by fanning out the rocks until they became hidden from sight.

"If they come in large enough numbers, we'd have a heckuva time turnin' them away," said Jake, who stood to take a turn with the rake. "Here's our problem."

He drew a line with the end of the handle through the dirt. Then he crossed the dirt and drew a line all the way to Stubby's piles of debris. Using the end of the rake handle as a pointer, he expressed his concerns. "Our problem is that we have our backs to the Tennessee River," started Jake, pointing to the first long line. Then, referencing the many piles of debris in the area Stubby identified as Memphis, he continued. "When these piles of human debris venture out in our direction, we'll be trapped with only one exit, the bridge into Savannah."

"I can assure you that we won't be welcome there," said Colton.

Stubby spoke up as Jake continued to push the small stones through the rich river-bottom soil. "I've known the Durhams and the Pussers my entire life. None of us will be welcome there, and Savannah will never be an option for us unless things change drastically. This leads me to my next point. While the threat from these pebbles is a potential future problem, the immediate concern I have is Ma and her son."

CHAPTER 4

11:00 a.m., September 28
The Grounds
Shiloh Ranch

Madison was in awe at the extent that Shiloh Ranch had changed from a weekend getaway into a fully operational farm complete with dairy cows. She no longer looked at Bessie as an older woman who was an expert in Southern cooking. This lady had skills learned through years of practice that would be critical to their survival.

"This is the garden," said Bessie. "It doesn't look like much now because we've harvested all of the spring and summer crops. We've just finished planting spinach, lettuce and radishes to produce a little somethin' during the early winter months."

"There are some things growing over there," said Madison, pointing toward three plots of the garden adjacent to the horse stalls.

"That'll be next week's project," said Bessie. "Our ground crops like potatoes, carrots and onions will be ready to harvest then."

"You seem very well organized," added Madison. "None of this was here before."

"Well, we did have the container gardens behind the house, but they were used primarily for flowers. Now, they are part of the overall growing program. Each one contains a variety of foods like tomatoes, peppers, and cucumbers. We use companion gardening so they all play well together."

A covered pavilion was in full use by some of the Allens' employees. Fires were burning, and a full-blown canning operation was underway.

"Come on," urged Bessie. "There's someone I'd like you to meet."

Madison followed along and watched in amazement as the vegetables were prepared and the fires were stoked. A woman wiped her hands on her apron and approached the group.

"*Hola!*"

"Hey, Maria, please meet our friends from Nashville," said Emily. The woman shook Madison's hand.

"I'm Maria Garcia," she said. "It is my pleasure to meet you." Madison noticed that Maria enunciated her words very deliberately. Although she had a heavy Spanish accent, she spoke slowly to use proper English.

"It's nice to meet you, Maria. I'm Madison Ryman."

"*Oh, bueno!* Your husband is a country star too, like Mr. Jake?"

Madison and Emily laughed. "Oh, no. Colton, my husband, only sings around the campfire. We'll leave the good singing to Mr. Jake. Goodness, it's very hot in here." The heat from the fires was staying within the pavilion, as there was very little breeze.

Maria smiled and nodded before walking back to a long concrete countertop covered with canning supplies. Ball jars, Tattler lids, and other tools were all in use, as Maria had a very organized crew performing the difficult task of canning without electricity.

"We have to keep the fires hot and at a fairly even temperature to keep the water at a rolling boil," said Bessie. "Before the lights went out, we could use the propane gas grills or even the kitchen stove to heat the pressure cookers. Propane is in short supply and we use the solar power primarily for refrigeration. Burning a fire makes more sense."

"There's no shortage of trees," said Madison as she looked around the perimeter of Shiloh Ranch.

"That's true, but we didn't cut enough wood in the spring to anticipate this," said Bessie. "Seasoned firewood may become a problem if we have a harsh winter."

"Can't you just cut more?" asked Madison.

"We can, but pine takes about six months to season and hardwoods like oak take as much as a year. Plus, there's the problem of fuel for the chainsaws. We don't have the manpower to send the ranch hands out foraging for gasoline. Stubby has plenty of diesel for the farm equipment, but gas is a scarce resource."

Madison shook her head as she looked around the ranch. "We had four extra cans of gasoline, but those fools shot holes in the cans and most of it drained onto the highway."

"You were shot at?" asked Emily, unaware of the details of the Rymans' journey to Shiloh Ranch.

"Emily, you've no idea what it's like out there. We've been shot at and we had to shoot back." Madison looked at the ground and became teary-eyed. Only the sight of Alex riding on the back of a beautiful spotted Appaloosa in the horse pen prevented her from becoming more emotional.

"Really?" asked Emily, appearing to be shocked at this revelation.

"Unfortunately, yes. It's a different world out there, Emily. It's a different world just across the river too."

The three women stood silently for a moment until Bessie suggested they walk over toward the horse pen. Madison regained her composure as Bessie, who sensed what Madison was feeling, comforted her and led her by the arm.

The guys approached from the other side and eventually all of them were watching Alex take the distinctive leopard-spotted horse by the lead as she walked her around the circular structure.

"Hey, Allie-Cat," shouted Colton. "Who's your new friend?"

"Hi, Daddy! This is Snowflake. She's an Appaloosa!"

"Javy, come on over," instructed Stubby. A Mexican man not much taller than Stubby removed his straw hat and joined the group. Stubby explained that Javier Garcia had joined the Shiloh Ranch a couple of years ago as a general ranch hand and ultimately brought his wife Maria to America to work as the Allens' housekeeper.

As the dairy operation grew, Javier, who preferred to be called Javy, added some friends from the mountain cattle ranches near the Mexican border of West Texas, who were most likely in the country illegally. Stubby didn't ask and didn't care. The men worked hard, were loyal, and asked that virtually all of their earnings be sent to their families in Mexico via Western Union. That proved to Stubby they were honorable and loyal.

"I gave up trying to understand the politics of immigration a long time ago," said Stubby as Javy returned to help Alex with Snowflake. "All I know is this. If I had to be in a foxhole again, any of these men would have my back."

Alex joined the group as they started back toward the house when a gust of wind shifted the breeze and a horrific odor into their nostrils.

"Whoa!" exclaimed Colton. "What the heck is that?"

"Ha-ha." Jake laughed. "We showed y'all the good stuff first, but we've saved the best for last."

"Ladies and gentleman," started Jake, removing his signature charcoal black snapback cowboy hat and using his best circus ringmaster gestures, "presenting the Shiloh Ranch latrine and composting facility. Take a whiff, friends!"

"Ugh," groaned Alex.

Stubby stepped forward and took over the presentation. "Jake can be a little dramatic at times. I think he'll be a mighty fine entertainer when he grows up. We have indoor plumbing in the main house, as you all know. Our water wells are scattered around the property and each of the pumps is outfitted with a small solar array providing it power. This keeps water running to the toilets."

"Is this the sewage treatment plant?" asked Madison as she burrowed her nose in her sleeve.

"Sort of, Madison," replied Stubby. "A septic tank and sewer system has been in place since the home was built. But this summer I added a manure compost pit to create manure tea."

"No way!" lamented Alex. "You guys are out of your minds."

"Take it easy, Alex." Stubby laughed. "It's not to drink. It is, however, simply the best organic concentrated fertilizer you can make. What you have here is a self-contained sewage facility for both human and animal waste designed to create liquid compost made from manure steeped in water, just like you'd steep a cup of tea."

"I used to like tea," murmured Madison under her breath.

"It's high in nutrients, especially nitrogen," added Bessie. "We put it on all our vegetables, especially the green leafy ones. The liquid manure really soaks into the soil and hits the roots."

"Gross," said Alex. "Will it make the vegetables taste like, um, poop?"

"No, honey," replied Bessie. "If anything, manure tea brings out the natural colors and flavors of organic vegetables. It's easy to make and we can create a fresh batch in about two weeks."

"Fresh?"

"Well, you know, a new batch."

Stubby led the entourage back towards the main house and away from the ripe stench of the compost.

"Well, I wouldn't want that job," said Alex, who quickly broke away from the pack to avoid the smell.

The covered porch of the main house wrapped the entire perimeter of the home. The group pulled seven rocking chairs onto the east deck. A cool breeze emanated from the Tennessee River, which could be seen in the distance through the now leafless oaks.

Emily and Bessie went inside and retrieved a pitcher of sweet tea and glasses for all. They tinkled with the sound of ice. The scene was reminiscent of any Southern home's porch in normal times.

"If my memory serves me correctly, I think you'll like this," said Bessie as she handed Colton his glass. "Do you still like an Arnold Palmer?"

Arnold Palmer, the golfing legend from the sixties and seventies, created his own Southern concoction consisting of sweet tea and roughly half lemonade. Palmer and his wife experimented with the mix at their home until it became his signature drink. In his memoirs, Palmer recalled how he ordered his favorite drink while in a Palm Springs restaurant and a woman overheard him place the order. She told her server that she wanted an Arnold Palmer and the simple drink became legendary.

Colton took a sip and smiled. "Sweet nectar of the South. Let's raise our glasses to the recently departed Arnold Palmer. God rest your soul, my friend."

As everyone raised their glasses, Colton continued. "I wasn't sure if I'd ever see an ice cube again. I have to say that you guys are very well prepared for the apocalypse."

Jake responded, "We owe it all to Stubby and Bessie. They had a homesteader mindset, which has translated into one heck of an operation, as you've seen. But, as you may recall, Stubby is a former Army Ranger. He understands weaponry and defensive measures that, frankly, never crossed my mind until the compost hit the fan."

Stubby laughed and then stood to sit on the rail, where he could face everyone. "Folks, all of the things that we have goin' for us here won't make a hill of beans' difference if we can't defend it. Simply said, *if you can't defend it, it isn't yours.*"

Madison nodded her head in agreement. The Rymans had experienced firsthand what desperate people would do to survive. They had defended their neighborhood and their home from depraved human beings who were willing to kill to take what they needed or wanted.

Madison set aside her glass of sweet tea and spoke up. "Listen, we've come here uninvited, but we can help. We want to be a part of your family and pull our weight. None of us knows anything about gardening or milking cows or composting, but we're willing to learn."

Alex chimed in, "Speak for yourself on that composting part, Mom."

"Maddie is right about that," added Colton, ignoring Alex's comment. He turned his attention to Jake but then looked directly at Stubby. "There is one thing we've experienced that only you've seen in your lifetime—the depravity of man. We'd appreciate some training in the use of firearms. We'll help defend Shiloh Ranch as well as make it a place where we can all live together without fearing for our lives. We'd like to make this our home too."

CHAPTER 5

Sunset, September 29
Cherry Mansion
Savannah

The Brumby Rocker was far from being in bad condition despite being one of the oldest pieces of furniture remaining in the historic Cherry Mansion. The white paint looked a little faded from its exposure to the setting sun, an event the Brumby had experienced since it arrived on the porch in 1933. Like its present occupant, the bones of the Brumby were pretty old, but they were still sturdy. Both the chair and Ma Durham had a steely resolve—hardened by years of weathering storms.

Creak, creak, creak.

The Brumby Rocker continued its back and forth motion as Ma slowly pushed it on the old wooden floorboards of the covered porch. She sat alone with her thoughts. Her boyfriend, Bill Cherry, the former president of the Hardin County Chamber of Commerce, was the owner of Cherry Mansion and a direct descendant of the original owners. Wild Bill, as he'd become known around Hardin County, had a penchant for partying, which Ma tolerated to an extent. Like so many other men in her life, Wild Bill Cherry was nothing more than a tool to advance her goals. She didn't care for alcohol but allowed Wild Bill his fun as long as he obeyed. It was a relationship that suited both parties.

Creak, creak, creak.

Ma, like the Brumby Rocker, was showing telltale signs of aging, including crow's feet, gray hair, and older looking hands. She stared down at her bony, wrinkled digits that resembled those of a much older woman than Ma's mid-fifties. She realized long ago that she was not a looker like many of the hussies she'd grown up around. Ma knew, however, that she had feminine wiles, a woman's power, which she covertly used to influence the men who needed it.

Men were weak in Ma's mind. For the most part, their minds were focused on one thing. Her ability to manipulate men when she was younger brought her into a position of power in Hardin County. After the solar flare brought the power down, she created a brilliant plan to control the horny fools of the county, including Wild Bill and her son the sheriff, Junior, to do her bidding.

She provided them sex but not from her, of course. There were plenty of others around to do the dirty work of servicing the menfolk within her charge. Initially, it was designed as a barter system of sorts.

"Everyone must pull their weight," she'd told the townspeople in those early days after the grid collapsed.

The young women of the town were told that they could either work at the Vulcan Quarry or they could do other, less strenuous work. Initially, many of the women were appalled at the suggestion. They would not sacrifice their morals by having sex with Ma's crew. But after several days of pounding rock at the quarry, the façade of chastity came crashing down. Brothels controlled by Ma sprang up around Savannah to service the men.

Not unexpectedly, the men would get out of hand from time to time, usually as a result of too much alcohol. They would abuse the women, and soon the brothels began to empty of able-bodied employees. The women of Savannah simply ran away.

This was bad for morale, in Ma's opinion, so a solution had to be reached. She needed new recruits, and she quickly developed a new plan of attack. She was proud of two major decisions she'd made related to the collapse of the power grid.

First, Ma considered herself brilliant for having armed men ready to secure all of the major retail stores around the town. She had a hunch the solar flare might cause more damage than the media let on. She was right. When it came crashing down, she instantly became the power broker she'd always dreamt of being. Controlling the government as mayor was one thing. But there were restrictions, rules, and *watchers*—prying eyes making sure she *did the right thing*. But after the collapse, she could run things the way she saw fit. Uninhibited. Lawless.

As this newfound unrestricted power took hold, Ma solved several problems with one brilliant plan. She used the Emergency Broadcast Network and the local radio station to invite folks from all over to join them in Savannah. The new residents needed to meet certain criteria. She was looking for working automobiles, muscle, medical personnel, and more girls for the boys.

Her invitations via the radio broadcasts worked. Cars began to arrive from far and wide, and they were greeted by Wild Bill. He would prescreen the occupants of the vehicles to determine if they helped fill the town's needs, and if they did, they were taken to the county jail for additional screening.

Their cars and belongings were confiscated. The men were told harm would come to their women if they didn't go to work in the quarry. The women were then placed into sexual slavery.

The newcomers didn't always cooperate and the result was the execution of the men in front of the women. The women were then turned over to Junior and Wild Bill, who *trained* them.

Creak. Creak. Creak.

Ma didn't care. She had a town to run and expansion plans in mind.

Nooooooo. Pleeeeeease. Nooooooo.

The screams could barely be heard over the creaking of the Brumby Rocker. If a stranger walked onto the front porch of the Cherry Mansion, they might have heard the muffled sounds emanating from the basement cells, which had been built during the Civil War. However, those strangers would be focused on the aging woman slowly rocking on the porch of this magnificent antebellum home as she watched the sun set on another day.

CHAPTER 6

11:00 a.m., September 29
Main House
Shiloh Ranch

Of course, Chase Allen remembered Alex from their visit four years ago. Back then, she was a standoffish preteen who was friendly enough to pal around with, but wasn't interesting enough to lose sleep over. As he rode up to the stables and saw her standing with her parents, his surprise at seeing them was quickly replaced by his astonishment at how beautiful she'd become.

"Well, I'll be dogged," said Chase as he approached the group and dismounted. "Hey, Alex. Hi, Mr. and Missus Ryman. I didn't expect to see you guys."

"Hey, Chase," said Alex as she walked up and grabbed the bridle. Chase dusted off his clothes before they shared an awkward hug. "We decided to come visit for a while. You know, things were getting a little *heated* in Nashville."

"I can imagine." Chase laughed. He shook hands with Colton and gave Madison a hug. "It's really great to see you guys. Sorry I'm such a mess. We went huntin' for a few days."

"I see that," said Alex, who studied the one-hundred-forty-pound white-tail deer draped across the back of Chase's horse.

Chase looked past everyone and hollered towards the barn, "Hey, Stubby, are you in there?"

Stubby and Javy emerged, wiping their hands on a couple of red shop towels. They had been working on an old Ford tractor used to plow the fields. Stubby immediately walked to the deer carcass and felt it.

"Still warm," he muttered. "She's good sized. How long ago did you bag her?"

"About an hour," said Chase. "We were fixin' to head home and I came upon her down at Childers Hill near the Wolven place."

Stubby took the reins and handed them to Javy. "Get them in the barn and we'll dress her. This will be an opportunity for y'all to learn how to field dress a deer. Follow me."

Javy led the group into the barn, but Chase and Alex lagged behind. "It's been a long time, Alex. You've, um, changed a lot."

"For the better, right?" asked Alex. Chase sensed she was flirting with him. *She is cute!*

"Yeah." He started putting on his best suave and debonair approach. "You're prettier and more polite than you used to be."

"You know what, Chase?" Alex bristled and then she hesitated. Her voice calmed. "I am pretty. Politeness is half good manners and half being a good liar. You're better lookin' and polite too. Chew on that." Alex kicked up some dust with her boots and strutted ahead of Chase. Alex had spirit in a sassy kinda way. He liked that.

Stubby began the tutorial. "First, you should always field dress your deer within the first two hours after the kill while it's still warm. The first step is to drain the deer."

Javy removed the deer from the back of the horse with the help of Stubby. They had a place set up in the barn for this purpose. A bed made of hay bales had been positioned near a galvanized bucket of water. The deer was placed onto the bales with its backside down and head elevated. This exposed the deer's belly and allowed for gravity to assist in the removal of its internal organs.

"Ladies, I know this is a new experience and you might be squeamish, but we live in a different world now and the meat market at the grocery store ain't around. I need you to stay with me as we go through the process, okay?"

"Okay," replied Madison, but Alex stood with her arms folded and didn't reply. Chase surmised that she wasn't comfortable with this.

"The key to safe and efficient field dressing is a sharp, sturdy knife," continued Stubby. He pulled a fixed blade out of a sheath on his leg. He rotated it for everyone to see and then gently ran his finger along the blade. "You'll wanna use a knife with a blade at least four inches long, a guard like this one, and a large handle. A small knife can turn sideways if the blade hits bone. You don't need something like those grossly oversized Bowie designs. I've had this knife a long time. It's called a Coyote Stag."

Stubby approached the deer and spread the fur from its belly to provide a clear view of his incision point. He began at the bottom, slowly cutting deep enough to get through the skin clear up to the base of the neck. Blood began to trickle out of the carcass.

Madison turned away, but Alex continued to watch. Chase was studying her to gauge her reaction. He was impressed that she didn't faint or do the usual girly backlash. Her eyes seemed unfazed. He began to wonder what she'd been through on the trip to Shiloh Ranch.

"Now, I have to begin to cut through the muscle and cartilage. Gutting a deer is more like precision surgery than it is barbaric brutality. It's a process that requires an orderly transition from skin to muscle, to ribs, and then organs."

Stubby methodically made his cuts through the belly muscle and then he maneuvered the knife through the ribs with a prying motion, which caused the crunching sound of cartilage breaking. Everyone winced, which was a natural reaction. Chase had done this many times, so he was unaffected.

"After you've made your way into the chest cavity, you can remove the esophagus by cutting it free. With that chore behind us, we can pull out all of the guts in one fairly continuous mass."

Stubby and Javy worked together to remove all of the inner workings of the deer into a galvanized tub. Javy then wrapped a leather strap around the deer's head and shoulders and hoisted it into the air. He quickly tied off the hind legs with a rope to drain out any remaining fluids from the body.

Alex pointed to the galvanized bucket. "What do you do with this?"

"Ordinarily, we'd discard the contents of the bucket and leave it for the coyotes," replied Stubby. "But food is a scarce commodity now. Meat is meat and the gut pile is no exception. Javy and Maria will remove the heart, liver, kidneys, and tongue and prepare them as a dish."

Chase stepped forward. "I promised Tristan Wyatt the deerskin. After she drains, I'll turn her upside down and remove the hide. We'll immediately butcher her afterward."

"Wow," said Colton. "This is amazing. How much meat will you get out of this deer?"

"Anywhere from sixty to eighty pounds, depending on size," said Stubby. "Hunting needs to be a big part of our daily activities. The deer population is limited around here, and we need to get what we can before it gets depleted by others."

Stubby wiped his hands off and led the group out of the barn while Javy and a couple of helpers finished off the gutting process.

"Chase, is that one of your daily duties—hunting?" asked Alex.

"Yeah, among other things," he replied. "I usually report to Stubby in the morning and see what he needs done. Hunting and scavenging are my favorite jobs."

"Speaking of jobs," started Colton. "We've had a day to get our bearings, and we're ready to start helping out. Do you have plans for us?"

Stubby stopped and looked around the vast open space that comprised the middle of Shiloh Ranch. "Our biggest needs are security and food gathering. Colton, how are you with weapons?"

"Not bad considering I've learned everything I know in the last few weeks," he replied. "We had a situation back home that required quite a bit of shooting. I got some training from a neighbor who was an NRA instructor. The session lasted all of five minutes. The rest was on the job, if you know what I mean."

"Well, we can certainly expand on that," said Stubby. Stubby turned to the group. "We're gonna get all of y'all some training, but in the meantime, let's do this. Colton, I'm gonna have you on daytime perimeter patrol and possibly hunting with Chase and Jake at a later point. Madison, you and Alex can work with Bessie and Emily on gardening and KP duty."

Alex stepped forward, and Chase thought she bowed up a little. "What's KP duty?"

"That's military terminology for kitchen patrol," replied Stubby.

"I can shoot," said Alex dryly. "I'm the best in our family."

Stubby was shocked at Alex's proclamation, and Chase saw the standoff taking shape. Apparently, Alex was not interested in KP duty. *Good*, thought Chase. He'd love to have her ride around on hunting trips with him.

"Okay, let's talk some more about that," said Stubby, who was clearly caught off guard by Alex's bluntness. "But first, we need to mount a recovery mission for that Jeep Wagoneer of yours."

CHAPTER 7

10:00 a.m., September 30
Glendale Road
Coffee Landing

"Well, buddy, you did a great job of burying the wheels out of sight," said Jake as he stood to the side of the Wagoneer, which had been the Rymans' loyal and faithful steed on the trip from Nashville. Jake dismounted and tied his steed to a tree.

"Yep," said Colton, he pulled a steel-handled shovel out of the saddle's scabbard. "I didn't even need one of these."

"At least nobody messed with our stuff," said Alex as she quickly dismounted. Chase followed suit and immediately took his rifle and surveyed the woods. "Daddy, Chase and I'll make sure we don't have anybody watching us. Plus, we buried stuff all over the place."

Alex and Chase began walking up the hill with their rifles in low ready as they surveyed the clearing and the pine trees.

"Wait," hollered Colton. "Don't forget the list." Colton had created a treasure map of the locations of their hidden belongings. He trotted to meet Alex, who thanked him and gave him a peck on the cheek. The two had grown closer since the collapse. *Cheating death will do that.*

Colton removed his backpack and retrieved the keys. He also took out the distributor cap and the plug wires. Then he and Jake retrieved the gas cans, which were hidden in the woods. The first order of business was to get the old horse running again.

Everything in place, Colton turned the Wagoneer's ignition. The two-hundred-thirty-horsepower V-8 roared to life, and the friends exchanged high fives.

"Never a doubt in my mind." Colton laughed.

"I had doubt," quipped Jake. "Now for the fun part. From the looks of the gravel and branches, it appears you gave it the old college try before."

"Yeah, the ground was just too wet. It was raining and water was pouring down this dry creek bed. It was hopeless. So whadya think?"

Jake walked around the Wagoneer and surveyed the situation. He tapped the ground behind the wheels. He took off his hat and set it on the roof. "I think it may be too soft to drive out, but we can probably dig out a trench behind all four wheels to make it easier."

"Let's do it," said Colton as they began the process of digging a one-foot-by-five-foot trench behind each of the tires. During this time frame, Alex and Chase returned with more of the Rymans' preps.

"You were carrying quite a load, Colton," started Jake. "I see a generator, gas cans, and all of this fishing equipment. This will be helpful out at the ranch. Were you prepared for this solar flare thing?"

"Not really. Madison and Alex were scrambling around the day the lights went out. We have a lot more, but we had to leave it behind."

Jake, who had stripped down to his tee shirt, continued to sweat. He wiped his brow with a bandana. "The truck will be a huge asset although we're low on gas. Let's put just enough in the tank to get us home. The rest we can use for the saws and small engine equipment."

"Do you have any ideas where we can find more fuel?" asked Colton.

"Diesel is easy," replied Jake. "Every farmer has a tank for his equipment. Gasoline will be hit or miss except Stubby has a solution."

"He does?" asked Colton as he moved the debris from the rainstorm away from the back of the truck. Once he got it going, he intended to bolt out into the clearing to avoid getting stuck again.

"It's simple, really, and your generator will help," replied Jake. "With all of our farm equipment, Stubby bought rolls of different size hoses to be used for irrigation, battling fires, watering, and as replacements on our equipment. He has a couple of pond pumps in the barn, which he uses to transfer water from the cattle ponds to the gardens. He thinks we could transfer gasoline out of underground storage tanks at gas stations with a portable generator."

"Hey, I remember a news report about something like that several years ago," said Colton. "We went to Disney for a week and read that they busted these guys in Ocala for stealing gas. They had a van that they pulled over the top of the tanks. Their pumps pulled out a bunch of gas before they got busted."

Chase and Alex returned with their last load and tied off their horses. "Daddy, that's everything."

"All right, cross your fingers," said Colton. He hopped behind the wheel and fired the engine again.

Colton eased down on the gas pedal, but the Wagoneer remained planted in the soft soil. He then put it into drive and pulled forward slightly, keeping his foot on the brake pedal until he was on a slight incline in the rut. He threw it in reverse and gave it another try.

The truck moved and threw up a little debris as Colton gave it more gas. As Colton freed the truck from its resting spot, he gave it gas and lurched into the clearing. He let out a *woot*!

"Great job, Daddy!"

"That's some fancy four-wheelin' there, hoss!" yelled Jake as he retrieved his hat from the ground. "C'mon, Chase. Grab half this genny and let's git her loaded up."

"I've got it, Dad," said Chase as he carried the generator to the back of the Wagoneer.

Alex joined Jake in carrying the gas cans out of the woods toward the truck. Jake whispered to Alex, "He's trying to impress you."

"Why?" she asked.

"Look, Chase is at that age when he thinks the sun comes up just to hear him crow," replied Jake. "I was there once, as was your dad. He's gonna work overtime to impress a pretty girl like you."

"C'mon, Mr. Allen," said Alex. "He wouldn't be interested in me. I'm sure there are plenty of girls back in Branson to keep him interested."

"To be honest, not really," said Jake. "My son has a big ego, but he also recognizes that a lot of these girls showed interest in him because of who I am. Of all the girls I've seen him with, you're the only one that isn't smitten with him because of his family."

They dropped the gas cans and walked back to the woods to bring another load while Chase helped fill up the Wagoneer. Alex shuffled along in deep thought before she spoke.

"He is kinda cute, and I've learned that country guys are more genuine than the boys I was around in school. But don't tell him I said that. Everything is, well, *weird* right now. You know what I mean?"

Jake laughed. "Oh yeah, I get it. It's hard to start a relationship under circumstances like these. But I think you guys can help each other through it. Chase and I are not close like you are with Colton. I was on the road a lot until the last couple of years. He got used to being without his dad, and Emily is not much on cracking the whip, if you know what I mean."

Alex stopped and looked to Jake. "He seems nice, Mr. Allen. I don't think he's a bad guy at all."

"Oh, Chase is not a bad kid. He just liked to test boundaries when he was growing up. All teenage boys are like that. My concern is how Chase will adapt to a world with no fences."

CHAPTER 8

1:00 p.m., September 30
Highway 64
Crump

They sat in the Wagoneer in silence for several minutes, observing the activity on the road. Just two days earlier, this highway was devoid of traffic. Now, the occasional old car would pass by their hidden position in the trees across from the bait and tackle shop where Alex had crossed the highway before.

"I feel like we should warn them about Savannah," said Alex as another vehicle crossed their field of vision. "They have no idea what they're headed for."

"We can't risk it," said Chase. "For all we know, these are Junior's people scoutin' around."

More silence.

Alex leaned back and put her feet on the dash. Chase fidgeted with the radio, looking for any station besides Ma's propaganda broadcast. After a moment, Chase became restless.

"You know, they won't be here for a couple of hours, probably. Let's go do something."

"Like what?" asked Alex.

Chase grabbed his rifle, jumped out of the truck, and locked the door. He slapped the hood twice and gestured for Alex to join him. She scrambled around and followed him back down the tree-canopied country road.

"C'mon, Alex," said Chase as he began trotting toward a mailbox with a hidden driveway.

Alex picked up the pace and finally caught up with him.

"What are we doing?" she asked, out of breath.

"Let's go see what we can find," said Chase as he barely allowed Alex time to recover from the jog. "Tristan and I do it all the time. It's fun."

"Are you talking about looting?"

"Nah, just lookin'. You know, window-shopping." Chase was off as he trotted down the driveway toward a stately two-story home. A two-car garage with a side building stood off to their right. As they reached the clearing of the home's front yard, Chase abruptly stopped and lowered himself into a crouch.

Alex joined his side and did the same. She raised her weapon and scanned their surroundings through its scope.

"I don't think this is a good idea, Chase," she whispered.

Chase ignored her. "Looks deserted to me. Let's run across the yard to the left side of the porch. Ready?"

But before Alex answered, Chase was tearing across the uncut lawn. He ducked under an oak tree's low-hanging branches and pressed his back against the wall below a bay window.

Alex, following his course, ran across the lawn and joined him. She was breathing heavy but not necessarily from being winded. She was starting to get the adrenaline rush of putting your life at risk. This was different from the defensive measures she had taken on the trip down the Natchez Trace. This reminded her of going into their neighbors' homes on Harding Place in those first days after the solar storm. *It was fun.*

"Do you think they're home?" asked Alex.

"There's one way to find out," said Chase as he picked up a four-pound river rock out of the landscaped bed and heaved it through the plate-glass window to the left of the front door. The glass shattered and the rock could be heard tumbling along a marble floor in the entrance.

They both held their breath, listening for any sound from inside. It was quiet. No sounds. No movement.

Chase led the way and reached through the broken glass pane to unlock the front door. He quickly moved into the foyer and readied his gun. He was carrying a Remington 700 bolt-action rifle, which was not made for this type of operation. Alex, who slept with her AR-15 resting at the nightstand, was better equipped.

"Let me lead the way," she said to Chase as she warmed up to the idea of breaking and entering. "Daddy and I have done this before. First, let's clear the house and then we'll look around."

They quickly made their way through the downstairs and then hit the bedrooms on the second level. The house was deserted. The master bedroom had an empty suitcase on the floor and some clothes neatly stacked on the bed. It appeared the family had gone away and hadn't had room for the additional luggage.

Chase shouldered his rifle and slid down the banister to the foyer. He stuck the landing and raised his arms triumphantly. "Perfect landing! Try it, Alex."

"No, thanks. I'll stick to the old-fashioned method." She quickly skipped down the stairs and walked into an oversized living space featuring a floor-to-ceiling stone fireplace. The walls were adorned with a variety of hunting trophies.

"These folks like to kill things," remarked Chase. "I don't even know what some of these critters are."

"They're trophy hunters," said Alex dryly. She was still uncomfortable with the prospect of hunting deer and hogs as a source of meat, but she understood why it had to be done. This was different. These people killed exotic wild animals to show off for their friends. She despised the concept of trophy hunting.

"Check out this moose," said Chase as he rubbed the trophy's nose.

"That's an elk," stated Alex.

"How do you know?"

"It has antlers. Plus, its nose is more pointed. Listen, maybe we shouldn't stick around too long."

Chase didn't respond as he headed into a family room, where there were two big-screen televisions and a pool table. "C'mon, Alex, let's shoot some pool. We've got plenty of time."

"No, Chase. You go ahead. I'm looking for something else."

Alex moved down a hallway and explored some of the other rooms in the house. There was a formal dining room and finally a large kitchen with a breakfast room overlooking a stagnant, algae-covered pool. She opened all of the closet doors but didn't rummage through them. She was on a mission.

Chase caught up with her. "What are you looking for?"

"Have you seen a gun safe?" she asked as she bounded back upstairs.

"Um, no."

"These people are hunters, or at least they pretend to be," said Alex. She worked her way toward the back of the house overlooking the pool and entered a study, which contained more exotic animal heads on the wall. A bar was nestled into the corner with several half-full bottles of liquor on the top.

"Now we're talkin'!" exclaimed Chase. "How 'bout a cocktail, ma'am? What's your pleasure?"

"I don't drink and neither should you right now," said Alex. "We need to keep our heads together because you never know when something might happen."

"Party pooper," mumbled Chase as Alex continued to walk through the study.

"This doesn't make sense, Chase. They should have a gun safe." Out of frustration, Alex crossed her arms and scowled. She leaned against a bookcase, and it gave way. A noticeable click accompanied the movement as the hidden compartment behind the bookcase revealed itself.

Alex caught her balance and pulled on the leading edge of the bookcase, revealing a comparable-sized space behind it. Chase joined her and peered into the opening.

"Bingo!" he said under his breath. "Attagirl, Alex."

Inside the hidden compartment were half a dozen hunting rifles, dozens of boxes of ammo, and another half dozen handguns stacked neatly on the floor.

"Why didn't they lock this up?" asked Alex.

"People don't worry about burglaries and such around here. Heck, most don't even lock their doors when they leave the house. They all know each other and crime just isn't an issue."

Alex simply shook her head and began pulling rifles off the wall rack. Chase left her to empty the closet while he retrieved the Wagoneer. The time for their rendezvous was upon them, and they needed to load this into the truck.

While she waited for him to return, Alex found some boxes used for storing video games and filled them with dry goods out of the family's pantry. She also emptied the medicine cabinets of first aid supplies and prescriptions. She didn't disturb anything else.

Alex did not consider herself a looter. After the first few days of the collapse, she considered herself a survivor. Survivors foraged. Looters were thieves. Desperate people might consider themselves entitled to help themselves to food and supplies necessary for survival. She was fully comfortable with what they would load into the truck. Food and weapons to ensure their security were clearly survival items. Money, jewelry, and electronics were off-limits in Alex's mind.

Before they left, they made one other stop at the home—the garage. Inside, the two found liquid gold in the form of three five-gallon cans of gasoline and several tools that Chase thought they could use.

The adrenaline rush was over and Alex realized that foraging through other people's homes might become a part of their regular routine. In a way, humanity had gone full circle from shopper-borrowers to hunter-gatherers again.

CHAPTER 9

9:00 a.m., October 1
Main House
Shiloh Ranch

"Thank you, Javy," said Stubby as his right-hand man left the room. Stubby asked Javy to retrieve the weapons that were not being used on patrol and bring them to the main house. He'd established weapons caches throughout the ranch. He didn't want to keep all of the guns in one location and they would be useful in their perimeter defense if they were readily available.

"This is just a portion of our weaponry and ammunition," started Stubby. "Some are buried in underground, waterproof containers for storage purposes. Others are readily available in outbuildings in case we find ourselves facing an overwhelming force."

"Why don't you keep them in a safe?" asked Madison.

Stubby walked to a closet door, which revealed a stand-up gun safe. "A traditional safe is hard to breach, but not impossible. If we are overrun, the intruders will find this and try to open it. Or they'll drag it to an operating vehicle and take it with them. I felt like it was a good idea to provide them something so that they wouldn't look for the rest."

Spread across the floor was a variety of weapons, including nearly two dozen handguns, a dozen hunting rifles, several shotguns, and two battle rifles in the form of M16s.

"Won't the guns buried underground rust?" asked Alex.

"Not the way I do it," replied Stubby. "I bought six-inch PVC pipes with caps from the Lowe's in Savannah. Each one of these holds a long rifle, a couple of pistols, and ammo for each. I oil them up real good, wrap them in towels, and place lots of desiccant packs in the tubes to absorb moisture."

"Desiccant packs?" asked Madison.

"Yeah, they're full of silica gel that helps keep items in shipping containers dry," replied Stubby. "It sucks the humidity out of the tubes. Once the tubes were sealed, I sprayed them with a flexible rubber sealant to repel moisture."

"Where did you hide these?" asked Alex, pointing to the several dozen firearms lying on the floor in front of them.

"I have secret compartments built into every structure on the ranch. Part of what we'll do today is assign these to you and then return the rest to their designated hidey-hole. All of us need to know where the underground caches are, as well as the locations of ammo stores."

"There are a lot of guns here," said Colton.

"Alex and Chase really helped by adding to the arsenal," said Stubby, smiling at Alex. "The additional weapons are nice, but the ammo is just as valuable. You guys did a great job finding these."

"Well, I'm not too thrilled by the risk-taking," interjected Madison as she reached to touch Alex on the shoulders. "You could've gotten hurt, honey."

"Mom, we were safe. It was no different than the times Daddy and I checked out the neighbors' homes."

"It's important to be careful when you make these runs," said Stubby. "Unfortunately, yesterday's haul proved that the risk can create a nice reward in the form of food and weapons. From now on, however, we'll do this with a little advance planning rather than on a whim."

Stubby gave each of the teens a stern look and then returned the Taurus nine millimeter handguns to the Ryman women together with new paddle holsters. "I cleaned these for you. One of the things I need to work with you both on is breaking down and cleaning your weapons. Keeping your guns well maintained will allow them to last for generations, but more importantly, they'll operate safely. Like any tool, simple cleaning and oiling will ensure that it functions properly."

"I'm going to keep using the AR-15," said Alex.

Chase spoke up. "If we go hunting, Alex, I don't think the AR is gonna make sense. You probably need to pick one of the rifles."

"But I'm comfortable with this gun," Alex shot back.

"So use it," said Stubby. "A lot of folks think the AR-15 is made for self-defense, as a battle rifle. It's perfectly capable of hunting different types of game from small varmints all the way up to deer and hogs. The size of the round is the key. Alex, your rifle is chambered for .223 Remington, or what's known as NATO 5.56 millimeter rounds. I have plenty of sixty-two-grain ammo to fit the bill. As always, shot placement is the key."

"I'm a good shot," said Alex.

"So I'm told," said Stubby. "I have an area set aside for target practice and to study your mechanics. Every day, in addition to our regular duties, we need to practice dry-fire drills in a wooded environment."

Stubby handed Colton his Kel-Tec Sub-2000 and then approached Madison. "Madison, I understand you used the AR-15 once. Are you comfortable with it?"

"Not really," she replied. "I don't know how much help I'd be out there. I want to contribute, but honestly, I'd be more of a liability if we had to start shooting at people."

Stubby smiled and put his arm around her. "Defense of the hacienda will be just as important as a battle in the woods. I have something in mind for you." He reached down and picked up a short-barrel version of Alex's rifle and handed it to Madison.

"It's small, like a pistol almost," said Madison as she weighed the weapon in her hands.

"This is one of two Trident Arms AR9s that we have. I bought one for Bessie and Emily, but Bessie is gonna let you have hers."

The compact AR9 was built similar to an AR-15, but the shortened barrel made it easier to handle. Chambered in nine-millimeter rounds, it was a perfect complement to Madison's PT111 and ideal for close-quarters defense. Most important to Stubby, Madison immediately became comfortable with the weapon. With practice, her confidence level would rise, which was the key to safe weapons use.

Stubby led the group consisting of the Rymans and the Allens to a shooting range he'd set up prior to the collapse. It was originally placed in a hollow near the river in order to prevent stray bullets from flying around. In the hollow, not only would the ravine act as a backstop, but the sound would remain within the dirt walls.

For the next couple of hours, Stubby gave everyone a common-sense tutorial on how to handle their weapons. He began to assess the strengths and weaknesses of each of the shooters. Colton and Jake were fairly accurate at mid-range shots of about two hundred yards. For Emily and Madison, he focused on shooting their pistols and the AR9s from ten to fifteen yards.

Stubby was impressed with Chase's accuracy in middle- to long-range shots of three hundred yards. His weapon of choice was the Remington 700. A bolt-action rifle, the Remington was one of the most popular hunting rifles produced since its introduction in the early sixties. Using .308 Winchester ammunition, this rifle would take down any type of game or predator.

In order to set up the long-range targets, Stubby moved the group deeper into the ravine toward the river. Tree branches began to impact their ability to hit their target, but Stubby wanted to test their abilities. As they approached four hundred yards, only Chase and Alex were able to hit the target on a regular basis. Five hundred yards was the limit of their shooting range within the ravine.

"Chase has hunted more than I have," said Jake. "We've learned that the bullet will drop as the distance from the target increases."

"We've sighted our hunting rifles the same, although in a perfect world we'd set each rifle up for the individual's capability," added Stubby. "Depending on the circumstances, we may all have to use each other's weapons. I've sighted the long-distance rifles in three inches high at one hundred yards. I know to aim three inches low at that distance and dead on at three hundred yards."

Chase shot a few rounds at the target five hundred yards away. At first, he missed low and then he'd overcorrect and miss the target high. After six rounds, he hit the target. He handed the rifle to Alex.

Alex rested the rifle on the bench Stubby had created for target practice. She adjusted the bipod and focused on the target. She took a deep breath and exhaled slightly before holding her breath.

She gently squeezed the trigger.

BOOM!

The shot echoed through the hollow.

"Hit!" shouted Stubby, who followed his trainee's progress through long-range binoculars. "Slightly high right."

Alex repeated the breathing process.

BOOM!

"Wow, dead on the money," exclaimed Stubby as he lowered the binoculars. "I think we've found our human range finder."

CHAPTER 10

9:00 a.m., October 3
Perimeter Watch
Shiloh Ranch

Javy was pleased to assign Snowflake, the Appaloosa horse, to Alex. The two had quickly developed a bond as Alex spent time feeding, grooming, and riding her around the ranch. This was their third day on patrol, and the two had grown at ease with each other. Alex studied Snowflake's body language. Javy said to pay attention to her legs, face, and tail to gauge Snowflake's attitude and comfort levels with her surroundings. Alex quickly learned that there was a lot more to riding a horse than jumping on a saddle.

She also was getting more comfortable around Chase. She understood that he was trying to impress her. Alex liked the attention and hoped that Chase would be himself rather than trying so hard.

The two rode in silence along the well-worn trail. Between the livestock and the horses, the path around the perimeter fencing of Shiloh Ranch allowed for an easy ride.

"I killed someone," Alex blurted out as the two rode down a gradual embankment and crossed a small creek.

Chase's head snapped in Alex's direction, and he applied a little pressure to his horse with his heels to encourage the stallion up the other side. He turned and waited for Alex. "Say that again."

"In Nashville, a man came after me, and I shot him. He died."

Chase didn't say a word for a moment, causing Alex to become uncomfortable. She didn't have a particular reason to inform him of the shooting. In a way, she was trying to make conversation.

"What was it like?" asked Chase as Snowflake made the climb to join him.

Alex shrugged. "It all happened so fast. I went over to this boy's house a few days after the power went out. I found his stepdad in the basement, beating on him. It was kinda dark, so I couldn't see that well. All of a sudden, he charged at me and I pulled my gun and shot him twice."

Chase stared at her for a moment and was speechless. Alex shook the reins and started down the path again.

"Were you scared?" asked Chase.

"Before I shot him, I was mad because he was beating up the kid. When his father came at me, I just reacted. I really never thought about what was happening. I drew the pistol and shot him."

"Could you do it again?"

Alex nodded. "I had to shoot at people on the way down here. Now, it's no big deal."

"Kinda like playing video games, right?" asked Chase.

"I guess so. The way I figure it, if someone is trying to hurt me, I'm gonna defend myself. I wouldn't shoot someone for the heck of it."

The two picked up the pace and rode in silence for several minutes. Loud, excited voices interrupted the two teens' thoughts.

"Come on!" shouted Chase as his horse galloped through a trail to their right and into an open clearing to the north.

"What's that?"

"Those shouts are coming from the Wyatts' place! Let's go!"

Snowflake held her head high and let out a neigh. Without prompting, the Appaloosa gave chase. Alex realized that she had a lot to learn about controlling her new companion. The sudden movement almost threw her to the ground.

More shouts of alarm could be heard through the woods. As Alex entered the clearing, several riders were coming at a fast pace from the middle of Shiloh Ranch. Javy led the way as the sounds of hooves pounding the soil approached and then raced past her.

The riders descended upon a gate connecting the ranch to the farm owned by John Wyatt and his family. Chase dismounted and opened the gate for everyone to race through. Another shout prompted Javy to dig his heels into the side of his gelding as the duo raced into the woods where several of the Wyatt farmhands had congregated.

A crowd encircled a dead steer in a small, grassy clearing amongst the pines and oaks. Alex couldn't get a look at the center of attention until Lucy Wyatt rode up and dismounted. Everyone stood aside as she worked her way past them.

Lying dead in the grass was one of the Wyatts' steers. But it was more than dead. It had been brutally attacked.

Lucy fell to her knees next to the massive animal's bleeding carcass and without hesitation put her hands in some of the gaping wounds.

"My God," she muttered. "Someone's taken a machete to this poor animal." She picked up a chunk of the dead steer's rear flank. "It's still warm. Y'all, this just happened. Stand back, everyone."

The crowd pushed away from the scene and pulled their horses out of the way. Lucy began to look through the grass and reached down to pick up a small tree branch.

"Fresh blood," she started. "Whoever did this just left and they're headed west towards the road."

"Let's get 'em," hollered Tristan Wyatt, the oldest of the Wyatt children.

Chase worked his way next to Lucy. "Mrs. Wyatt, Javy and our boys will help too."

"Thanks, Chase, we'd appreciate it."

Chase turned to Javy and nodded his head. Then he looked to Alex. "C'mon, let's go hunting. I've got a hunch."

Alex returned to Snowflake and followed Chase as he doubled back to the farm gate. He didn't bother to close the red steel gate as he cut the corner and raced along the fence row that separated the two properties.

When Chase had to slow his horse to navigate a dry creek bed, Alex caught up. "Whadya think?"

"There's a busted-up cabin in the clearing where an old wagon road was carved out years ago. I put in a gate so we could ride four-wheelers through their woods. If somebody had a hideout, that deserted cabin would be it."

Alex followed Chase down the trail as it narrowed and the tree branches began to overtake them. Suddenly, Chase stopped and held up his hand. He jumped off his horse and tied him off to a single rotting fence post.

She dismounted and joined him. They worked their way up to the gate and Chase directed her attention to the blood on top of the pine railing. Alex's eyes got big and she leaned in to whisper to Chase, "Should we get the others?"

"No time," replied Chase. "They might get away. Be ready." Chase slowly lifted the gate latch and moved through the opening into a thick patch of rhododendrons until the two could get a better view of the cabin.

"I see smoke," said Alex as she raised her rifle and studied the clearing through her scope. "It's on the back side of the house. Are they having a cookout?"

"Low-down scum," muttered Chase as he moved to his right along the edge of the clearing. As the two made their way through the woods, muffled voices could be heard.

Two men wearing jeans and sweatshirts stood over the fire. The machete used to attack the steer rested on a tree stump. A fire was roaring, and the men took turns placing pieces of raw meat on the end of a pitch fork, which created a makeshift skewer.

The two began laughing loudly, when Chase accidentally stepped on a twig, producing a loud crack. This caught the men's attention, and one of them reached for the machete.

"Who's out there?" hollered the man holding the pitchfork.

Chased raised his gun and pointed at the man closest to the machete.

"Chase," whispered Alex, "let's get the others."

"No time," said Chase as he pulled the bolt and chambered a round. The sound startled the man with the pitchfork and he immediately ran in the opposite direction. The other man instinctively lunged for the machete.

BOOM!

The loud report of the Remington reverberated through the clearing and into the woods. The man fell in a heap and onto the stump before he could reach the machete. He was dead.

Alex was stunned and stood in shock for a moment. Chase bolted into the clearing and began running after the other man.

"Crap," Alex said to herself as she pulled the charging handle of her AR-15 and carefully entered the clearing, scanning from side to side. Chase ran around the house to the right, so Alex went left.

She cautiously approached the corner of the dilapidated structure in time to see the other man running down the dirt driveway toward the road. Chase stopped, took a shooting stance, and chambered a round. He shot and missed. He tried again. Another miss.

Alex trained her weapon on the fleeing steer killer and focused her sights on his back. She gently flipped off the safety and slid her finger onto the trigger. With a deep breath, she paused and then lowered the weapon. She wasn't going to shoot a defenseless man in the back no matter what he'd done to that poor steer. That was crossing a line she wasn't prepared to cross.

CHAPTER 11

1:00 p.m., October 4
Front Gate
Shiloh Ranch

Jake and Stubby rode their horses to the front gate, where two ranch hands held a carload of men at gunpoint. The vehicle, an early seventies Chevy Kingswood Estate station wagon, was filled with boxes in the rear and four men who were standing at their doors. One of the men wore a uniform—Sheriff Junior Durham.

"What can we do for you, gentlemen?" asked Jake. Stubby stayed to Jake's left, keeping his hand near his pistol. Stubby knew that Junior brought trouble. Also, he feared that the escaped marauder had identified Chase as the killer of his partner. Chase had explained that the killing of the man who attacked the steer was in self-defense, but Stubby didn't buy the explanation. Alex hadn't wholeheartedly endorsed Chase's summary of the events either. Stubby suspected she was holding back or protecting Chase.

"We're lookin' for some folks," started Junior. "Have any strangers approached y'all in the last several days?"

"Nope," Jake curtly replied.

"Well, now, don't you want me to describe them to you?" asked Junior as he approached the gate. Jake took a step forward while Stubby inched his hand closer to his 1911. "Better yet, how's 'bout you let me take a look around. They may be hidin' out on your land, Mr. Allen. You can't be too careful."

"Listen, Sheriff. I've already said we haven't seen any strangers."

Junior removed his hat and ran his fingers through his thinning hair. Despite his diminutive frame, he stood tall and walked with confidence as he approached Jake's towering body.

"Here's the thing, Mr. Allen. We followed these folks north out of town and learned they crossed over the river into Saltillo using this old man's ferry. We plan on visiting Percy to discuss this, but we were down your way today and thought we'd check around here first."

Jake, unruffled, stood toe-to-toe with the law. "Seems to me, Sheriff," he said sarcastically, "that you're lookin' in the wrong part of the county. Last time I looked, Saltillo is way up towards Jackson."

"Mr. Allen, you leave the investigation to me. We intend to pay those folks a visit as well to see what they know. But we've got an eyewitness from the other day placing a Jeep Wagoneer that matches the description of the fugitives' vehicle crossing 64 and headed in this very direction."

Stubby decided to intervene before Jake's temper got the better of him. A physical confrontation with Junior and his men wouldn't end well. It would also bring the wrath of Ma Durham to their front door.

"Okay, Junior," started Stubby, "we appreciate your concern, but I can assure you we haven't seen any strangers, fugitives, or Jeep Wagoneers. I didn't think cars ran anymore. This big old Chevy is quite a sight."

"Stubby, these people are dangerous. They shot up my town and tore up a bunch of the county's property. Fella said his name was Joshua Dalton. We don't want to make any trouble for you or the Allens, but I ain't gonna stop lookin' until I find this guy and the two women ridin' with him."

It didn't take much of a conversation with Junior for Stubby to recognize that he had a burr in his saddle. From the Rymans' recounting the events in Savannah, they'd embarrassed Junior and the boys a lot. Stubby also knew that if he couldn't convince Junior, the next group of visitors might be led by Ma and a dozen men. He decided to give Junior something with the hope that it would deflect attention elsewhere.

"Okay. We had an incident yesterday over on the Wyatts' farm. A man attacked one of the Wyatts' steers with a machete and tore it up like some kind of crazed maniac. We helped the Wyatts track the guy down."

"What happened?" asked Junior.

"One of our guys, and I'm not sayin' who, found the fella over at the old cabin on the back road to the bridge. He went for the machete and our man killed him."

Junior studied Stubby and asked, "Was the man alone?"

"No, there were others, but they ran off before our people could catch them. We didn't even get a good look at 'em."

"Women?" asked Junior.

"Don't know. They took off through the woods and then up the gravel drive. Do you know the old cabin I'm referrin' to? It's the old Skelton place from years ago."

Junior nodded his head. "Where's the body?"

"We left it to rot. We've got no use for strangers, especially cattle killers."

Junior studied Stubby and Jake for a moment before returning to his car. As he entered the driver's seat, he shouted, "Who shot him?"

"Now, Sheriff, we're not giving up our people over a cattle rustler, and it seems to me that you've got plenty to deal with runnin' all over hell's half acre chasing your fugitives. We'll keep our eyes open. You can count on that."

Junior backed the Chevy Wagon up the driveway and drove off through the tree-lined entry. As soon as he was out of sight, Stubby pulled the men around him.

"Javy, take a man up to the Skelton cabin and keep an eye on Junior. If he crosses the fence onto the ranch, come find me. Jake, let's ride up to the Wyatts' place and let them know about this little get-together. Alex was up there yesterday, and a slip of the tongue could cause us a lot of trouble with Ma and Junior."

Stubby was raised knowing that you couldn't run from trouble. Eventually, it'd catch up to you.

CHAPTER 12

2:00 p.m., October 4
Lick Creek
Shiloh Ranch

The western half of Hardin County was primarily rich bottomland broken up by several rivers and streams feeding the Tennessee River. Its history stretched back to the days of the Mound Builders, inhabitants of North America from thousands of years ago, who constructed large earthen structures as a tribute to their gods. Several of these platform mounds dotted the landscape of Hardin County and were used by Union soldiers during the Battle of Shiloh as observation posts.

One of these structures was built near the confluence of Lick Creek and the Tennessee River, where the old homestead of J.J. Fraley stood. The Confederate Army occupied the Fraley home as a rear command post and first aid station. As the Battle of Shiloh turned for the worse for the boys in gray, the Fraley house and yard became full of wounded men and the blood of dying soldiers.

Local historians wrote about the blood of the Confederate soldiers soaking into the ground and mixing with the remains of the Mound Builders. As the story goes, Lick Creek, which created a distinctive serpentine shape as it wound its way through the fields, was haunted with the blood of the dead.

"Hey, Alex, do you remember this place?" asked Chase as he led his hunting party consisting of Alex atop Snowflake and three bluetick coonhounds.

"I sure do. Is the rope swing still here?"

"Yep," said Chase. "Go on, guys, take ya a swim. The water's not that cold yet." The coonhounds, an athletic and hardy breed, didn't need to be told twice. In addition to being an outstanding hunting dog, their obedience and ability to stay happy made for a great pet. Their love of swimming was rivaled only by the Labrador retrievers.

Alex dismounted and laughed as the dogs flew off the bank into the small lake. Their deep voices echoed up and down the creek for the second time that day. The first was when they'd treed a raccoon, whose life was saved by Alex's insistence. The critter was cute and she wanted to convince Chase that he didn't have to kill everything because he could.

"How did you come up with their names?" asked Alex as she found a large rock to sit on overlooking the pond. The rock served as the launching pad for the rope swing they used years ago. The rope still hung over the lake, frayed from weather and use.

"My oldest, Smokey, is the big guy with the tan muzzle and the bluetick blaze across his head. I named him for the most famous bluetick coonhound of them all—Smokey, the mascot of the University of Tennessee."

"What about that one?" asked Alex, pointing to a completely bluish-black dog with the distinctive bluetick markings on his mush.

"He's Huck. You know, short for Huckleberry Hound the cartoon character."

"I don't think I've ever seen a Huckleberry Hound cartoon," said Alex. "You have a girl in the mix too."

"The third one's named Ol' Red. There's an old George Jones song that mentions her. Blake Shelton did a remake of it a few years ago. She's unusual because her ears and face lean toward a brownish red. I usually just call her Red."

Alex sat quietly for a while and enjoyed the frolicking of the dogs in the pond. She had had a heated conversation with her parents the night before regarding her outings with Chase. Her mom was concerned for her safety, naturally, and insisted that Alex stay closer to the main house from now on. Her activities with Chase had escalated from breaking into a home to shooting a defenseless man.

Her dad was a little more understanding because he had seen the other side of Alex when they scavenged through the homes of Harding Place. Alex confided in her dad that Chase meant well, but he needed guidance. She understood enough about teenagers to know that if his parents tried to rein him in, the exertion of control would either break his spirit or cause him to rebel. Colton presumed the latter would occur, so the Rymans agreed to keep their opinions to themselves.

Alex received permission to continue working with Chase on security, scavenging, and hunting because they trusted her level head. She also promised to talk to him about the events of the last few days and establish some ground rules. Alex opined that Chase wanted to hang out with her and would check himself in order to continue.

She picked up a few stones and tossed them aimlessly into the water. The dogs came out of the pond in unison and shook water all over the banks. They took up positions behind Alex in the sunshine. They were a team.

Chase, who was always restless, removed his shirt to enjoy the above-average temperatures. He was very handsome and well built. Chase was not as tall in stature as his father, but stood six foot one nonetheless. While they made small talk, Chase practiced throwing his knife into the trunk of an oak tree.

At first, Chase positioned himself around fifteen feet from the tree. He'd turn his left shoulder in line with the target and step forward with his left leg toward the tree. He threw it hard and it stuck each time. The entire technique looked like a baseball pitcher winding up and throwing a pitch.

Thump!

"The key, according to Stubby, is you gotta throw it so hard that the tree's ancestors feel it."

Chase took the knife by the grip and threw it again. Each time, he'd step a little further from the tree to make the toss more difficult.

"You're good at that," said Alex.

"You wanna try it?"

"Maybe, in a minute," replied Alex. She gathered up the courage to broach the elephant in the room. "Listen, about what happened at the cabin ..."

Chase retrieved the knife and wiped the blade off on his jeans. He rolled his head on his neck and shoulders. "Alex, before you say anything, let me explain. I wasn't going to take any chances with those guys. I didn't want them to get away and I certainly wasn't going to give them a chance to get a jump on us."

"I know," started Alex. "I don't disagree, but—"

Chase interrupted again. "We were in a tough spot and I wanted to make sure you were safe. If I took out the guy with the machete, I figured the other one was unarmed. It turns out that I was right."

Alex shifted uneasily on the rock. She didn't want this conversation to be confrontational, but she had to assess Chase's attitude. If he didn't take it well, she'd pull herself out of the situation and stay close to the main house. It wasn't the best way for her to contribute to the group, but it was the safest.

"A lot of things turned out right about the other day," said Alex forcefully. "They didn't have guns. They didn't have friends inside the cabin. The other guy tucked tail and ran. All of those things could've gone the other way."

"But they didn't," interjected Chase. He went back to throwing his knife, but this time with sufficient force to wake the dead for miles.

Alex decided to finish her point and hopefully diffuse the situation. "Chase, neither one of us asked for this crappy world, and a month ago neither one of us contemplated killing anyone. Now we both have a notch in our belt."

He stopped at the tree and thought for a moment before dislodging the knife from the trunk.

Alex continued. "We're partners now. We've got to have each other's backs, which means you and I are equals. We make decisions together, including whether or not to go in guns blazin' or simply walk away. Sometimes a situation might be too dangerous. I need you to agree with me, or I'm gonna have to be stuck at the house like my parents want."

There was an awkward silence as Chase fiddled with his knife.

GGGGRRROWWWWL!

The dogs began to utter deep growls. Their alarm turned into full-blown anger as they began to bark uncontrollably. The three hounds scrambled off the bank and charged toward Alex. She instinctively pulled herself into a ball as they stumbled down the embankment.

Ol' Red lunged first and caught something with her mouth. She yelped and rolled down the bank as Smokey took a turn.

"It's a copperhead!" exclaimed Chase as he scrambled towards the fray.

Alex remained still on top of the rock. She couldn't move fast enough to avoid the snake's lunge.

Huck grabbed an end and bit into the snake's torso. Smokey followed suit as the two coonhounds yanked and pulled at the hissing copperhead with the intent of pulling it apart. As the five-foot snake was pulled between the two growling animals, Chase threw his knife, cutting it in half.

Smokey shook the fanged end of the copperhead back and forth before flinging it into the pond.

Alex jumped off the rock and rushed to Ol' Red's side.

"Was she bit?" yelled Chase.

Alex was frantically checking her skin for puncture wounds. She couldn't find any blood and there was no sign of swelling. Ol' Red was panting heavily, so she was in some type of distress.

"C'mon, honey," said Alex into Ol' Red's ears. "Let's try to get you on your feet. Chase, can you bring us some water?"

Alex helped the dog on her feet and she seemed to stand okay but was favoring her left front paw. Alex felt around her leg. Ol' Red didn't flinch as Alex felt for a broken bone. Alex continued her examination and one of the coonhound's paws revealed the source of the pain.

"Look at this splinter," said Alex, showing Chase the wound. A two-inch piece of wood had pushed its way between the pads of her paw. "It must've caused her enough discomfort to let go of the snake."

Chase rubbed Ol' Red behind the ears. "I think you'll live, old girl. This looks like a job for Mom and Bessie."

"Thank goodness," said Alex. "They saved my life, Chase. There's no way to treat a snakebite wound out here. The hospital in Savannah is even less safe for us."

Alex collapsed back into a seated position on the ground. Her eyes began to well up in tears as the emotions of the last few days took hold.

Chase sat down next to her and wrapped his arm around Alex's shoulders, pulling her head to his chest. He whispered into her ear, "Alex, I promise you. I've got your back."

CHAPTER 13

8:00 a.m., October 5
Main House
Shiloh Ranch

"We're gonna try somethin' new today," announced Bessie as she came out of the kitchen, followed by Maria with several plates of breakfast fixin's. "Maria wanted to try out a new venison recipe using some of her garden specialties and cheddar cheese. Take a deep breath, everybody. We're callin' this dish Deer Holler."

Each plate had an open-faced biscuit with quarter-inch slices of deer meat. Melted cheddar cheese and fried pickles covered the top. The dining table was set for ten this morning. Javy, Maria, Stubby and Bessie joined the Rymans and the Allens at Stubby's request. There were some developments to discuss.

"I don't know, y'all, but this looks good," said Jake. "I'm so hungry I could eat the north end of a southbound goat." Jake fixed his serving like a sandwich and took a big bite. He began to chew and then his eyes started to water.

The table burst into laughter as, apparently, the joke was on him this morning. Colton slid the pitcher of water in Jake's direction to refill his glass.

"Here, Colton," said Stubby as he slid a farm bottle of fresh milk down the table, "give him a glass of milk. It'll give him some fast relief."

Jake finally recovered and glared at Stubby on the far end of the table. "Look at you, grinnin' like a possum eatin' a sweet tater. You know what they say about payback."

"I hear ya." Stubby laughed. "We've been gettin' even with each other for a lotta years now. You've gotta get up early to get one up on me."

After the laughter died down, nobody was eating. Finally, Bessie encouraged everyone to get started. "More of Maria's habanero peppers found their way onto Jake's plate somehow. Y'all are good to go."

Hesitantly, the rest of the morning breakfast crowd dug in and Maria was rewarded with lots of accolades—every chef's dream. After some small talk, Stubby explained the reason for getting everyone together.

"I talked with John Wyatt and Lizzie Hart, who owns the farm on the other side of Federal Road from the Wyatt place. They're both concerned about the increase in refugees coming on their land. Lizzie said two men broke into her chicken coop and stole eggs the other morning. They tried to catch the chickens, who led them on a chase through the briars. She found torn shreds of clothing on the stickers."

Chase glanced toward Alex and added, "It serves them right. Is she alone up there?"

"She's got her twenty-three-year-old son, who made his way home from Memphis. He apparently walked the whole way, which was a miracle 'cause the boy's pushin' three hundred pounds."

"Can he protect the place?" asked Jake.

"I dunno," replied Stubby. "He may have bigger problems. He's got diabetes, and he's out of his medicine. Lizzie's scared for him. His vision is failing, and his feet are causing him problems."

"Those are classic signs of untreated diabetes," said Emily. "He needs insulin, which is only available at the hospital in Savannah."

"They tried that already," said Stubby. "The Wyatts loaned them a couple of horses and a wagon to travel into town. When they met Junior's men at the other end of the bridge, they were turned away."

"That's awful," added Madison. "They have to take care of sick people."

"Well, according to Junior's men, they didn't have anything to trade," said Stubby. "To make matters worse, they confiscated the horses and the Wyatts' wagon. The Harts barely made it home before the young man's feet gave way."

Madison joined Maria in clearing away the dishes. Colton squeezed his wife's hand and gave her a reassuring smile. He turned his attention to Stubby.

"I suspect there's more to talk about," said Colton.

"Yes," started Stubby. "The Hart boy reported that groups are making their way out of Memphis, just as we suspected. They're breaking into every home along the way. Just as we discussed a few days ago, it's a matter of time before we'll have to deal with them."

Jake, still recovering from the initial bite of Deer Holler, knocked back the last of the fresh milk. He began to create a makeshift map on the table, using unused knives and forks. "I can't say for certain, of course, but I don't think we need to be concerned with any threats coming from our south," said Jake as he drew a finger along the tablecloth. "Did Mrs. Hart indicate how far off the road these refugees are wandering? There's a pretty good ways between us and the highway."

"She didn't say," replied Stubby, "but I think we have to be prepared for more visitors. Like those two from the other day."

"Not to mention that one of them got away," said Chase. "Who knows where he ran off to?"

"Right," replied Stubby. "I think we need to expand our security perimeter to include patrols around Federal Road where it passes between the Wyatt and Hart farms. I think we even need to patrol up towards Pittsburg Landing."

"Wow," said Jake. "That's a lot of territory. I don't think we can defend that much."

Stubby stood and walked into the kitchen to retrieve a map he'd drawn on a poster board. The Tennessee River, Savannah, Crump and Highway 64 were all clearly marked. He also had a Sharpie to add to the sketch.

"Here at the house, it's about ten miles to Highway 64," explained Stubby. "The Wyatt farm, at its northernmost fence row, is eight miles, and Lizzie's place is even closer than that. If we can keep them from coming down Federal Road, we might be able to *encourage* them elsewhere."

"Do you have a plan?" asked Colton.

Stubby wrote *Five Ds* on his poster board and circled it. "After the visit by Junior's men the other day and the increased activity of potentially dangerous refugees, I decided we need to beef up our security. In the military, it's referred to as the five Ds of perimeter security."

He slouched back into his chair and set the poster board on the table. Stubby studied the faces of the civilians surrounding him. Women, teenagers, and two men with no military experience returned his stare. He wondered if they could all understand the threats they faced from an overwhelming force, whether with guns or sheer numbers. He decided to lay it out in the simplest terms.

"Preparation without security is meaningless. We're way ahead of our neighbors in terms of food storage, defensive capabilities, and medical supplies. As some of us have experienced, the world is no longer full of unicorns and rainbows. Unless you're prepared to give up all of this, or even your lives, we need to put together a bigger security plan."

Colton looked around the table. "Tell us what we need to do."

"First, we need to give the appearance that we've put together a defendable perimeter. I propose we block all roads coming into Federal Road from State Road 22. This will prevent future visits by Junior and his men or anyone else with an operating vehicle."

"What if we need to get out in the Wagoneer?" asked Madison.

"There are plenty of trails through the woods," replied Jake. "If not, we'll make trails with the Wyatts' old Ford tractor. Plus, I think I know where an old Bobcat skid steer is located. If it runs, that'll be worth its weight in gold."

"How do we block the roads?" asked Alex.

Stubby sat up in his chair. "The easiest way will be to drop trees across them, using our chainsaws. The gasoline you found the other day was a huge help, but we'll need more."

"Alex and I will find some for us," chimed in Chase.

Madison shot Colton a glance. Stubby surmised that mama didn't want her daughter foraging around the countryside, but unfortunately, she was good at it. He might as well address the issue.

"That's exactly what I hoped you'd say, Chase," said Stubby. "You two are excellent shooters and have experience. I am going to place one nonnegotiable provision on your scavenging duties."

"What's that?" asked Alex.

"Recon," replied Stubby. "When you guys go out, I want you to take plenty of time to do surveillance of the properties you plan on entering. I want you to understand scavenging, foraging, looting, or whatever term you choose has the inherent risk of *reciprocal fear.*"

"What do you mean by that?" asked Alex.

Madison reached for Colton's hand and squeezed it. Stubby doubted she'd ever get comfortable with Alex's role within the group. He hoped he wasn't making a mistake, as he'd grown fond of the young woman.

"Reciprocal fear is the compounding of each combatant's fears of what the other combatant fears. Sometimes, the term is used in relation to surprise attacks. If a nation is afraid the enemy is about to launch a surprise attack against them, they might initiate hostilities first—out of fear. As events occur, a multiplier effect takes hold, ensuring that a hot war occurs. The same applies to this situation. If Alex and Chase are afraid they might be fired upon and the occupants of a house have the same fear, this will most assuredly lead to a gun battle."

"So we'll keep our heads together, right, Chase?" said Alex.

"Yeah, of course," replied Chase.

Stubby moved to clarify. "Here's what I'm saying. First, don't get cocky out there. You've had some success, but every situation is different. Second, don't get in a hurry. Take all the time you need to guarantee the property is vacant. If you're not one hundred percent positive, move along. There will be other opportunities."

"Okay, no problem," said Chase.

"One more thing," added Stubby. "We're on a specific mission right now. Focus on weapons, ammo, and fuel. Don't worry about food although you could make a list or, better yet, hide it away. We can go back and get it later. For now, we need to focus on security."

"Okay, General." Chase laughed. "When do we get started?"

"Hold on there, cowboy," said Stubby. "The cutting of the trees will form suitable barricades to both deter and deny vehicles access. I propose that we also create signs warning people away. Most security companies will tell you that the first line of defense is their security signs. They'll tell you that depending on whether you have a gun-shy or a brazen burglar, simple signage will turn them in another, less defended direction."

"We'll look for spray-paint cans too," interjected Alex.

"What if they slip past the log barriers and walk through the woods?" asked Emily.

"Good question, Emily. That relates to the third D, which is detect. Except for Chase's blueticks, which perform an important hunting function, we're going to deploy all of our dogs from the three farms to the outside perimeter. They will detect any strangers and create a barking alarm system. There might be false alarms, but our patrols will be all over it. Also, a barking dog has a strong deterrent effect."

Jake nodded with approval. "I like it. It's like defending a castle except we don't have a moat."

Colton laughed. "We could expand the latrine and compost facility to surround the house. That'll keep the marauders away."

"Zombies, too," added Alex.

"I suppose we could reassign the youngest among us to dig several new latrines to create a moat," said Bessie.

"Forget it," insisted Alex. "I'd rather fight the zombies."

"The house is in the clearing and over a thousand yards from the woods," said Stubby, who attempted to get the discussion back on course. "Only an expert marksman with a high-powered sniper rifle could shoot at us from that distance, and I suspect they'd have better things to do with their skills."

Stubby pushed away from the table and tossed the Sharpie on top of his poster board. "Jake and Colton, I'd like you guys to ride up to the Wyatt place and inform them of our plans. Javy and I will supervise cutting trees at the points farthest away from Shiloh Ranch near State Road 22."

"What about us?" asked Chase.

"I have a list for you two. Follow me."

CHAPTER 14

Noon, October 5
Hamburg-Purdy Road
Shiloh

The horses' hooves clapped the asphalt as Alex and Chase methodically made their way towards the first homes on the list. Much of the area surrounding Shiloh Ranch was part of the Shiloh National Military Park. Located to the north of the Wyatt place, closer to Pittsburg Landing, the park would provide an additional buffer from stray travelers. Other than the area surrounding the visitors' center, much of the park was heavily wooded and wouldn't lend much to intruders. Once the roads were blocked, Stubby felt it was likely they would turn around and push east or north along the river.

His plans for Alex and Chase involved visiting known residents along Hamburg-Purdy Road. Stubby knew the owners and expected them to be home. He also knew that the folks on this list were not dangerous. They had been longtime residents of the Shiloh area, including several who'd been around for generations. He asked the teens to act as ambassadors as well. They would check on their neighbors and exchange information.

But he admonished them to be careful. *Things are not always as you might expect, and a misread of first appearances might get you in trouble.*

They crossed the Sherman Road intersection and approached the first home, which belonged to Mrs. Denise Keef. Her deceased husband had been a longtime family friend of the Crumps, and Stubby regretted not checking in on her sooner.

They tied off their horses and walked the last hundred yards toward the house. It had been so quiet that it would've been easy to let their guard down. Alex vowed to be diligent as they moved forward with their plan. In a way, she felt like she had to protect herself and Chase—from himself.

The fallen leaves provided very little cover. Chase led them down a four-wheeler trail, which dumped them out into a clearing about two hundred yards from the front door. They remained in position for fifteen minutes, studying the surroundings through binoculars and their rifle scopes.

"Do you see a car or anything?" asked Chase.

"No. The carport is empty and the two small buildings to the rear don't look like they're big enough to hold a vehicle."

"Whadya think?"

"Chase, I know what I said before about recon, but there are absolutely no signs of life around here. It sure seems deserted."

"Good enough for me," he said. "Let's go check it out and then retrieve the horses. I'd be pissed if someone ran off with them while we're lying in this field."

"Me too. Let's go." They began to run across the field toward the home, using large mature oak trees to conceal their approach. Taking turns, they darted across the field from trunk to trunk. Despite their disagreements in the past, Alex and Chase were on the same page and maneuvered accordingly.

They fanned out and worked their way through the tree-lined perimeter. A dog began barking in the distance to their west. If someone was inside, it didn't stir their interest. At the rear of the house, Alex caught up with Chase and they crouched behind an old bass boat.

"I don't think anybody's home, but maybe we should knock before going in," said Alex.

"Lead the way."

Alex ran toward the storage building and poked her AR-15 barrel into the open door first. It was uninhabited, but she did catch a glimpse of two gas cans. She left the building and met Chase at the back door.

"My building had an old four-wheeler in it and some tools," whispered Chase.

"Kinda the same for me. Old boat parts and a couple of gas cans. Should we knock or what?"

Chase nodded and ran past the back door so they could cover both sides. He steadied his rifle and pounded on the door.

"Mrs. Keef? Are you home? Stubby Crump sent us to check on you."

They waited for a moment and Alex strained to pick up any discernible sound. It was quiet. She looked to Chase and nodded. *Do it again.*

He thumped the half-wooden and half-glass door. Sheer curtains obstructed their view of the interior.

"Mrs. Keef? My name is Chase—"

Hisssssss! Reeeeeaaaaaar!

Two cats bolted out of the small swinging pet door installed in the rear entry. Startled, Alex shrieked, and Chase fell to his knees. They both recovered quickly and began scanning the yard with their guns until they fell into a fit of laughter.

"That's one heckuva welcoming committee!" exclaimed Chase.

"Yeah, they were not happy about us pounding on their door."

"I'm guessin' that Mrs. Keef isn't home," added Chase. "Let's go in."

Chase took the buttstock of his rifle and broke out a single pane in the top of the door. He carefully reached in and opened the bolt lock, allowing them to enter.

"Whoa, what's that smell?" whispered Alex.

"I dunno, but we're fixin' to find out," replied Chase. "Follow me."

They cleared the kitchen and breakfast room and started down the hallway when two more cats rushed past their legs and through the back door. The house was a one-story rancher with all of the rooms connected by a common hallway. The ten-foot walls reached a peak in the ceiling held up by wooden post and beam construction. A large stone fireplace capped the end of the living area, and the master suite anchored the other end of the home.

Each room was methodically cleared by Chase and Alex. Inching along the dark hallway with their backs pressed against the wall, they approached the closed door to the master suite.

Alex covered her nose and mouth with her sweatshirt sleeve. Chase pulled out a bandana and did the same. The smell of death was emanating from the room and Alex was afraid of what they'd find inside.

She raised her weapon and used it to wave Chase to open the door. He flung it open and Alex immediately moved in to fill the void. The stench hit her in the face, but there were no dead bodies except for a lone fox carcass lying at the foot of the bed.

"It must have been chasing the cats and got stuck in here," said Chase. "And from the smell, I'd say it was recent."

"Ya think the fox found its way through the trapdoor?" asked Alex.

"Yup, and then somehow closed the bedroom door on itself." Chase looked behind the door and found the remains of a cat. "Here ya go. He caught the cat behind the door and accidentally shut himself in."

Alex dropped to a knee and looked under the bed. Another dead cat was pushed up under the bed skirt.

Chase opened the two forward-facing windows while Alex opened the rear sliding glass door. The slight breeze and cool air from outside provided welcome relief to their nostrils.

"I'll run and get the horses while you open up the house and get started," said Chase as he started for the front door. "When I get back, I'm gonna see if I can get that four-wheeler started."

"Cool."

Alex opened several more windows and then she immediately sought out the cat food. She wasn't sure how they were surviving, but this would be a gourmet meal for the Keef cats this afternoon.

She quickly started the search for hidden weapons. She found a Marlin .22 rifle in a closet, with a brick of ammunition. In the nightstand, she found an old Smith & Wesson Model 10 .38-caliber revolver and a box of bullets. On top of a shelf in a closet, she rummaged through some shoe boxes and uncovered a Glock 17 pistol. Another shoebox revealed nearly five hundred rounds of ammo.

Pleased with herself, she began to stack her finds on top of the kitchen table. The Keef cats returned home and were chowing down on Little Friskies when the sound of a horse whinnying signaled Chase's return.

"Find anything good?" asked Chase as he entered the breakfast room.

Alex was emptying the cupboards of canned goods to pick up on a future trip. She remembered her instructions—*hide the food.*

"A few guns," she replied. "We'll find a place to stash this food where no one would think to look. I need to retrieve the gas cans from that storage building."

"I'll get the gas," said Chase. "What else?"

"This ammo is heavy and we need to divide it up between our saddlebags."

"Maybe not," said Chase. "Give me a minute. I might be able to get that four-wheeler started. It looked like an old Yamaha Banshee. My dad used to have one when I was born. Mom made him give it up."

Alex continued to gather canned goods out of the pantry as well as spices and condiments. Earlier, Bessie had reeled off a wish list of items that Alex made a mental note of.

The high-pitched whine of the engine indicated Chase's success. An ATV was a major score and would help expand their patrol area. This immediately reminded Alex of the importance of gasoline, so she made her way to the storage shed to speed things up.

One gas can was half full and the other smaller can contained a fuel-oil mixture. A chainsaw hung on the wall and a large jug of Husqvarna Bar and Chain Oil sat underneath it. These were both good finds. Then, remembering their usefulness during their watch patrols on Harding Place, Alex searched the bass boat for its emergency kit. She was pleased to find two air horns that were still in their original packaging. She'd show Stubby how they could be used for perimeter communications.

Alex reviewed Stubby's wish list and then waved Chase down, who'd accelerated around the yard, creating donuts.

"Let's go, hot rod, you're gonna attract attention," said Alex. "Do you think this thing will make it back to the ranch?"

"No doubt about it. Look, I can strap those gas cans on the rear fenders and lay the weapons on my lap. If there's any food, we can fill the saddlebags. This is an excellent haul!"

While Chase loaded the four-wheeler, Alex returned inside and took one more look around. She began to feel like she was violating people's privacy by foraging through their homes. Only a month ago, this lady would probably watch TV and do crossword puzzles. Occasionally, she might have a friend over to play gin rummy and drink coffee. She probably missed her husband and now her home missed her.

CHAPTER 15

Noon, October 6
Graham Chapel Methodist Church
Savannah

Pastor Bryant closed the hymn book and walked to the front of the sanctuary so he could face his congregation to give the Benediction. He adjusted his gold braided stole and bowed his head.

"May the Lord bless you and keep you. May the Lord make his face to shine upon you and be gracious to you. May the Lord lift up his countenance upon you and give you peace—through Jesus Christ our Savior. Amen."

The organ began playing as the half-full sanctuary of congregants gathered their belongings and began to shuffle toward the narthex of Graham Chapel. Suddenly, the heavy wooden entry doors burst open and a group of uniformed sheriff's deputies brusquely entered the church.

Pastor Bryant held his hands up to calm everyone, but then another group of men entered the church from the rear, forcing a group of women who were preparing food in the back to come into the sanctuary.

"Please, everyone, stay calm," implored Pastor Bryant as he looked at the congregation. His wife, Leslie, sat in the front row, staring back at him. The two of them had discussed their role in the community many times. The Bryants feared the time would come when Ma and Junior would discover their involvement in the secret underground activities of Coach Joe Carey and his Tiger Resistance. He gave her a reassuring smile and then immediately sought out Carey, who sat on the opposite end of the front pew near the fire exit. Pastor Bryant often wondered if Carey sat there each week in preparation for this eventuality.

Fortunately, per their protocols, the Tigers were not present. After the early days when many of the teenage boys were arrested and forced into working at the quarry by the Durhams, Carey instructed his players to stay in hiding. They were of no use to the Tiger Resistance if they were stuck at the Vulcan Quarry, pounding rocks.

Junior strode to the front of the sanctuary and discreetly pushed Pastor Bryant to one side. He addressed the crowd. "Ladies and gentlemen, I'm sorry to interrupt your church service, but I need to discuss a matter of uttermost importance."

Pastor Bryant snickered to himself as the mental midget, Junior Durham, continued to bastardize the English language even upon growing up.

Junior continued. "It's been about a week since a carload of strangers came into our fair little town and wreaked havoc. They destroyed county property, attempted to murder my duly lawful deputies, and generally took our offer of hospitality for granted. They returned the favor by shooting at me, wounding several members of law enforcement, and fled."

The congregation took their seats and began mumbling between themselves. The entire extraction mission was conducted by Coach Carey and the Tiger Resistance. Very few of the townspeople knew who participated except for the mothers and fathers of the young men involved.

Over the last few weeks, Pastor Bryant had counseled them and assured the parents that their sons were in good hands. They were not provided any additional details and didn't care as long as the boys were out of the evil clutches of Ma and Junior. As far as many parents knew, their sons had fled Hardin County to get away from the Durhams' post-apocalyptic form of indentured servitude.

The same was true for the parents of teenage girls from Savannah. Most of them fled with their mothers as soon as it became apparent what Ma's plans were for the local females. Many were not so lucky and had lived to regret it, mostly. The majority of the women fled south towards Mississippi but were stopped at the Pickwick Dam by the military. To their credit, the women of Savannah resisted the urge to return and had remained hidden in the homes of friendly folks in the small towns of Pyburns and Nixon.

Junior's men began to walk through the aisles of the sanctuary as a show of force. Junior was intentionally intimidating and it began to anger Pastor Bryant. He took a chance and decided to challenge Junior.

"Junior, you know that I've asked my congregation for information regarding that day just like I promised you. Nobody has come forward, but if they had, you would've been the first to know. I really don't see a need to disrupt our—"

"Shut up, old man!" yelled Junior, his face turning red with anger. "I waited patiently outside while you finished up your prayin' and now it's my turn. Another word and your preachin' days are over! Do you hear me?"

"Mark," muttered Leslie as she rose to join her husband before being forced back into the pew.

"Same goes for you, Mrs. Bryant," hollered Junior. "We go way back, but this is serious police business and I won't have any interference. Got it?"

"Please, Leslie, sit down," urged her husband. Pastor Bryant was very much aware of Junior's anger issues from his wife's days as his guidance counselor in high school. His newfound power as sheriff, under Ma's tutelage, provided him the legal authority to be bad. A post-apocalyptic world without rule of law made Junior dangerous. Pastor Bryant elected to remain silent, hoping that Junior would simply blow off steam and then leave.

Junior began to walk down the center aisle between the pews. He made eye contact with virtually everyone except those who hid their contempt by staring downward.

"Kathy Austin, where's that pretty cheerleader daughter of yours?" said Junior as he pressed himself past an elderly man sitting next to the aisle. "Huh? What was that? Where's your kid?"

Mrs. Austin began to cry and shook her head and buried her face in her hands. "I dunno."

Junior smelled blood. "Where is she? We got some work for her, you know? Where did you send her off to, dangit!"

"She just left. She got up in the middle of the night and rode off on her bicycle. I don't know where, I swear!"

He picked up her hands and held them up for everyone to see. "Do you see how rough this woman's hands are? She's been workin' in the quarry, helping out. Now, I could give her a much better job if she'd just tell me where her daughter ran off to, but she refuses."

Junior threw Mrs. Austin's hands back down and strutted down the aisle once more. He began to return to the front of the sanctuary when he bellowed out, "Hey, where is our championship-winning coach of the mighty Hardin County Tigers? How about it, where's the great Coach Carey?"

Carey slowly pushed himself up with the assistance of a cane. The cane was a useful prop to create the illusion that he was too disabled to work in the quarry. Thus far, Carey was able to pull the wool over the Durhams' eyes. If not, with a twist of the handle, a dagger would emerge, which would allow him to go down fighting.

"Yes, sir, Sheriff," said Coach Carey, allowing his voice to drag out the word *sheriff*. Pastor Bryant shot him a glance, begging him to behave.

"Coach Carey, winner of championships, why didn't you let me play on your great football teams?" asked Junior.

"Well, Sheriff, you were just too mean. I didn't want you to hurt or frighten the boys from the other schools."

Junior cocked his head as he determined whether this was an insult or a compliment. On this day, Junior was full of himself, so he chose the latter.

"You're right, Coach. Back then, I was too mean. Today, I've mellowed considerably, wouldn't you agree, boys?" Junior turned to each of his deputies, who grinned at their boss.

Junior continued his questioning of Coach Carey. "So, Coach, where's that star quarterback of yours and the two orphans, the Bennetts?"

"Now, Sheriff, you might remember that the boys drove to Nashville earlier that day to watch the Cowboys on Thursday Night Football. I'm sure they're probably walking back home as we speak."

"I'm sure they are, Coach," said Junior as he got very close to Coach Carey's face. Then he whispered, "Where's the rest of 'em?"

"Rest of who?"

"Who? The whole dang team, that's who!" yelled Junior. "Where oh where did the whole frickin' football team go?"

Junior caught the coach off guard and kicked his cane out from under him. Carey had the presence of mind to stumble and fall to his knees. He'd passed Junior's test, but his face was hot red with anger. Pastor Bryant saw a scrap comin' and ran over to aid the leader of the Tiger Resistance.

Pastor Bryant whispered in Coach Carey's ear, "Remember, hold your temper, Joe. Nobody can make you angry but yourself."

Coach Carey nodded and allowed Pastor Bryant to help him up. Carey whispered back. His words would be remembered by Pastor Bryant for years to come.

"You don't have to participate in every argument you're invited to—just the important ones."

CHAPTER 16

9:00 a.m., October 8
Pickwick Dam
Near Hamburg, Tennessee

Brown, mud-filled water splashed against the banks below them. The rushing current and the waves were typical of those created by barge traffic on the Tennessee River—except there hadn't been any boat traffic since the power grid collapsed.

"What do you think is stirring all of this up?" asked Colton as he dismounted into the slushy field.

"Two days of solid rain may have something to do with it, but I've never seen it this swift," replied Jake. He tied his horse off to a tree and stepped closer to the edge of the embankment. His large frame caused his boots to sink into the mud.

"Check out the erosion of the banks across the way," added Colton. "The water is getting near the porches of those two old houses."

Part of the riverbank at Jake's feet gave way as mud crashed into the water. He quickly jumped back as large clods of sod slid down as well.

"I can't imagine that the Corps of Engineers would open the spill gates at Pickwick this much," said Jake as he retrieved his horse. "They're gonna wash us out if they don't cut back on this volume."

"How far is it?"

Jake mounted up and replied, "Maybe five miles if we hug the river. There are several homes along the way as we approach Rock Pile, so we'll need to keep our eyes open."

"Rock Pile?"

"Yeah. When TVA built Pickwick in the thirties, they had to reduce the width of the river in areas downstream. Just below us here, they built up a thirty-foot-tall retaining wall, using limestone quarried from east of Savannah."

Colton mounted up and followed Jake as he headed south along the river.

Jake continued. "Several small houses were built on top of the wall and were rented to TVA employees working on the Pickwick project. Eventually, a restaurant and bar was opened and the tiny community of Rock Pile, Tennessee, became a permanent fixture."

"How many people live down this way?" asked Colton. "Should we bring a couple of Javy's men with us?"

"Nah," replied Jake. "I rode down here with Chase after the power went off to check on things. Most of the property is rented out to summer visitors who clear out by Labor Day. Of course, I know the folks who run the bar. We'll pay them a visit on the way back, you know, to wet our whistles."

The two men rode in silence as they made their way back to Leath Road, which took them to within viewing distance of the dam. As expected, the properties along Rock Pile were shuttered for the winter.

The tiny town of Hamburg showed little activity. It was settled by a group of German immigrants in the eighteen hundreds, who named it after their hometown in Northern Germany. Hamburg Landing, as it was known during the Civil War, was used as a rear logistics headquarters for the Confederate Army. Riverboats would travel up the Tennessee River from Alabama with troops, horses, and cannons in preparation for the Battle of Shiloh.

They stopped twice to speak with a couple of kids playing in an overflowing creek and an elderly woman who was harvesting pumpkins from a field. Jake and Colton were primarily interested in learning about suspicious activity and strangers. There was none to report.

This southernmost portion of Hardin County that adjoined Mississippi was sparsely populated. As they say, *you can't get there from here.* In a post-apocalyptic world, Jake and Colton agreed that these residents were better off being desolate.

The road took them back towards the river, where the effects of the flooding was more pronounced. A dozen homes were built on the west bank of the river near Chambers Creek. Although they were elevated on ten-foot stilts, the water was rushing under them.

A bass boat had been washed inland along with a couple of Jet Skis. The soybean fields were under water. The river was wider at this point than at Shiloh Ranch, and the west bank was at a lower elevation.

"Those homes have to be abandoned, right?" asked Jake. "I mean, how long can they last with the water beating against their pilings?"

"In Galveston, they used to bury the pilings ten to twelve feet," replied Colton. "I don't know if they go that deep here, but most of those homes in Texas could withstand a pretty strong storm surge, except for Hurricane Rita, of course."

"Rita? Don't you mean Katrina?" asked Jake.

"No," replied Jake. "Hurricane Rita came three weeks after Katrina back in '05. It was a true Category Five when it made landfall, unlike Katrina, which was a Category Three."

"Wow, I had no idea," yelled Jake over the roar of rushing water from the dam, which came into view. "Let's go up on top of this hill."

Jake urged his horse up an embankment to the top of one of the many mounds constructed thousands of years ago. This provided them a view of the dam from a thousand yards away.

Stretching across the Tennessee River for nearly two miles, the Pickwick Landing Dam's twenty-two spillways were all dispensing water to the Tennessee River sixty feet below.

The immense power of the river was breathtaking when viewed from this perspective. Water gushed through the spillways at the rate of seven hundred thousand cubic feet per second, creating a deafening roar. The crashing of the water below created a massive amount of turbulence and whitecapped waves that crashed onto the shore on both sides.

Across the river, travel trailers had been dislodged from their vehicles and parking spaces. They were moved inland for hundreds of feet before they rested against the edge of the woods. Homes were destroyed and the Historic Botel, constructed from an old houseboat built on a barge, lay on its side against a stand of trees.

Jake took out his binoculars to get a closer look at the dam and the vehicles on top of it. He handed them to Colton, who nodded.

"It's just like we were told," said Colton. "The military has a pretty big presence up there. In fact, it looks like several of them are looking our way and at the destruction they've created."

"I can't believe they'd allow the dam to open up like this. Normally they control the flow of water so that it doesn't have such a big effect. Look around, everything on this side is destroyed."

The men dismounted and led their horses to an indentation in the ground where rainwater had accumulated. The horses readily drank the cool water.

"Colton, I think we can add a new threat to Shiloh Ranch. We've got Ma and Junior rattlin' their swords in Savannah to our east. We've got groups of marauders, probably both large and small, headed our way from Memphis to the west. Now we've got potential floodwaters coming from the south. From the north, who knows what might be brewin' in Jackson."

"It's just like Nashville," said Colton. "For several days, I honestly thought we could ride out the collapse and make a life for ourselves until the government could get it together. Then the neighbors got ugly, opportunists in the form of gangs began to move in, and the fires burned out of control. It was too populated and the powder keg was about to explode."

"You guys got out just in time," added Jake.

The men climbed back on their horses and took one last look at the millions of gallons of water rushing in their direction.

"Do you get the sense that the walls are closing in on Shiloh Ranch?" asked Colton.

"I do, my friend. I do."

CHAPTER 17

6:00 p.m., October 9
Main House
Shiloh Ranch

The fire crackled as the water and steam trapped inside exerted its pressure on the burning oak. The intense heat caused the water to vaporize, demanding that the freshly cut logs give way to allow its escape.

POP! POP!

"Yikes," exclaimed Alex as sparks flew out of the campfire and sailed over her shoulder. "I like the warmth, but maybe I should scoot back a little bit."

The group was exhausted from a long day of harvesting the remaining crops. The rain-soaked soil aided in the retrieval of the root vegetables, but the muck made it difficult to maneuver. They were rewarded with a meal of pork barbeque courtesy of a feral hog shot while rooting around in the mud of Lick Creek.

Madison was mesmerized by the flames. So much had happened in the short span of six weeks. Her mind recalled the thirty-six hours leading up to the solar flare. She regretted not listening to Alex early on. After living at Shiloh Ranch for a week and a half, she'd made a mental list of the things she could've purchased or brought from home.

Yet, they'd made it. They'd survived the trip down the Natchez Trace and now were trying to make a life for themselves. Everyone else seemed deep in thought as the fire continued to emit the *snap, crackle,* and *pop* sounds that could put Rice Krispies cereal to shame.

"Alex and I used to enjoy watching *Survivor* on CBS," said

Madison, breaking the silence. "Jeff Probst would say that *fire represents life*, and when someone was voted off the island, their torch would be snuffed out. It was symbolic of their being removed from the remaining survivors."

A few heads nodded and Madison, feeling philosophical, continued. "There was a time back in Nashville that I was prepared to give up. I almost asked Colton if we wouldn't be better off in one of those FEMA camps. My breaking point was when the smoke filled the air from the fires burning to our west. I knew that it was a matter of time before we'd have to leave the home that we loved."

She had the group's attention now. Colton added, "A major substation had exploded due to the overwhelming power surge caused by the solar storm. There weren't sufficient resources to put the resulting fires out and the dry, windy conditions at the time whipped the blazes into a frenzy."

"One day, I reconciled that our home might be lost eventually," continued Madison. "I gained strength from Colt and Alex. All of a sudden like, I hitched up my big-girl panties. I survived because the fire inside me burned brighter than the fire around me."

"I remember, Mom," added Alex. She reached for a broken tree branch and stoked the fire, causing sparks to rise into the clear, cool night sky. "Daddy and I joined Mom for dinner and it looked like Thanksgiving, with grilled Spam, of course."

The group laughed. Madison described the meal of grilled Spam topped with pineapple slices. She had wanted to make a nice meal before the family made a critical decision.

"Yeah, Mom simply said, 'I think it's time for us to leave,'" said Alex. "Daddy and I didn't really argue. I guess, deep down, we knew it might happen eventually."

"Is that when y'all decided to come down here?" asked Chase.

"Yes. We really didn't have any other options. Along the way, we'd spot a place and consider it, but you didn't know what might greet you at the end of those long country driveways."

Jake stood and grabbed several logs for the fire, which was starting to die off. As he returned, he whispered to Chase, who immediately fetched some blankets from the house.

"I think I speak for everyone in saying we're very lucky to have you all at Shiloh Ranch," started Stubby. "You bring a lot to the table, and as circumstances continue to develop, I'm not sure we could've done it without you."

"Thanks, Stubby," said Madison. "You guys seem to be very well prepared. Did you scramble around like I did that last day, or have you always been ready for something like this?"

Stubby adjusted his hat and then turned up the collar on his coat as a cold breeze passed over them. "Madison, I've experienced a lot in my life. Did I ever tell you that I started out playing professional baseball?"

"No, really?" asked Alex as Chase wrapped a blanket around her. She smiled and thanked him.

"That's right. I played a couple of years in the St. Louis Cardinals' minor league organization after high school. That was a lot for a young man who was still wet behind the ears. Fortunately, Bessie saw what a wonderful catch I was and caught me at the altar one Saturday afternoon."

Bessie began to laugh before slugging Stubby. "Keep it up, old man. If you don't watch out, I'm gonna jerk a knot in your tail."

"She means it too," said Jake, laughing.

"Well, anyway, we got married and I gave baseball another year. Back then, they didn't pay you a rookie salary in the six figures. In the minors, they paid you and you immediately spent it on room and board. You pretty much played for free just to have the opportunity."

"Is that why you quit?" asked Madison.

"Not really. A lot of the fellas around here were joining the military to fight the Vietnam War. In a rural area like we're in, there isn't much opportunity for a young man growing up. You might get a job in the quarry, or you could run 'shine out of Mississippi. Mostly, I decided to join the Army because I needed a job, not necessarily out of a sense of patriotic duty."

"Did you like it?" asked Alex.

Stubby laughed and leaned back on his tree stump, almost losing his balance. "I had these visions of wearing a uniform and shooting fancy guns, you know, mowing down the Viet Cong right and left. I'd seen too many war movies, I guess."

"It wasn't like that at all, was it, dear?" asked Bessie as she rubbed her husband's shoulders. Madison was touched by the show of support and affection. She casually reached for Colton's hand and gave it a squeeze. She wondered what their life would be like after fifty years of marriage.

"Bessie's heard all these stories many times over the years. After boot camp, I was assigned to the 3rd Ranger Battalion at Fort Benning. I was hell-bent on becoming a Ranger, and after sixty days of the most physically demanding work in my life, I was officially an Army Ranger and on a plane for Cambodia."

"Is that what you expected?" asked Madison.

"The destination, yes. The conditions on the ground and in the minds of my fellow Rangers was very different from what I expected. Cambodia was brutal. It was a soppin' wet hell-hole of a jungle with the VC hiding behind every palm tree. They were brutal fighters and our guys were not really up to the task."

Stubby seemed to become uncomfortable with the conversation and Madison wondered how her question had led them down this path. It was clear that the horrors of war were always on Stubby's mind so that every event in life circled back to those dark days.

Stubby continued. "The 3rd Rangers and two other Ranger battalions participated in Operation Fishhook and Operation Parrot's Beak. During this period in the war, Washington began to make battlefield decisions based upon political pressures at home. We'd be deployed on these operations only to be pulled back as the fight would begin. Soon, the orders received from command required us to break away and avoid shooting back in order to conserve our forces. The problem was the Viet Cong didn't get the same orders. During Fishhook, we had a fierce firefight with the North Vietnamese that only ended because we lit up the jungle with napalm. We lost two-thirds of our unit."

Stubby hung his head. Bessie comforted him as he gathered the strength to continue.

"Stubby was awarded a Silver Star for what he did that day," said Bessie.

The group sat silently for a moment as Stubby gathered himself. When he regained his composure, he looked each of them in the eye. "We weren't mentally prepared to fight. And by *we* I mean from the White House all the way down to those of us soaking our boots in the Cambodian swamps. After that day over forty years ago, I made a pledge to myself and Bessie that I'd never approach any challenge unprepared or uncommitted. I love my life, and I love my wife. I'll be darned if I let anything cut our time together short. As I watched the napalm scorch the earth, that's when the fire of survival began to burn in me."

CHAPTER 18

1:00 p.m., October 10
Horse Barn
Shiloh Ranch

Alex followed Javy's instructions with Snowflake by gradually fading out the pressure she used with her hand commands on the reins and increasing the leg pressure to perform basic tasks such as stopping, moving backward and forward, and changing the pace of his gait. Through practice together, Snowflake was now responding to Alex's commands to change her speed from a walk to a trot and a full-speed gallop. Stubby called the training—*extinguishing*—the process fading out hand commands in favor of a more forceful leg command.

"Good girl," whispered Alex into Snowflake's ear as she rewarded her with a piece of apple picked from the orchard near the front gate. "I think you and I make a great team, Snowflake." Snowflake agreed with a long, proud whinny to her fellow horses. As the sole Appaloosa on the farm, Snowflake probably felt special already. With Alex on her back, the difference was noticeable.

"Nobody has bonded with her except you, Alex," said Stubby as he scruffed Snowflake's forehead with his fingertips. "Continue practicing this every day. As your scavenging runs with Chase increase, you'll find your hands full more often than you realize. Simple tasks like opening and closing gates can be done with leg commands. A well-trained horse is an incredible asset in the situation we're in."

Alex dismounted and rubbed Snowflake's muzzle and the horse immediately responded happily. "You mentioned some other things we need to teach her. What are they?"

"You've done most of the common tasks already. We've taught her not to get spooked around flapping objects by riding her when the wind is blowing tarps, flags, and sheets. She's comfortable trusting you to lead her through flowing creeks. You've got her dragging objects and leading another horse, which, believe it or not, can be a challenge."

Alex dusted off her jeans and added a few other common tasks she'd accomplished. "I've taught her to be comfortable with me mounting on both sides and carrying two riders. I think it's time for the final two difficult tasks."

"Noise and fire," added Stubby. "In the old westerns, you'd see the cowboy sending his horse at full gallop across the prairie, firing his revolver next to the horse's ears. That's not realistic. Nothing spooks a horse like a loud, sudden noise and fire."

"Will it be hard to train her around fire?" asked Alex.

"Fire is a horse's natural enemy," replied Stubby. "Having her hang out with us last night during our campfire was a start. I don't want to set too many fires intentionally for this purpose because the smoke can draw unnecessary attention to the ranch, but every time we cook over an open pit or burn trash, we'll include her. She'll eventually get used to it."

Snowflake pushed her muzzle into Alex's shoulder and seemed to smile.

"She knows we're talking about her," quipped Alex.

"Maybe." Stubby laughed. "Horses are considered social creatures but more so toward each other. The debate about whether horses have feelings toward their rider is second only to the intense debate as to which gun is better, an AR-15 or an AK-47."

"AR-15," stated Alex dryly.

"Have you ever shot an AK-47?"

"No," she replied. "But it doesn't matter. AR-15 is the best."

"All-righty then," said Stubby. "AR-15 wins again. This leads us to how to turn Snowflake into a mounted shooting horse. It's not impossible to teach your horse to accept having firearms fired from the saddle."

"Where do we start?" asked Alex.

"With you, actually," replied Stubby. "You're gonna find it extremely difficult to shoot your beloved AR-15 while riding Snowflake. You'll fire wildly and might even hit a target that you didn't intend to shoot. For that reason, I'm going to suggest that you practice with your sidearm."

"Okay," said Alex. She patted the PT111 in her saddle holster. Everyone carried a long rifle and pistol at all times.

Stubby continued. "The other factor is noise. Your AR-15 has a muzzle brake attached, which helps with the recoil of the weapon, but it also has a tendency to direct sound and pressure waves back towards you. This will be harder on Snowflake's ears. Over time, we might get lucky and find a suppressor for your gun, but in the meantime, practice using your handgun."

They began walking toward the barn together, where Javy was preparing to feed hay to the horses in their stalls. He took the reins from Alex and got Snowflake settled in with the others. Stubby advised Javy of the plan and then he led Alex out of the barn. He grabbed Mrs. Keef's Marlin .22-caliber rifle off the wall as they left.

"We're gonna work this into our training regimen for Snowflake and all of the horses," explained Stubby. "We have plenty of spare .22 rounds, so we'll use them for this purpose."

When they were roughly fifty yards from the barn, Stubby aimed into a dirt mound ahead of them and fired a single shot. He whispered a count of *one, two, three* and then fired again. The horses appeared to be a little agitated, but Stubby said he'd seen worse.

He repeated the process until he'd emptied the Marlin of its fourteen rounds. The whole process took less than two minutes. Javy walked out of the barn toward them.

"How'd they react?" asked Stubby.

"Okay," replied Javy. "After six rounds, they ate and didn't care."

Stubby smiled and handed Javy the spent rifle. "Let's continue this with every feeding daily. We want to do this every day so the horses begin to associate the gunfire with food. When they remain relaxed and keep their heads in the feed, then we can move on to the next step.

"In a couple of days, we'll move closer to the barn and shoot from a location where Snowflake can see you," Stubby continued. "Eventually, if she barely glances in your direction while the feeding and firing process takes place, we'll be ready to start mounted and dismounted training."

Javy turned and left for the barn. Stubby placed his arm around the taller Alex's shoulders and led her toward the house.

"You're a fast learner, Alex, and I suspect Snowflake is as well. In the next few days, we'll have you practicing dry-fire routines with her. You'll show her the weapon and allow her to sniff it. Over a week or so, in the same way you desensitized her to sheets blowing in the wind and crossing creeks, you'll have her comfortable with carrying you during a gunfight."

"Sounds good to me."

Stubby stopped dead in his tracks and looked Alex in the eye. "Does it?"

"Does it what?"

"Does being in a gunfight sound good to you?"

"Well, um, no. I mean …"

"Gunfights are not glamorous, Alex. People get hurt and die. It's not something anyone should look forward to." Stubby didn't appear to be angry with Alex, but rather he was concerned.

Alex was ashamed at her poor choice of words and looked at the ground while she was admonished by Stubby. "I know that." She finally spoke in her defense as tears welled up in her eyes. "I've killed someone. I've shot at others several times. Stubby, I can't think about the fact that I'm taking another human's life or I won't be able to do it. I just want to be ready so they don't kill me."

Stubby gave her a hug like he would his granddaughter if he had one. Alex broke down her façade for the first time since her arrival at Shiloh Ranch. The two shared a bonding moment that would give Alex the strength to survive in the weeks to come.

CHAPTER 19

4:00 p.m., October 12
Wyatt Farm
Shiloh

The smell of fresh bread hovered through the air as Bessie and Maria showed Madison the art of survival bread making. Hot loaves adorned the picnic table outside the pavilion, where Alex and Chase took turns cutting off a hunk and dipping it into fresh farm butter.

"That's bannock bread, Alex," said Bessie from behind the open fire. She was holding a heavy cast-iron skillet to flip over another loaf. "The Scots began making bannock a thousand years ago and it's one of the easiest campfire breads to make. Really, the only trick is to make sure you don't burn it."

It was time for Madison to give it a try. She mixed two cups of flour with a couple of teaspoons baking powder. Two tablespoons of shortening and water allowed her to create a smooth consistency.

"We use pork fat from the hogs we hunt to oil the cast-iron pan," said Bessie. Maria held the frying pan as Madison poured the mixture into the sizzling skillet. Maria placed the skillet on the grates and everyone watched for the next few minutes as the bread browned.

"Wow, this is heavy," said Madison as she flipped the bannock bread over the first time.

"You guys use every part of the hog, don't you?" asked Alex.

"Pretty much," replied Bessie. "Everything has a use, including the charcoal created by these fires. We use it as an additive to the compost and the livestock feed if they're having digestive problems."

"It also has medicinal value," added Emily. "Activated charcoal is used for things like food poisoning, bee stings, and relieving trapped gas."

"Great," said Alex. She turned her attention back to Bessie, who was flipping the bannock bread in the skillet.

"If it flips nice and clean, it's almost ready and you can remove it from the heat," said Bessie. "It's a fairly simple recipe and cooking process. We also use the same recipe to make bread on a stick. We wrap the dough around a small tree branch and cook it the same way except we add sugar in the mixture, and afterward we might add a little salt. It makes for a pretty good pretzel-style treat."

Alex took a bite of the bread on a stick. It was incredible.

"The last thing we'll make are some hoe cakes," continued Bessie.

"What?" asked Alex as Chase snickered. She gave him the *look*, admonishing him for making fun of her.

"Hoe cakes in the real world are simply known as cornbread." Bessie laughed. "You see, back in the pioneer days, garden tools served multiple purposes. A cast-iron hoe could be used to bake cornbread."

"Oh, I see," said Alex. "You said *hoe*."

Bessie retrieved a wooden-handle hoe that had been parked by the fire in the center of the pavilion. The hot iron was smoking then began to sizzle as Maria dropped a thick clump of the mixture of cornmeal, flour, buttermilk and eggs onto the tool.

"You can also use an axe," said Bessie.

Pop—pop—pop!

"Did you hear that?" asked Chase.

"What?" asked Alex.

"It sounded like gunshots coming from the Wyatts' place."

"It might've been the fire. I didn't hear—"

"No, swear, I heard it," he shot back.

Pop—pop—pop!

BOOM! BOOM!

Pop—pop—pop—pop!

"No doubt about it," said Chase. "C'mon, Alex!"

Alex began running toward Snowflake, holding her paddle holster to keep it in place. She'd almost reached her horse when the unmistakable wail of an air horn reached their ears.

"Trouble!" yelled Chase.

Javy and a ranch hand sped past them in a full gallop toward the northernmost part of Shiloh Ranch. Both the Wyatts and the Allens were given the air horns found by Alex and told them to use them only in the event of a gunfight. The alarm meant all hands on deck.

Alex and Chase were halfway to the gate when one of the Wyatts' farmhands greeted them.

"Please fetch Miss Emily. We've got a man down. Please hurry!" He immediately turned his horse and raced back in the direction of the Wyatts' west gate.

Pop—pop—pop!

Pop—pop—pop!

Chase looked at Alex, who nodded back. "You go. I'll go back and get your mom. Be careful!"

"Thanks!" he shouted back to her as he brought his horse up to full speed.

BOOM! BOOM!

It sounded like a war zone!

"C'mon, Snowflake. We need to fly!"

Snowflake took off at a full gallop, ears pinned back and air filling her nostrils. She didn't slow as Jake and Colton sped past them from the east.

"Whoa, whoa!" urged Alex as the high-spirited horse had difficulty slowing down.

"Emily!" shouted Alex. "The Wyatts have a man down. He's been shot. Hurry!"

Emily and Madison ran to the main house. Alex shouted to Maria to fetch Emily's horse from the barn. Snowflake continued to dance around out of excitement. Alex was trying to calm her, but the Appaloosa was feeling strong and alive. In the moment, Alex made a mental note to ride her mare at full speed from time to time. She had a little thoroughbred in her.

Her mom and Emily emerged from the house, carrying a trauma

bag and a backpack with more supplies.

"Do you need me?" asked Madison.

"No, there'll be plenty of hands up there to help," replied Emily. "Lucinda is a vet and will have medical experience too." Maria helped Emily mount and Alex carried the trauma bag.

It took seven minutes of hard riding to reach the Wyatts' main gate, where a crowd had gathered around one of the Wyatts' farmhands stretched out on the ground. Lucinda was already there, applying a chest compress.

Jake cleared the area to allow Emily and Alex inside the circle. Alex surmised that the shoot-out was over because the gunfire had stopped and everyone appeared to be there, including Chase. She glanced around for any other wounded or dead bodies.

Emily ran to the victim's side and Lucinda immediately began to fill her in. "He's alive, but he has heavy bleeding. His breathing is labored, but I don't see any signs of a collapsed lung."

Lucinda lifted the cloth over the chest wound and blood began to seep out. She reached behind her and John provided her another folded-up tee shirt to be used as a compress.

"Has he been conscious?"

"No."

"Exit wound?" asked Emily as she rooted through the trauma bag to pull out some large gauze patches. She quickly applied them to the open wound and placed Lucinda's compress back in place.

"I forgot to look."

"Okay, real easy like, let's roll him slightly so I can see," said Emily. The man, who was wearing only a plaid felt shirt, began to revive as Emily searched for a hole in his back. He then lost consciousness again.

"Crap, no exit wound."

"Jake, Colton, I need you down here to help hold this man still if he wakes fully," said Emily. "We don't need him panicking and wigglin' around."

Jake and Colton took up positions on each side of the victim.

"Alex, grab me a blanket and some water."

Alex looked around and asked one of Javy's men to use his wraparound baja. The man didn't hesitate and offered it to Alex. Water bottles were offered up from several sources.

"Chase, go find out what kind of bullet the shooter used."

"I already know. It was a .270."

"Does anyone know whether a .270 fragments easily?"

"Probably thirty percent," replied a voice from the back of the crowd.

Emily wrapped the man in the blanket to help avoid shock and then cut away his bloody shirt. She removed the tee shirt compress and irrigated the wound, immediately replacing clean gauze over it. The blood was oozing out of his chest slowly.

She rechecked the flow of blood and asked Alex to look into her trauma bag for the Celox.

"What's this for?" asked Alex.

"Celox is used to control bleeding in a trauma situation like this one," replied Emily. "It's used by military medics around the world. Good stuff."

After a moment, the bleeding slowed and Emily applied a generous amount of antibiotic ointment to dress his wound. She strapped tape across the gauze and relaxed somewhat.

"We need to get a stretcher and take him to the house. An interior door will do, with some blankets as padding. Bring a pillow also."

Several men mounted their horses and took off for the Wyatts' farmhouse. The others began to pepper questions in Emily's direction.

"Aren't you going to remove the bullet?"

"He's going to be all right, isn't he?"

"It's just a shoulder wound."

She stood and removed her latex gloves. "Listen up, everyone. Nothing is gonna happen out here on this gravel road. He's stabilized, but I need to get him inside to a warm, clean environment. There is no exit wound, so the bullet is still inside his shoulder area. Because I don't know which direction the bullet entered his body, I can't go rootin' around looking for it. That might make matters worse."

"Like I said, it's just a shoulder wound. That's good, right?"

"Well, let's hope so," started Emily. "What folks don't realize is that there are a lot of huge blood vessels around the shoulder and collarbone. If they're not damaged, he should be fine by leaving the bullet inside his body. But if those vessels have been punctured, that's life threatening."

The sounds of horses returning from the house caused the onlookers to stand back to make room.

Emily continued. "He's bleeding but not profusely. That's a good sign."

Lucinda gave Emily a hug. "Thank you, Emily."

"You and I have made part of our lives the ability to save another's life. Let's start with this gentleman right here. Whadya say?"

"Deal."

CHAPTER 20

10:00 a.m., October 15
Hog Lane
Hurley, Tennessee

"I don't know, Chase," started Alex, lowering the binoculars and handing them back to Chase. The two remained in a prone position. "Those horses look well fed. Besides, they told us not to cross over Highway 22. That's why we blocked the road, remember?"

Chase let out a sigh. He liked to be alone with Alex, but sometimes she was too much of a rule follower. He preferred the thrill of the hunt. "Of course breaking into people's homes is risky, but if we don't take the risk, we won't get what we need and someone else will," replied Chase. "Look around. This guy must run a lawn service. I mean, how many riding mowers do you need? Also, do you see any cars or trucks?"

Alex shook her head. "No."

"That means that nobody's home and the welcome mat has been laid out for us. Let's go."

Chase took off before Alex had a chance to argue. *He who hesitates is lost, or something like that.* Out of habit, he looked both ways before crossing the street and ran behind a large oak tree. Alex quickly joined his side.

"Should we check out the garage first?" asked Chase, nodding toward the oversize white structure, which was adorned with vintage signs bearing the names Esso, Gulf Oil and Quaker State.

"I doubt anyone is in there," replied Alex. "The same is probably true of the barn. Let's try the house first."

"Okay. Let's skirt the perimeter like always and meet at the back door. I'll poke my head in the barn on the way, just in case," said Chase.

Chase darted between several trees and rounded an overgrown row of boxwoods. Alex methodically moved from oak to oak toward the left rear of the red brick rancher. An American flag continued to wave from a thirty-foot flagpole in the middle of a flower bed. The home had been well maintained prior to the collapse.

The barn was a typical gambrel design with a hay loft door in the upper level. It was gently swaying on its rusty hinges as Chase pressed himself against the wall. The sound of a horse inside spiked his adrenaline and he immediately readied his bolt-action hunting rifle. He wanted an AR-15 like Alex's, and although he never said it to her, that was the primary reason he wanted to scavenge so much. He understood that the ranch had certain priorities, but his was a prime battle rifle like hers.

The wind blew from the north and his nostrils caught a stench similar to what they had experienced at Mrs. Keef's place. Death. Chase walked around to the backside of the barn, upwind, and slowly looked through a six-inch crack in the barn doors.

Movement!

His heart raced as a shadow crossed the opening. It was too small to be a horse, yet somehow it was out of place. It slowly crossed again. Someone was inside, probably pacing the floor.

"Chase, where are you?" he heard Alex say in an under-the-breath whisper. She repeated herself with the sound of concern in her voice. "Chase!"

The shadow crossed the opening again. He had to do something. If he shouted back to Alex, she'd be exposed at the rear of the house and he would give away his position. He had to use the element of surprise.

Chase moved back to the front of the barn along the side closest to Alex. He waved to get her attention and put a finger to his lips, indicating she needed to be quiet. With hand signals, he instructed her to take cover around the side of the house.

A horse was exiting the barn. Casually, hoof after hoof, a black stallion emerged without a care. He turned toward the adjacent field to join three others. Chase wiped his brow. He'd never encountered anyone in their homes on their prior runs. He'd thought this home was empty, and he was wrong.

His mind raced. Should he sneak off and get Alex out of this situation? Should he catch the homeowner off guard and shoot him? There wouldn't be any witnesses, and he could swear the other guy drew his gun first. This house had horses and probably plenty of gasoline. There might even be guns for the taking—like an AR-15.

He inched closer to the door and heard a creaking sound. He looked up to see if the noise was coming from the loft door. It was still, as was the wind. Chase caught a glimpse of Alex peeking around the corner of the house. *It was time.*

Chase gathered his courage and burst into the barn. He pointed the barrel of his rifle wildly in all directions, intending to shoot anything that moved. His sudden movements startled a flock of barn swallows. Dozens of the small blue birds, which had nested in the barn, swooped down toward Chase and passed him on their way through the barn doors. Chase lost his balance and fell backward into a pile of loose hay and horse manure.

That was when he saw the source of the movement. High above him, swinging from the rafters, was the body of a dead man. The creaking sound was made by a rusty pulley, which was probably used for lifting motors out of old cars or farm equipment. The old farmer, dressed in his Sunday best, had opted out.

Chase studied the body for a moment as it gently swayed and swirled from the noose holding it a dozen or more feet off the ground. He wondered how long it had been there. The body was thin and the man's face was barely recognizable. His black suit and white shirt were soiled from dust and the droppings from the swallows nesting in the rafters. It was a rude way to treat someone who was so distraught that they were willing to take their own life.

He stood and exited the barn, kicking rocks in the dirt as he left. He quickly debated whether to tell Alex. They could look through the home and then the garage. He could lie and tell her the barn was empty, but she was too stubborn to accept his deflection. *Besides*, Chase thought to himself, *it's written all over my face.*

Alex emerged from the corner of the house and walked up to Chase. She noticed immediately that something was wrong.

"Hey, you okay?"

"Yeah, well, not really," Chase replied. "I found a dead body."

Alex raised her weapon and began to scan the surroundings.

"No, he's been dead awhile. Suicide, I think."

"Oh, God," exclaimed Alex. "How sad." She gave Chase an unexpected hug and he held Alex close to his body. They'd never had this much physical contact before and it felt *right*. He and Alex had become partners in their foraging and security activities. Of course he was attracted to her. She was beautiful and a real *guy's girl*. But the circumstances prevented him from trying to take it to another level. Besides, the Rymans and Allens were like family. Until this moment, he'd looked at her more like a little sister than someone he would fall in love with.

She broke their embrace and started for the back door. "Let's make sure the house is empty and then let's give him a proper burial. Whadya say?"

"Yeah," replied Chase sheepishly. He couldn't figure out why this man's suicide affected him so much.

The two entered the small home and went through their routine. Pictures of the man and woman were found on the fireplace mantel. He wore United States Navy dress whites together with his gloves and a sword. His lovely bride was dressed in a beautiful wedding gown.

Photo frames filled with smiling kids and grandkids were displayed throughout the home. The youngest of the children were photographed riding ponies. This was a happy family before tragedy struck.

A shotgun and a .38 revolver were found in the couple's bedroom. Chase found this odd because a handgun was certainly an easy method of committing suicide. For some reason, the man couldn't bring himself to use it.

The master bath was filled with a variety of medications that neither Chase nor Alex could identify. Several prescription bottles were scattered on the bathroom countertop. Names like Xeloda, Trexall, Zofran, and Fentora were prevalent, but all were empty.

After the two solemnly swept the home for anything of value, they retrieved the horses, two colts and a couple of ponies, and led them back to the barn. Alex suggested that they close the ponies in the barn with plenty of hay and water. They'd be fine until retrieved later. She thought the ponies might become unruly being led by Snowflake and Chase's horse.

For the next half hour, the two saddled up the man's horses and loaded them down with supplies and fuel cans. Other than the tragic find of the body, this had been a good haul for Chase and Alex.

They dug a grave in some soft dirt under the American flag in the front yard. Chase insisted and didn't care that they were exposed. The man had been in the military and deserved a proper burial.

In the barn, Alex helped Chase lower the man's body into a wheelbarrow. They contemplated burying him in his naval uniform, which they found in the closet, and decided against it. If this gentleman had wanted to die in his dress whites, he would've worn them in the first place.

"He didn't want to disrespect his service," concluded Alex as she cut the noose from his neck. "Maybe that's why he didn't use a gun."

Chase positioned the decaying body into the wheelbarrow and then spotted a piece of paper sticking out of his shirt pocket. He pulled it out and then glanced at it. It was a suicide note.

"Should we read it?" asked Alex.

"What do you think?"

"He wrote it for a reason," she replied. "Do you want me to do it?"

"No, let me."

Chase gulped and unfolded the one-page piece of faded parchment. It was stationery probably used by his wife in writing letters to family or friends. Embossed at the top of the page were the words *From the hearts of John and Emma Young.*

Dear God and our family. Please extend your hands of forgiveness to me for taking my life. I will proudly stand before you and be held to account, but at this time I am too weak to continue.

My dear Emma has passed, as the cancer consumed her body. Her life was devoted to loving me, our children, and grandchildren. She was devoted to your Son and the Church. I've prayed for her and look forward to joining her in Heaven.

God, you gave me life and purpose. Throughout, I put my life in your hands. When I strayed, I asked for forgiveness. As I forsake you once again by taking the life you've given me, I beg you to understand. This is not a life for me. I am alone. My feelings of despair consume me daily. I wander this empty home, begging for my Emma to return. I cannot live life without her.

You have been my strength since her passing, but I can no longer survive. I hope that you will find it in your grace to forgive me and allow me to join the love of my life beyond Heaven's Gate.

Your humble servant in this life, and beyond. John Young.

CHAPTER 21

5:00 p.m., October 15
Cherry Mansion
Savannah

Creak—creak—creak.

The Brumby Rocker moved methodically atop the decking. Ma Durham, wrapped in a wool blanket, stared across the river, which had finally receded after several days of flooding. The Tennessee River flowed in front of Cherry Mansion at a steady pace. Like life, the river dictated that you go with the flow. Ma believed going against the flow took effort. Throughout her life, she'd learned that deciding to walk away from a problem or persevere was difficult. She'd only walked away from a problem once—the night her home burned down with her drunk husband Leroy on the sofa. That decision worked out for the best. Now she faced another choice. *Sometimes, going against the flow was necessary.*

"The problem we have now is lack of weapons to support the number of new *deputies*," said Wild Bill Cherry as he continued his assessment of Ma's operations. She was a quiet woman and maintained a steady nerve. She was not known for vocal outbursts. When you made her mad, you'd know it from the steely glare her gray eyes provided you. People feared Ma, not because she was a menacing physical presence, but because they knew she was capable of administering any form of punishment without compunction. Those within her charge toed the line.

"Have we had any defections?" she asked in an expressionless, raspy voice.

"Not really," replied Cherry. "Some of the boys got rough with

girls at the Walnut House, but we fixed her up at the
e slipped out one night and we haven't found her. Other
he guys that matter have stuck around."

"How's the quarry production since the heavy rains?" she asked.

"Fine, except for the accident. We sent the new men to shore up a wall that was compromised by the flooding. A mudslide triggered a rockslide, and seven of them died."

Creak—creak—creak.

Ma remained impassive, unemotional. "That's a cost of doing business."

Creak—creak—creak.

Cherry nodded and lit a cigarette. Normally, he wouldn't smoke around Ma, especially inside. He stepped into the yard, where the smoke wouldn't pass near her, and continued. "I need to talk with you about Junior and his obsession with this family that tore up the town a couple of weeks ago," said Cherry.

"What about it?" Ma bristled. Cherry wasn't family and she didn't care for his tone.

"Junior is expending a considerable amount of time and resources searching for this Dalton fella, his wife, and daughter in the western part of the county."

"Is it slowing down our operation any?" asked Ma.

"Well, no," replied Cherry. "It's just that he's taking our best men and—"

"Does Junior think those people are still around?"

"Yes. He's taking a contingent up toward Saltillo in a couple of days. He found an old man near Clifton who remembered the family. He thinks they may have taken the ferry across the river."

"Percy's? Is that old man still alive?"

"Maybe. Junior is gonna have a word with him as well. I'm just sayin' this is a lot of galavantin' around chasing ghosts."

Ma stopped rocking. "Look here, Bill. These folks made Junior *and you* look bad. You should've taken their guns when ya stopped them at the checkpoint. Heck, you shoulda just cuffed 'em and thrown them in the back of a truck from the git-go. I hear the women were real lookers. They're in short supply around here."

"I know, but they said they were headed toward Memphis and—" started Cherry before being interrupted again.

"That's a load of crap," said Ma. "They wouldn't run away from Nashville just to head to Memphis. Junior's got a hunch and he's followin' it. That's what a good law enforcement officer does. We can't look weak to these people in Savannah. That family got away, which might have given some folks around here the same idea. No, that Dalton fella and his women need to be brought to justice. So you leave Junior be and focus on your own stuff."

Neither spoke for a moment and only the sounds of a flock of birds headed south could be heard.

Creak—creak—creak.

Ma started up the Brumby again.

"Have you made a decision about expansion?" asked Cherry, quickly changing the subject after the stinging rebuke.

"The east side of the county has been exhausted. You've pushed as far as Waynesboro and collected everything there is to collect. How about towards the dam?"

"It's a real mess down there," replied Cherry. "The Corps can't control the river levels. They say the problems started upriver from Muscle Shoals to Decatur and then all the way up to Chattanooga. A lot of the riverfront homes are destroyed, leaving only trailer parks. They don't have anything worth pursuin'. As the rainy season hits us in November, there'll be more flooding."

"Going across the bridge into the west part of Hardin County will pose risks for us," Ma began. "For one thing, those ranchers don't like me. They didn't vote for me and don't consider me, as mayor of Savannah, to have any authority over them. Secondly, the good people of Adamsville and Selmer remember the Pusser legacy. They will stand up to us."

Cherry took another draw on his Marlboro and allowed a deep exhale of smoke. "Junior thinks the ranchers may be binding together. He was looking for the family that tore up the town and questioned several of the folks down in Shiloh. He was greeted with a lot of men with rifles."

"Well, you can't blame them for protecting their farms," said Ma. She waved her hand past her nose twice, indicating to Cherry that his smoke break was over.

"We can outgun them if we're strategic about it," said Cherry as he ground his cigarette into the lawn. "It won't be like the eastern half of the county, where we'd roll up with a couple of trucks and eight heavily armed men. These farms are large and they're fenced. I think we should avoid them and move directly into Adamsville and Selmer."

Ma contemplated this for a moment. The ranches offered so much in the way of food resources. Plus, she'd like nothing more than to knock those high-and-mighty rich folks off their perches. But there'd be time for that. She had some scores to settle in McNairy County first.

A chill swept over her as the sun began to set across the river. She stared at the part of her life that had passed many years ago. She remembered the rotten eggs breaking on her children's heads as the good people of Adamsville screamed for her to get out of *their* town. That was a lot of years ago, yet it was just the other day.

"Then it's settled," said Ma. "Get with Junior and come up with a plan. I want to send a sizable force into Adamsville and clean it out like a swarm of locusts. We're gonna send a message."

"Will do, Ma."

"Bill, when you're done, I want you to burn it down."

"Which part?"

"I don't care, just send a message that's loud and clear!"

CHAPTER 22

9:00 a.m., October 17
Tennessee River
Shiloh

It had been nearly three weeks since his family had arrived at the front gate of Shiloh Ranch, full of hope and excitement, only to face the guns and spotlights of their greeters. Over time, Colton and the girls had assimilated into the everyday activities of the ranch easily. Life was much safer than what they'd experienced in Nashville and along the Natchez Trace.

The solar storm and the loss of power set America back two centuries into a world where the basic necessities of water, food, and shelter were important. Colton laughed when he thought about the *important* headlines prior to the collapse: *Group Demands Removal of Nativity Scene from Courthouse—Colorado rejects Prayer in School—49ers Quarterback Shuns National Anthem, Then Given Spirit and Inspiration Award.*

The average American didn't know what life without luxuries entailed. A world without power brought reality to everyone's doorstep, including the Rymans. Before the collapse of the grid, the question of the day was *where are we going to dinner tonight?* After the solar flare brought America to her knees, the question became *are we going to eat tonight?*

Stubby added four more ranch hands that approached the front gate yesterday. These men had worked for the Allens three years ago when they built the pavilion and other outbuildings designed by Stubby. They were part of a Mennonite community in Whiteville, which was sixty miles west of Shiloh. Their entire community had

109

been overrun by gangs working their way out of Memphis. All of the small towns along Highway 64 were being looted and the residents—either murdered or disappeared.

The men brought their wives and children as well. The debate yesterday between Javy, Stubby, and Jake was not argumentative, but the conversation was mostly out of frustration. Taking in the families meant more mouths to feed, fifteen to be exact. Shiloh Ranch could use the help for security, food preparation, and maintenance of the livestock.

One of the biggest points of contention was the Mennonites' refusal to take up arms. They simply could not use firearms as part of their contribution to Shiloh Ranch. Javy pointed out that their ability to tend to the horses, the gardens, and construction of barriers would free up all of the existing ranch hands to perform security functions. In essence, the ranch could double up their security.

The next problem was where to house them. The main residence was overflowing and the ranch hands occupied the modest guest cabins. It was decided that Javy's men and their families would move into abandoned homes on the perimeter of Shiloh where the road blockades had been established. They would be closer to their security posts and the Mennonite families would be near the confines of the main house and the barns.

"I think we made a good decision," said Jake as he handed out fishing gear to Colton, Alex and Chase. "Stubby will get them settled today and assign responsibilities. These folks are trustworthy and hard workers."

"I agree," said Colton. "Plus, they brought us some valuable information as well. They're coming from the cities at a faster rate than we initially thought. I expected a few stragglers here and there, but the stories they told yesterday were about groups of nearly a hundred at a time."

The four fishermen spread out along the western shore of the river. Bank fishing was popular in Tennessee and an effective means of catching fish without a boat. Shiloh Ranch had a canoe and an aluminum skiff that was only stable for two. Chase and Alex said they'd go upriver toward Rock Pile and look for abandoned fishing boats. Several might have broken free during the flooding.

They spread out along the shoreline, utilizing unique features like fallen trees, rocks jutting out of the shallow water, or stumps, which might be interesting to the fish.

"Stay back from the shoreline, Alex," said Jake. "Fish are very sensitive to sounds and shadows. When you cast, start close to the bank and then work your way out toward deeper water. This part of the river is full of catfish, so you'll wanna keep your bait toward the bottom."

The group began to cast and initially didn't get any bites. Then Chase reeled in the first channel cat of the day. Jake followed with a black crappie. Soon, their five-gallon Lowe's buckets were filling up with dinner.

"Daddy, will these people from Memphis come down our way?" asked Alex.

"I don't know, Allie-Cat. They might decide to move into a town and stay there."

"That's right, Alex," interjected Jake. "There are several places for them to get settled like Bolivar, Selmer, and Adamsville. At some point, I'd think they'd stop traveling east."

"Or they might look at Savannah as the big prize," added Colton. "It's the biggest city in the area except for Jackson, and it's on the river."

"I seriously doubt that Ma and Junior will let 'em in," said Chase.

"That's the problem," said Colton. "When they're turned away at the bridge, what will they do?"

"Maybe they'll go back toward Memphis?" said Alex inquisitively.

"Or they'll fan out along the west banks of the river," replied Jake.

"That might push them our way," said Alex.

"Yup," grunted Chase. "What if we join up with Junior to fight them when they get here?"

Jake removed another large catfish from his hook and dropped it into a bucket of its own. "Out of the question," he replied to his son. "I wouldn't trust Junior to even approach him on the subject. Listen, the Durhams are crazy. They have a small army across the way. They may fight these hordes, or they may make a deal with them and point the masses in our direction."

"I'm just sayin' it might be worth a try," insisted Chase. "What other options do we have?"

"Not many," replied Colton.

CHAPTER 23

7:00 a.m., October 24
Adamsville, Tennessee

The 1968 Cadillac Coupe de Ville roared along Highway 64 towards Adamsville. The four-hundred-seventy-two-cubic-inch engine pushed this two-ton Tessie at a steady clip, forcing its driver, the town's psychologist, to slow at times for the rest of the caravan to catch up.

When Junior discussed his plan with Cherry and his ma, the consensus was that there was no real plan. Phrases like *shock and awe*, *pillage and burn*, and *take no prisoners* constituted the plan.

Junior's men were hungry for a fight and were getting bored. Ma had admonished him for allowing the guys to get rough with the women. Raiding Adamsville served a number of purposes. It would allow the guys to blow off some steam, have their way with the ladies without fear of reprisals, and get even in a way he and his brother, Rollie, could only dream about in those years after being run across the bridge into Savannah. He wished Rollie were there to join in the festivities.

"Doc, what do you make of these refugees streaming out of Memphis?" asked Junior as he lit up another smoke. "I mean, I'm sure the city sucks right about now. But these folks walked nearly a hundred miles. What exactly are they looking for?"

"I tell ya, Junior, when I was getting my doctorate at Memphis State years ago, we studied human migration throughout history," replied the psychologist. "The nomads of many years ago traveled from place to place with a plan to settle in a new locale."

"What if they have no place to go?" asked Junior.

"Migration is very different," the psychologist replied. "Humans

113

are creatures of habit and will only move if something forces them to. Sometimes migration is voluntary, but most often it's not. Throughout history, people have fled their homes because of natural disasters, political conflict or economic disaster. In the case of a catastrophic event like this one, the city has probably descended into anarchy. I suspect they are roaming in many directions, including toward Savannah, the next largest town."

"Doc, I know you're on board with our little program," started Junior as they roared past two elderly men walking in the opposite direction. "It's just business, you know, with what we do. What makes those two old men think that we'd welcome them with open arms?"

"They've probably experienced the dangerous conditions and competition for resources like food and water. In the populated areas, their options are few. They roam into the countryside based upon the false hope that they'll be taken in by a farmer or a smaller town. Unfortunately, false hope is a very dangerous emotion that rarely offers a reward—not immediately, nor with the passage of time."

Junior tapped the dashboard and pointed toward the sign that read Welcome to Adamsville, Home of Sheriff Buford Pusser.

"Well, ain't that sumptin'," sneered Junior. "They run his only kin out of town, but they're proud to have a sign with his name all over it. My grandpa would roll over in his grave if he knew how we were treated. I also think he'd be proud of how I plan on cleaning out these vermin."

Junior gestured toward the AmeriGas parking lot. The dozen cars behind them pulled in as well as fifty men, who climbed out, all carrying battle rifles. They all gathered around Junior and the Caddy.

"Listen up, y'all!" shouted Junior. "We've set this up for a few days now. We've watched their routines, which ain't much. They've put all of their efforts on the west side of town, turning away refugees. Today is no different."

Junior started walking through the crowd, looked each man in the eye, and patted his newly created deputies on the chest or back. Over the past several weeks, he'd earned the respect of his men and bonded with each of them. People's opinions of Junior changed dramatically after the solar storm. Now, they were prepared to fight for him. He continued.

"The east side of town will have very little resistance. Just mow through them. By the time the rest of their defenses learn we're there, it'll be too late."

"We're ready, Junior," shouted one of the men.

"Yeah, let's do this!"

More shouts of encouragement surrounded Junior as the men raised their weapons into the air and worked themselves into a frenzy.

"All right!" exclaimed their sheriff. "You all know your assignments. Remember, you take out every threat, which means any man capable of killing you. No need to ask permission, just do it. Second, we gather things of value—guns, cars, and gasoline, in that order. After the town is secured, we'll have a little party with the rest, if you know what I mean. Now, let's get down to bidness!"

The roar of the vehicles and the men shouting obscenities while firing their weapons into the townspeople of Adamsville was a scene straight out of a Mad Max movie. The massacre rivaled any known heinous event in American history.

The shock and awe approach that Junior employed worked. The citizens of Adamsville were not prepared for the depravity of Junior's men. By the early afternoon, hundreds of men, boys, and elderly residents were murdered. Homes were burned and women were brutalized.

Junior only lost one man—the psychologist, who was accidentally shot by friendly fire. Junior didn't consider the doc's death much of a loss. In his opinion, Savannah wasn't much in need of a psychologist anymore.

CHAPTER 24

2:00 p.m., October 27
Cherry Mansion
Savannah

"What are you gonna do with all of these people," asked Ma. A hundred people had gathered on both sides of the Harrison-McGarity Bridge crossing the Tennessee River into Savannah. "Where the heck did they come from, Adamsville?"

The Durhams' destruction had unexpected consequences for Savannah. Residents from the surrounding neighborhoods, who relied upon the slight semblance of order provided by Adamsville's leaders, were looking for a new source of security. Refugees fleeing Memphis now continued eastward on Highway 64 to the next largest town after Adamsville—Savannah.

"It started yesterday," replied Junior. "They don't have nothin', so we can't use them. If a moving car does approach the bridge, they can't pass because these people have the road blocked. We've tried to move them off the road into the homes in Bridge View Estates, but the residents started shooting at them."

"Good," shot back Ma. "Let them deal with the problem."

"It won't last for long," said Junior. "Those people in Bridge View ain't got a pot to piss in and soon they'll run out of ammo. They'll be overrun."

Ma sat back in her rocker and let out a sigh. "Good. What else?"

Cherry spoke up. "We're continuing to run the radio broadcasts, but our *recruits* are not as frequent as in the past. With the bridge blocked, our only major route into town right now is from the east. The Pickwick Dam is still blocked by the National Guard, and the

116

bridge at Clifton is supposedly blocked by a bunch from Decatur County. They've got their own little toll booth program set up."

"Are you talkin' about at Nance Bend where Highway 641 crosses?" asked Ma.

"Yeah," started Cherry. "The county line is in the middle of the bridge. They're blocking folks coming and going unless they're problem children. They're dumping them into Hardin County."

Ma bristled. She turned to Junior. "You knew about this?"

"Well, yes, ma'am. I learned about it when I sent the boys huntin' after that Dalton fella. I figured we had enough to deal with. Plus, they stayed on their side of the bridge."

"Gentlemen, let me get this straight," said Ma. "We're broadcasting as far north as I-40 and the only road down to us is being blocked by a bunch of good ole boys running their own shakedown? Put an end to that crap, do you hear me?"

"Yes, ma'am," replied Junior. "Well, we've been needin' to have a talk with old Percy and also I need to pay a little visit to Saltillo. I'm hearin' they're doin' real well up there. I think it's time they pay taxes to contribute to the coffers, don't ya think?"

"You betcha," said Cherry.

"And I'm certain that Dalton family snuck across the river using the old man's ferry," continued Junior. "That means somebody up there knows somethin' and I intend to find out what that somethin' is!"

"Okay, Junior, you do that," added Ma. "However, young man, we don't need a repeat of Adamsville."

"But, Ma, you said—"

"I know what I said, but in hindsight it wasn't a good decision. I let my hatred for those people get in the way of business." She pointed at Cherry's chest and then added, "I need you to speak up when I do that. You know my temper, but you can't let that get in the way of making good decisions."

"Ma, they had it comin', and if those folks in Saltillo helped that Dalton family, they'll have it comin' too."

"No, Junior. Our partners in the minin' operation let me know in no uncertain terms that Adamsville was too much. They'll tolerate our form of discipline and control, but burnin' towns will get the attention of the feds, who, if you recall, just moved into Jackson to set up another big FEMA camp. We don't want them down here sniffin' around, do we?"

"No, ma'am," replied Junior.

"How did our partners in Pulaski find out about Adamsville, a town nearly a hundred miles away?" asked Cherry.

"Well, Bill," started Ma in a sarcastic tone, "obviously someone in the Vulcan operations ran their mouth during a delivery. I expect you to take care of that. In fact, make a big to-do about it at the mine. Send a message to all of them. *Keep your dang mouths shut!*"

"Okay, Ma," replied Cherry. "We've increased our production, and they've really filled up our pockets. They're about ready to sell the lignite coal to those small towns around Tullahoma to fire up their electricity. They'll also have plenty of heating fuel for the winter."

"Bully, bully for them," said Ma. "We all know what they really want out of that quarry—the ammonium sulfate byproduct."

Cherry reached for his pack of cigarettes out of his shirt pocket, but Ma gave him the stink-eye. She'd thought about getting him hypnosis to kick the habit, but Junior got the psychologist killed. She'd just take the cigarettes away instead.

"How much of that explosive do the Klansmen want?" asked Junior.

"They've got big plans and deep pockets," replied Cherry. "They call it the *cleansing*. They've not told me specifically where this cleansing is gonna take place, but all I know is they said to keep the ammonium sulfate comin'."

"Fine by me," said Ma. "In business, I've learned that morality gets in the way of profit. Government is no different. Look how those fools in Washington ran this country. They didn't care about us. They looked for more power and wealth. Now, it's our turn. Who are we to judge the Klansmen? We'll mine the lignite and give 'em their ammonium sulfate. They pay us handsomely, which allows us to ride this horse for as long as we can. What happens after that is none of my business."

CHAPTER 25

1:00 p.m., Halloween
Saltillo

"Well, Mr. Mayor, the first annual Apocalyptic Hootenanny has been a real success," said Russ Hilton to the mayor of Saltillo, Jimmy Snyder. Kids were running up and down Main Street, picking up candy from makeshift booths and playing the various carnival games that remained from the Labor Day events prior to the solar storm.

"Listen, Russ, it's no secret that the entire community looks up to you and considers you the real mayor of Saltillo," said Snyder. "Since my legal troubles came to light, I've lost quite a few friends around here. Please don't tell anyone I said this, but this whole grid-collapse thing was just what the doctor ordered for me. Life's a lot simpler now, and I don't miss the stresses accompanying the *real world*. No, sir, not one bit."

"I get it, Jimmy. You and I have been friends since the day you welcomed me into this community. There are only a few hundred folks, and they all have bonded through this experience. Maybe a reset of our country wasn't such a bad thing?"

"It makes you wonder," replied Snyder. "All I know is that I've got a fresh start and people who disliked me are coming around. This Halloween festival was a great idea. We don't have much to give the kids other than some stale candy and several bushels of apples from the surrounding orchards, but they sure are enjoying themselves."

"Hey, Daddy!" exclaimed one of the Hilton kids, who was standing proudly by a Skee-Ball game. "I just hit the fifty-point ring twice in a row!" A couple of the local carpenters had created a Skee-Ball game using luan plywood, a variety of PVC plumbing pipes and some flexible plastic landscape edging. The holes were cut for the various point levels, and pipes were inserted in corresponding dimensions. With a Sharpie, they identified the points levels and the game was ready to set up. It was a big hit and was made completely out of scrap materials.

Another popular game, especially with the adults who enjoyed a friendly wager, was cornhole. One out of five households in Saltillo owned their own custom cornhole platform. The concept was simple. Each team had four sets of bean bags, filled with corn kernels if they were homemade, which were tossed towards a platform nine yards away. A bag in the hole earned three points and a bag landing on the cornhole board earned one. Just like darts were played in the big city pubs, a cornhole game was a mainstay of the Southerner's backyard.

"Tell me about this afternoon's show," continued Snyder as they walked through the three hundred locals of all ages enjoying this beautiful autumn afternoon.

"We've got the usual band, but we're also blessed to have some of the ladies from the Shady Grove Church put together a program of gospel music. You know how they are when they get wound up. Boy, there will be a lot of *praise the lord* this afternoon!"

The men laughed as they walked to the westernmost part of Main Street. Suddenly, shouts came from toward the river.

Fire! There's a fire by the river!

Russ took off toward Shoreline Lane to investigate the ruckus. Most of the mothers in attendance gathered their children close while the men ran towards the west bank of the river. Russ reached the shoreline to watch the last of Percy's home collapse within itself. The old wooden structure never had a chance against a hot fire.

The wind had picked up and the black smoke blew across the river, temporarily obstructing his view. But he heard the distinctive sound of Percy's ferry chugging through the water. Snyder's portly frame finally caught up to Russ.

"My gosh, Russ," said Snyder. "Poor old Percy. Do you think he's all right?"

"I don't know, Jimmy, but this may be him comin' now," said

Russ as he pointed to the ferry as it emerged from the thick black smoke, which quickly spread across the surface of the water.

CHUGA—CHUGA, CHUGA—CHUGA, CHUG.

The bow of the boat revealed several sets of legs and the barrels of rifles. When the ferry was less than twenty yards away, the picture became clear to Russ. Armed men, at least half a dozen, were coming their way.

"Run!" he exclaimed. "Everyone, go back to your homes. Now!"

"Russ, what do we do?" asked Snyder.

Before Russ could answer, shouts and screams came from town. He immediately thought of Lisa and the baby. He charged up the hill as the roar of a loud muffler could be heard from north of town on Route 69.

"C'mon, we're under attack!" he yelled as he bolted up the hill with his pistol drawn. He was greeted by women and children screaming as they ran away from Main Street.

"Stop! Don't come this way!" shouted Snyder. Several dozen people crashed into each other as they looked in all directions for an escape route.

"Go home," said Russ. "Go home and lock your doors!"

His neighbors scattered in all directions and Russ ran up a side street only to reach Main in time to observe the results of the onslaught. Several pickup trucks were roaring through the small town coming close to, but not hitting, the women and children who huddled on the sidewalk. They didn't hesitate, however, to run over the cornhole boards and destroy most of the carnival games the children had enjoyed in the middle of Main Street. The Apocalyptic Hootenanny was over.

Russ couldn't decide if he was frightened or furious. Their small town had been isolated from the world because of its remote location. Their only real contact with outsiders had been the Rymans. Colton had told him about the run-in with the Durhams in Savannah, and Russ's immediate thought was this might be related. When he saw Junior jump out of the front seat of an old Cadillac, his fears were confirmed.

"Who's in charge of this little party?" hollered Junior.

The only sounds that could be heard were the idling of the vehicles' engines and the crying children holding their mothers. Snyder looked toward Russ and hid behind the bigger man's body. Russ understood that Snyder wouldn't take the leadership role. He was all too happy to avoid law enforcement.

"Last chance! My name is Sheriff Durham, sheriff of Hardin County. Somebody needs to step up and talk to me, or my deputies are gonna have to find someone to speak for you."

The entire town stood still, reminiscent of a scene in an old western. Russ took a deep breath and stepped out of the crowd toward Junior. He realized he still held his sidearm, so he quickly holstered it. *Let's not get shot because of a misunderstanding, don't you agree?*

"This here is my party, Sheriff," said Russ respectfully. "Now, I apologize for not getting a permit from the county, but we didn't expect that y'all would send in the SWAT team." Russ chuckled and several of Junior's deputies did as well until he shot them a death stare.

"This is official county business, mister," started Junior. "State your name."

"I'm Russ Hilton. I think I can speak for the entire town. What can we help you with, Sheriff Durham?"

"There'll be a lot of things that *you can help us with*, Hilton. First off, are you the country singer? You look like him."

"Yes, sir."

"Okay, good," said Junior as he walked up to Russ. The height differential between the two men was remarkable as Russ looked down almost a foot upon the shorter Junior. But what Junior didn't possess in stature, he did possess in *cajones*.

"I guess you've gone from a big country star to runnin' this little town. Ain't you in high cotton."

Russ ignored Junior. He continued to analyze their surroundings. Saltillo was not prepared for a confrontation like this. They took their isolation for granted and should have known the ugliness of a post-apocalyptic world would knock on their door at some point. They'd be ready next time, if there was a next time.

"How can we help you, Sheriff?"

"Well, *Mayor Hilton*," said Junior sarcastically. "We're looking for information first. Have you seen a family come through town named Dalton? Man, wife and a perky teenage daughter?"

Russ knew it. He hesitated as he thought of an answer, a mistake that might destroy his opportunity to cover for Colton and the girls. *Think! Tell the truth, sort of.*

"Yeah, I remember them comin' through nearly a month ago. They rode Old Man Percy's ferry across. What's happened over there? Is Percy okay?"

Junior stood as tall as he could and pointed his finger in Russ's face. "That old man's none of your concern, but from the looks of that smoke, I'm guessin' my boys felt like he wasn't cooperating with law enforcement as he's supposed to. Listen up. We'd be glad to bring a lot more of that smoke down Main Street, startin' with the Hillbilly Hilton over there, unless you tell me what you know."

"Fine. They came through about a month ago. They were scared and hungry. We fed 'em, let them sleep one night, and sent them on their way. It was the decent thing to do."

"Did they tell you they were fugitives from justice?"

"Of course not. If they had, we would've turned them away. We don't want any trouble from drifters or troublemakers."

"What did they tell you?" asked Junior.

"They said they were headed toward Memphis. We pointed them west out Highway 69 and they were gone."

Junior studied Russ's face for a moment. Russ thanked God that Colton didn't tell him where he was really going. *Plausible deniability.*

"Okay, Mayor, here's what's gonna happen next. We can't have you folks armed. None of your people, to their credit, opened fire on us. Other towns were not so cooperative and it cost 'em. I need you to voluntarily give us your weapons and ammo, starting with yours."

Junior held his hand out for Russ's gun. Russ stood defiantly for a moment until Junior pointed at his holster and wiggled his fingers.

"Fork it over, Mayor, or I'll get this party started again, but it'll be my way."

Russ handed over his weapon and then nodded to his friends in Saltillo, indicating that they do the same. Junior smiled at Russ.

"Very good, big man. Now, we're gonna go street by street. I want you to tell all of your constituents to run along and gather their weapons. I wanna be back in Savannah before dark and my men get real awnry if they miss their afternoon happy hour. Unless, of course, you'd rather let them stay the night."

Russ wanted to grab this idiot by the neck and choke him like a chicken. Apparently, his face was getting red and his anger was readily apparent.

Junior got right up in his face. "You got something to say, *Mayor*."

"No, *Sheriff*, not a word."

"Good, we'll be seein' ya, then!"

Junior turned and marched off toward his Cadillac. He swirled his hand in the air and the people of Saltillo hustled off to their homes, and Junior's men began to canvass the streets. Saltillo had dodged a bullet in more ways than one, but somehow Russ knew they'd meet up with Sheriff Durham again.

CHAPTER 26

7:00 p.m., October 31
Shiloh Ranch

The evening routine continued to include a debriefing of the day's events. Stubby and Emily, who worked closely with the new Mennonite families, advised the group on their progress assimilating the new residents into Shiloh Ranch. The plan to house the Mexican families in areas away from the main house created some logistical issues for Emily and Madison. They needed to devise some form of taxi service to pick up Javy's people each day or assign a horse for every member of the Shiloh Ranch group. Alex and Chase assured everyone that horses and another wagon was high on the priority list. It was a shame that the Mennonite families didn't have their own, but in the end, the hardworking families were well worth the short-term inconveniences.

The subject of Alex and Chase's activities came up often because they'd become the group's eyes and ears outside their security perimeter. Madison had gradually accepted Alex's role as intelligence gatherer and part of the lead scavenging team. It was hard for Madison not to look at her beautiful young daughter as the smart, golf-loving teenager of two months ago. Alex had matured and was becoming fearless. Madison now wondered if Chase should be the one to hold Alex back when they made their runs.

"We learned a lot today," started Alex. "We agreed it was risky, but we approached a couple of women and their children near Crump. We found them hiding in an abandoned house at River Heights."

"Were they armed?" asked Madison.

126

"No, Mom, and we were very careful, as always," replied Alex. "They had traveled all the way from Memphis on bicycles. When they arrived yesterday, their husbands approached the bridge to find out why it was blocked. Junior's men beat one of the men and the other man turned and rode his bike back to Crump."

"Why did they beat the man?" asked Emily.

"'Cause they could," said Chase dryly as he tossed an apple core into the fire. "From what we're told, Junior is clearing people off the bridge. There are campsites all around the area, created by the homeless out of Memphis. Junior won't let 'em into Savannah, so they simply take up residence wherever they can find a place."

"A lot of those homes up there are trashed and empty," added Alex. "There isn't much to scavenge except down along Catfish Lane on the river."

"The RV park," interrupted Chase. He chomped on another apple. Madison wondered if he'd ever understand that he needed to curb his appetite. There were a lot of mouths to feed now.

"We'd like to find a boat to make it easier to fish and maybe some small propane tanks for Maria to use when canning," said Alex. "We learned something else. If the information is correct, it's horrible."

"What is it, Allie-Cat?" asked Colton.

Alex took a deep breath and took a long drink of water out of a fresh bottle of Evian she'd found during the day. "They told us that Adamsville was destroyed."

Stubby sat up in his lawn chair. "Whadya mean by *destroyed?*"

"The women we spoke with today said the men of Adamsville were slaughtered and, in some cases, their dead bodies were still lying around," replied Alex. "Also, a lot of the businesses and government buildings had been burned down."

"Who did it?" asked Stubby.

"Junior and them," replied Chase. He polished off another apple and was about to reach for a third when Jake picked up the basket and offered them to everyone else who sat around the fire. There were no takers, but Jake placed the basket out of Chase's reach. Chase glared at his dad and shook his head before continuing. "It must've happened recently. The women told us folks from Adamsville were walking up 64 towards Savannah. It makes sense."

"Why's that?" asked Madison.

"Like we said, the bridge is surrounded by people," replied Alex. "I would estimate three or four hundred refugees. They were denied access into Savannah, so they just copped a squat."

"We heard gunfire on the other side of the bridge," said Chase. "Apparently Bridge View Estates is firing on the refugees to protect their neighborhood."

Madison nervously rubbed her hands together as she received this information. She was uncomfortable with Alex interacting with these potentially dangerous people. The Ryman family had seen enough on the trip down from Nashville.

"I think you've done enough foraging up that way, don't you agree, Colton?" asked Madison.

Before Colton could answer, Alex interrupted. "Chase and I came to the same conclusion, which is why we're only going to make one last trip tomorrow. We saw a couple of small boats near the RV campsites. There may be gasoline and propane tanks. We're gonna go up to Catfish Lane for that one purpose, and we'll move on to another area."

"Plus, there are a couple of farms down there to check out," added Chase. "We need horses, so hopefully we can hit a home run."

"Hey, I'm the only one that hits home runs around here." Stubby laughed. "Except if I'd hit a few more, I might have played pro ball longer."

Madison stared at Colton, looking for help. Alex did not always respond to Madison's parenting very well, but she seemed to always follow Colton's advice. She finally decided to blurt it out. "Colt, maybe you can ride with the kids in the morning. They have a lot on their plate and you could help bring back a load. Right?" *Daddy would just be a helping hand.*

"Yeah, sure," replied Colton. "I haven't burglarized any homes with my daughter in a while. It will be like old times. Plus, I'm a little rusty on my B & E techniques."

"Very funny, Daddy. You can ride along. If we find a boat, we'll lead the horses back and you can bring the boat upriver."

The group grew quiet as Stubby stood to get everyone's attention. He put his hands in his pockets to warm himself as a brief gust of cool night air rushed over the group.

"I believe we've put together a pretty decent defensive perimeter for our three farms," started Stubby. "It's designed to address all threats from outsiders. With the growing numbers of refugees amassing at the foot of the bridge and the residents on the north side of the highway turning them towards us, it's a matter of time before we've got a horde of people at our doorstep."

"Yeah, you're right," said Jake. "They may not be armed, but their sheer numbers could overrun us."

Stubby stoked the fire and tossed on a couple of logs. The moist wood cracked and popped, throwing sparks into the air. The light from the flame illuminated the concern on his face.

"We aren't going to change our tactics, but I'm beginning to wonder which is the greater threat right now. Is it a few carloads of Junior's men or hundreds of desperate and hungry refugees?"

CHAPTER 27

Noon, November 1
Catfish Lane
Crump

"Did you hear all that gunfire this morning?" asked Chase as he and Alex ambled along the trail that hugged the Tennessee River. The paths had been cut through Pittsburg Landing many years ago by visitors to the Shiloh National Military Park. They agreed to stay off Route 22 when they traveled north toward the bridge to Savannah. Other than their Jeep Wagoneer, the only operable vehicles they'd seen belonged to Junior. Vehicles were not the issue—dangerous packs of refugees were.

"Yeah," replied Alex. She gave Snowflake a little pressure to encourage her up the bank of Snake Creek. They'd be in an open field now, but elected to hug the tree line in case of an unexpected threat. "At first, I thought I was dreaming about fireworks. It reminded me of when we stayed at Disney World one time. We had driven all day and my parents were exhausted. We went to bed early and then the fireworks at Hollywood Studios got started. It scared me."

Chase trotted past Alex to lead the way. She'd never taken this trail before and Chase, not wanting to frighten her after the encounter with the copperhead the other day, wanted to come upon any other slithery marauders before Alex. His horse was better trained and he could take a fall better than Alex.

"Let's get in and get out today, do you agree?" asked Chase.

"Yeah," replied Alex. "I wish my dad could've come with us. He and your dad took off before breakfast this morning to check on

130

something at the south end of the ranch. I mean, it's no big deal. We know what to do anyway."

"Let's avoid most of River Heights," said Chase. "I do have a package of food to give those women and their kids. That won't take but a minute though."

"I don't think that's a good idea, Chase," protested Alex.

"Why's that?"

"I think we should avoid them altogether," replied Alex. "Yesterday, they didn't see which direction we came from. Today, they may notice. If we give them food, they'll really pay attention to us or pressure us into taking them in."

Chase shrugged. He didn't get it. *Why wouldn't Alex want to help these women out?*

After a moment, Chase persisted. "We'll tell them no. What are they gonna do, chase us down?"

"Chase, I saw a woman lying on the asphalt, bleeding all over the place," replied Alex. "My mom and I decided to do the right thing and help her. It almost got us all killed. You can't trust anybody, and unfortunately, the people you are trying to help may be the ones who kill you."

"I get it, Alex. You guys went through a lot and that's BS. But not everybody we meet is a killer. You gotta trust somebody."

"No, I don't. I trust my parents and then you guys. After that, I'm always hyperaware that someone might turn on me. I mean, seriously, Chase, why risk it?"

"Fine," replied Chase. He gave his horse a little giddyup and led them past the side street that led to the vacant house where the women were holed up. Chase craned his neck to look for signs of movement as they rode past. As they entered Catfish Street and took notice of their surroundings, Chase began to feel uneasy. Something was wrong and he couldn't put his finger on it. "It's nothing," he muttered aloud.

"What?" asked Alex.

"Nothing. It seems really quiet around here."

"It was quiet down this way yesterday too," said Alex. "Most of the activity was near the bridge."

Chase stopped his horse and held his fist up. He quickly dismounted and led them to a patch of woods at the start of the RV park. They tied off their horses. A flock of geese flew aimlessly above their heads, flying south along the shoreline. Other than their occasional honk, the air was still and deathly quiet. Chase shrugged it off and they worked their way through the travel trailers.

One by one, they found them to be empty and looted. Clearly, a group had been through the entire RV park, looking for food or anything of value. Fortunately, the refugees were not interested in propane or small boats.

They quickly walked through the rows of RVs and found nine tanks, which Chase gathered at the entrance to the park. He then found an inline pressure gauge and installed it to the cut-off valves. Most standard propane tanks held twenty pounds of fuel. Chase found four that were close to full. These would be a big help to the canning operation.

Next, they searched for boats. There were quite a few, but they were on trailers and attached to vehicles. This part of the river was not allowed boat docks, so people had to use one of the numerous boat launches found up and down Catfish Lane.

They were within view of the bridge into Savannah and Alex cautioned Chase against getting too close. "We're pretty much out in the open here, Chase. If Junior's men have a good set of binoculars, they'll see us. They've got a clear, unobstructed view from the entrance to the bridge."

"Okay, let's check this last boat launch," said Chase. He picked up the pace and Alex had to jog in order to catch up.

"Whadya see?" she asked.

"Check it out. See that S10 pickup. It's parked on the incline with the boat on the trailer."

Chase ran ahead and reached the rig first. A twelve-foot aluminum-hull boat with a small fifteen-horsepower outboard motor sat on a single-axle trailer. He wasn't sure, but he thought the electronics were minimal on a motorboat like this.

He fetched a bucket of water from the lake and placed the propeller inside it. He pulled the cord on the motor, hoping it would crank. On the third attempt, it fired up with a high-pitched whine. After less than a minute, Chase cut it off and gave Alex a high five.

"This is awesome!" he exclaimed. "Now we can do a lot of fishin' and even go to the other side of the river."

"How are we gonna get it in the water?" asked Alex.

"Easy," he replied. "I'll let off the emergency brake, throw the pickup into neutral, and ease it into the water. We'll be good to go!"

"Now?" asked Alex. "Maybe we should bring our dads to do this? I mean, there's a lot to handle and the motor makes a lot of noise. What if someone—"

"Shhhh," interrupted Chase. "Listen."

The sound of a vehicle on the highway startled them and they both dropped to the ground. The roar of the engine was getting louder. *How did they get here so fast?*

VVVRRROOOOMMMM!

The motor roared on the 1968 Chevelle as it tore down Catfish Lane just beyond where Chase and Alex hid behind the S10 pickup.

"We've gotta hide!" exclaimed Chase.

"What about the horses?" asked Alex.

"They'll be fine. If they try to steal them, they've gotta ride past us to get out. We'll take them back."

Without hesitating, Chase darted out into the open and crossed the field toward one of the lakefront stilt homes that doubled as a bait shop. He turned for a moment to look for Alex, who waited by the truck.

Just as she started to run for the house, the Chevelle slammed on the brakes, throwing it into a skid. Alex stopped to return for her rifle, which she'd left leaning against the fender of the pickup.

"Alex, come on!" yelled Chase.

She froze.

The roar of the Chevelle pouncing on Alex like a lion made him sick to his stomach. He locked eyes with Alex and the realization came over them both. She had no way out.

CHAPTER 28

3:00 p.m., November 1
Shiloh Ranch

Her eyes plead for help, but Alex mouthed the word, *Go*. Chase steadied his rifle and thought about picking them off. There were only two men, but the car skidded to a stop between Alex and Chase's hiding spot under the house. He could kill the driver, but the other man easily tackled Alex as she tried to run towards her gun. Chase's mind raced and there were no good options. Anything he tried, whether disabling the car or attracting their attention toward him, could get Alex killed.

The men wasted no time attempting to tie Alex's hands behind her with zip tie cuffs. She wriggled loose once before being slammed to the ground, causing her to yell out in pain. Chase looked under the Chevelle and could see that Alex was putting up a fight. Once again, he considered rushing the car and shooting the men while they were distracted with Alex.

He rose to his feet and began to bolt past some overgrown shrubs when he dropped to the dirt once again. The men wrangled Alex into the cuffs and hoisted her off the ground.

Alex was covered in grass and dirt and appeared to be in pain as they forced her into the backseat. She looked out the window one last time as the Chevelle roared to life and lunged toward the bridge, throwing dirt and grassy sod into the air.

The Chevelle hit Highway 64, screeching the tires, and roared across the bridge. Then it became completely silent. The entire abduction took less than three minutes.

Chase began to cry, something he hadn't done since his dad's tongue-lashings when Chase mouthed off as a kid. Jake never struck him, but when a man the size of Jake Allen towered over a young child and screamed, it felt like Godzilla roaring in the young boy's face.

No, Chase cried now because he was scared for Alex. He felt responsible and helpless. His emotions brought him to his knees.

"What have I done?" he moaned aloud. The tears poured out of his eyes. Then he vomited, repeatedly.

After a few minutes, Chase got it together and grabbed Alex's rifle. In the melee, the thugs hadn't seen it against the truck. He quickly considered using the boat to get back to Shiloh Ranch. Alex was right, it was noisy and it would probably grab the attention of Junior's men. Plus, he was unsure of its reliability and fuel levels. Now was not the time to take a chance getting stuck in the middle of the Tennessee River. Nor should he get caught. Then nobody would know what happened to them.

He took off for the horses, running as fast as he could. He made sure Snowflake was tied off and he laid some apples on the ground for her that he'd planned on giving the women hiding in the abandoned house.

"We'll come back for you, girl, but first we have to rescue Alex," said Chase quietly, attempting to calm the horse, which sensed the excitement. He gave her another rub of the muzzle and scruff behind the ears.

Chase flew like the wind along the river and through the Wyatt farm. Tristan attempted to flag him down, but Chase didn't stop.

"They captured Alex! Junior's men have Alex!"

"I'll tell my parents!" Tristan shouted back.

Chase approached the boundary fence between the two farms and waved his arms at one of the ranch hands.

"Open the gate! Open the gate!"

One of the young Mennonite boys quickly obliged and Chase raced through, his stallion's nose high in the wind. Rider and horse continued the final stretch to the main house, where Stubby was giving instructions to Javy and two of the new guys.

"Stubby! Stubby!" yelled Chase before he dismounted. He pulled back on the reins, bringing his stallion to a halt. Chase jumped off too soon and tumbled several times through the dirt.

"Chase, what is it, son?" yelled Jake, who came running from the house.

Chase lifted himself off the ground and bent over, attempting to catch his breath. He took a deep breath and replied as Jake and Stubby helped him stand upright. "They've got Alex. We got ambushed at the RV park and two men grabbed Alex and took her to Savannah."

"What?" asked Madison. She'd walked over to Chase from the pavilion, where they'd been canning apples.

Madison stood alone, wiping her hands on an apron. She frantically looked around. Tears were flowing down her face and Jake moved to comfort her.

"Madison, we'll get her—"

"Where's my daughter?" screamed Madison, continuing to look in all directions. "Alex! Alex! Noooooooo!"

She collapsed to the ground and buried her face in her apron. Her crying wails brought tears to virtually everyone as Madison begged God to help her and Alex.

A horse came from around the barn. Madison immediately looked up, eyes full of hope that it was Alex.

It was Colton. He ran to her side. "What's happened? Where's Alex?"

Chase quickly ran through the events. When he was finished, Madison began to berate him.

"Why did you let them take her? You should've done something!" She was angry and let her emotions overflow.

"Mrs. Ryman, I thought about it, but I couldn't take them both out and Alex would've been hurt."

"Whadya think is gonna happen to her now? It's probably already happening!" Madison was shouting in between sobs.

"I'm so sorry," said Chase as he hung his head.

"Son, what were you doing so close to the bridge?"

"We found a boat, Dad. It ran too. I fired up the outboard just to make sure. I swear it ran less than a minute."

"That's probably all it took," muttered Stubby.

Madison pushed Colton away. "Why didn't you go with them? What was so important that you couldn't be there to protect your daughter?"

"Maddie, I'm so sorry. They've done this so many times. I just thought it was a routine—"

Madison tore off her apron and threw it to the ground. "You take all of this in stride. Just another bump in the road. No big deal. The world has gone to hell! People are killing each other over a pair of shoes or a bushel of apples. And now our daughter is in the hands of rapists and murderers. Do you hear me? Our daughter, Alex, is probably gonna die!"

She collapsed to the ground again and cried uncontrollably. Bessie and Emily moved to her side and looked towards Colton. A sadness enveloped the father's body as the stinging words soaked into his core. He not only had to deal with the loss of his daughter, but his wife placed the blame squarely on his shoulders.

Stubby stepped forward. First, he turned to Chase. "Young man, I want you to get your horse some water and then ride up to Lizzie's place and tell her what happened. We'll need her new men to help. On the way back, stop by the Wyatts' and tell them the same thing. Explain that it will be only for tonight and it's a security risk we'll have to take."

Javy moved into the group with one of his guys. Stubby provided him similar instructions. "Javy, pull all the men off the perimeter and bring them to the main house by dark. Tell them to bring their families." Stubby wanted to hunker down in the center of the ranch for the night.

Then he turned his attention to Madison and crouched in front of her. "Madison, please look at me."

She whimpered and raised her head to Stubby's face. Bessie pulled her hair back, and Emily dabbed her tears with her sleeve.

"Now listen here, young lady. God didn't bring you and your

family through this storm just to drop one of you in a puddle. God will protect Alex while she's in danger. He will guide us as we get her back too. Do you believe that?"

Madison nodded her head.

Stubby took her hands in his and smiled. "Sometimes God calms the storm, and sometimes He lets it rage and calms His child. You stay calm, Madison. Pray for her safety and pray for all of us as we get her back to you."

Madison smiled again and looked past Stubby towards Colton, whose face was covered in tears. She stood on her own and opened her arms to him. The two parents embraced. They'd been through so much and now the young girl they'd brought into the world, the precious child they'd held in their arms since she was born, and who they promised to hold in their hearts forever, was in trouble.

Madison and Colton needed to find strength in God, and each other, to weather this storm.

CHAPTER 29

5:00 p.m., November 1
Shiloh Ranch

The barn was filled to capacity. Stubby didn't realize how many men he had within his charge until they were all gathered in one place. They were platoon strength in terms of numbers, but they were far from a fighting force. These men who were ready to risk their lives to retrieve Alex had the fortitude of any Army Ranger Stubby had served with.

Prior to formulating a plan, he debated the magnitude of his attack. Chase was not entirely wrong in his assessments during the moment Alex was taken. One wrong move could've easily resulted in her being killed by Junior's men just to be rid of the extra baggage.

Likewise, if he came on too strong this evening, Junior might react and kill Alex out of spite. Stubby had visions of her body being dumped into the Tennessee River to take the fight out of the enemy. Demoralizing your attacker was an excellent defense in guerilla warfare and he didn't doubt that Junior would employ the tactic.

Stubby decided to use subterfuge as his plan of attack. Success would depend on predicting Junior's reaction and the ability of Colton to reunite with his friends—Coach Carey and the Tiger Resistance.

"There are several aspects of my plan to save our girl," started Stubby, addressing Colton, Jake and Chase, who were sitting on a fence rail next to Snowflake. Javy had taken two men to scout the area where Alex was taken and to retrieve her prized horse. "We have to get you three across the river safely. Unfortunately, that depends upon the reliability of a boat sitting on the back of a trailer up at the

RV park. Chase assures me that it runs, and we need enough fuel to get her across the river."

"I've got a five-gallon can here," said Jake. "However, I have no idea what the ethanol mix is. It may be bad for the outboard motor."

"If it's E10, ten percent ethanol, it should be fine," offered John Wyatt. "E15 might lead to engine failure or damage to the components over time. I don't think it will seize or anything like that. You should be good for a couple of trips."

"I think it's fine," said Stubby. "We live in the country, where folks don't care about stuff like ethanol content. Most of the gas pumps around here are still pumpin' the good stuff."

Stubby had created a map of the area from Shiloh Ranch up to the bridge crossing to Savannah. The deteriorating wood barn board was spray painted in black, indicating roads and boundaries, and then there were several white arrows added. Stubby pulled a machete off the wall to use as a pointer.

"The Wagoneer will act as a diversionary tactic here," said Stubby, pointing to the white arrows leading across the bridge and facing Savannah. "We'll approach the checkpoint, and after I exchange signals with you guys, we'll open fire to engage Junior's men."

"Won't they recognize the truck?" asked Madison, who had entered through the back of the barn unnoticed. "If they haven't already, they'll instantly associate our Wagoneer with Alex. They might kill her."

Stubby approached Madison. "I've thought about this. Junior's pissed off at all of y'all. If he puts two and two together, which in Junior's world equals three, Alex will become a bartering tool rather than another conquest for the Durhams' evil ways. I think this might help keep her alive because he will use her as a bargaining tool to get to you guys."

"Okay, I want to go, then. Let them see me and maybe I can trade myself for Alex. I'm the one that drove that day. It's me they want."

"Madison, I'm sorry, but that ain't happenin'. They want all of you, and then they'll want to get at us for helping you. Let's not compound our problem by putting you in the middle of this mess."

Madison hung her head and then looked toward Colton. She nodded and allowed Stubby to continue.

"After you guys give me the signal, we'll open fire. This will draw Junior's men to the western part of town. Also, I plan on giving you enough cover to get the boat across and up Mud Branch to Riverfront Drive. You'll ditch the boat and find your way by following Town Branch. You remember where to go from there, right, Colton?"

"Yes. Based upon what you've described to me, Town Branch was the creek I followed before I stumbled onto the Carey property. It makes sense that it would meander all the way to the river. This will give us cover and a path to the right location."

Jake and Chase, anxious to get started, jumped off the fence. Stubby handed out the two-way radios that the Rymans had brought with them, as well as a couple of his own.

"Tell me again how you plan on communicating with this Coach Carey fella," said Stubby.

Colton took the radio and began to scroll the dials. "I've been trying to pick up chatter on the radio this afternoon, but we're too far away. Coach Carey has Tigers everywhere. They watch Junior and his men virtually twenty-four seven. If they saw the Chevelle with Alex in it, they're probably mounting a rescue of their own."

"We don't want to trip over each other," said Stubby.

"That's why I insisted on going after Alex now," continued Colton. "I realize it would make more sense to sneak up on them in the early morning hours, but time is not on our side."

"Tell us about their radio communications system, Colton," said Jake.

"Each day, a different channel is selected based upon a player's jersey number. The decision is made by Coach Carey and communicated to all the Tiger Resistance by one of his boys, Beau, Jimbo, or Clay. They've divided the town into four sections. North of Highway 64 is blue and south is deemed red. West of County Road 128, where their headquarters is located, is referred to as left, and the east side is right."

"So red left would be the southwest corner of the town where you'll land with the boat," said Stubby.

"Exactly. Now, after that, I know very little. They had a safe house on Twenty-Fifth Street, which was labeled *25*. If they plan on creating a diversion at a specific location, they use the term *pull trap*."

"What does that mean?" asked Jake.

"Coach Carey explained it to me. In football, it means that the offensive guard is going to step behind the line and move down the line to block for a running back. In Coach Carey's scheme, it means that the diversions will pull Junior's men away from the real location of their operation."

Stubby stuck the machete in a log next to his map. "Brilliant. We'll pull Junior's men to the west entrance of town. Coach Carey and his Tigers can pull them in any number of directions. All we need to do is locate Alex."

John Wyatt stepped forward. "There are two logical places to start. The first is the County Jail. Junior hangs out there most of the time and coordinates his men. The other, which is also likely if they figure out who Alex is, would be Cherry Mansion."

"What's that?" asked Madison.

"Cherry Mansion is a historic, antebellum home that's been in Bill Cherry's family since before the Civil War," replied Stubby. "Rumor has it that Ma and Bill took up with each other and she moved in the place."

"That's what we've heard too," said Wyatt. "It's just over the bridge and sits high up on a bank overlooking the river. Beautiful place."

"I know where it is," said Jake. "Emily and I went on a tour there when we first bought the ranch. It's a beautiful home."

"Well, now it's occupied by Ma and it could be a place they might hide Alex," said Stubby.

Colton stepped forward and held up the radio. "Once you start shooting at the checkpoint, we'll hurry across the river. I'll monitor the radio for chatter from the Tigers and you should do the same. Remember the codes they use and think football. You'll figure out what they're up to."

"Colton, how are you gonna get home?" asked Madison. She hugged her husband and looked for reassurance.

"The same way we came, or we'll cross somewhere farther south. We'll be home, all of us. I promise."

CHAPTER 30

6:00 p.m., November 1
Hardin County Detention Center
Savannah

The administrative wing of the Hardin County jail contained Junior's offices. The jail, or the more politically correct title of Detention Center, was also part of the complex. On any given day prior to the collapse, several hundred inmates would be held within the complex. Most were serving short-term prison sentences of less than one year for minor crimes. Others were awaiting their trial date without bond. The complex would be bustling with activity as inmates were booked or released, and lawyers hustled in and out of meetings with their clients.

On that fateful night when zero hour came and the nation was thrust into darkness, the jail had been emptied. All the prisoners' sentences had been commuted by Sheriff Junior Durham in exchange for an oath of loyalty.

Those who were serving out their short-term sentences for petty crimes were provided the opportunity to continue their activities as employees of Sheriff Durham. They were given a free pass, so they looted for the sheriff. The entrance to the Detention Center began to resemble a successful Second Harvest food donation drive. Junior had to feed a new army of deputies, and the townspeople needed to donate to the cause. Besides, their hunger would create a dependent class of citizenry who were useful in many ways.

Junior also utilized the worst of the inmates within his charge. The Hardin County judicial system had its share of violent criminals as well. Virtually all men, these inmates had charges that included some form of violence or use of a weapon. They were either awaiting trial, sentencing, or transport to a higher security facility within the Tennessee State Prison system.

Politicians and leaders in law enforcement often discussed ways to reduce the rate of recidivism—an ex-con's potential to relapse into criminal behavior. The recidivism rate in the United States was nearly eighty percent. Four out of five ex-cons returned to a life of crime prior to the collapse. The rest were seen as success stories.

Sheriff Durham crafted his own solution to the high recidivism rate—do away with the laws. "It's quite simple," he had quipped. "*No laws, no criminals.*"

The night the solar storm was hurtling towards earth, Junior conducted employment interviews in each of the jail cells of his violent inmates. These men swore allegiance in exchange for freedom. Junior announced they'd become newly appointed Hardin County sheriff's deputies.

And just like that, the Hardin County Detention Center was emptied of its prisoner population. It was the single biggest act of pardons and commutations since the departure of the last U.S. president from office.

Junior studied the whiteboards hanging in the conference room adjacent to his office. One of his assistants kept close tabs on the city's residents. Junior wanted to have information on everyone, and he frequently used his newly minted deputies for this task. They were not shy about kicking open doors and counting heads, or bustin' them as necessary.

The workforce at the Vulcan Quarry totaled seven hundred, give or take. As their partners in Pulaski insisted on increased production, some of the women in town who ordinarily worked the fields were being used to quarry the lignite. He held back the younger women, of course, for his deputies' entertainment.

One board contained a hand-drawn map of the county with its dozens of small, unincorporated municipalities. This whiteboard constituted his search grid for the family that caused him embarrassment and loss of respect with some of his men. He was always aware that those within his command might make a play for power. He had to keep a pulse on his army of miscreants, or one night his throat could be slit, along with Ma's.

"Let go of me!" shouted a female voice in the hallway. Junior quickly turned to the sound of the commotion. A teenage girl, a pretty one, tried to wiggle away from two of his scouts assigned to the western part of the county in the search for what he knew as the Dalton family.

"Shut up, girl. Show some respect for the sheriff of Hardin County."

"Well, boys," said Junior. Junior walked closer to Alex and pretended to smell her. "Looks to me like you caught a wildcat and a pretty one at that. She's not gamey like the others. Well kept."

Alex backed away from Junior and he began to laugh. "Well, there's some fire in this one. She'll need to be housebroken, if you know what I mean." The men laughed as Alex continued to writhe in their grasp.

"Whadya want us to do with her?" asked one of Alex's captors.

"Shift meeting is comin' up and we need to finish cleaning those refugee vermin out of those homes on the west side. Let's get everybody rollin' on that and then we'll examine our new friend a little closer. Get to know one another and all, right?"

"You got it, Sheriff. We'll put her in the holding cell down the hall."

Junior returned to the conference room, where the leaders of the operation were gathering to exchange notes about their progress. Junior had finally tired of the constant stream of refugees approaching the western checkpoint, begging for food and shelter. Ma didn't like her view of the Tennessee River being spoiled by a bunch of homeless in tents and cardboard lean-tos.

That morning, just before dawn, a couple dozen of Junior's men conducted a sweep of the two small neighborhoods on both sides of the bridge on the west bank of the river. There were no specific orders other than to run them off or kill them off. It didn't matter to Junior.

"Let the refugees go pester the ranchers and farmers for food," he'd said. "I'm sure they've got plenty."

The meeting was under way, and the consensus was that they could mop up the remaining stragglers by the end of the next day. As for the future, this was the second step in taking control of West Hardin County with its abundance of farmland and livestock. The first step was burning out Adamsville. A clear message in the spirit of cooperation, *Durham-style*, was sent on that day.

"If we can clear them out of Bridge Water Estates too, then we can seal off the intersection of 64 and 22 …"

The words trailed off as Junior's mind wandered to the confrontation with the Dalton family that day. He had been driving the old sixties model Ford Galaxie 500 toward the intersection. They were going to intercept the two women who'd evaded his deputies' pursuit, which landed one of their cars in a swimming pool.

He visualized speeding toward the intersection when the lead chase vehicle spun out of control and hit a tree. *No matter. I was in position and ready to take the shot.*

"We'll rendezvous at the western checkpoint at oh-six-hundred and finish the job. Now, boys, no drinkin' or carousin' tonight. We need clear heads in the mornin'."

Junior recalled starting to draw his pistol. He'd planned on shooting out the windshield, causing the driver to crash. He'd wanted them alive—to administer his own form of punishment.

It was the blonde hair flowing out of the passenger-side window that caught his eye first. Then it was the muzzle of the assault rifle spitting round after round into the old Ford. He'd ducked beneath the fender but managed to make eye contact with the driver. The exploding front tires of the Galaxie caused Junior to hit the pavement, but he followed the Wagoneer with his eyes as it eased past the wreckage. The passenger of the Wagoneer had turned and looked in his direction.

"I'll be dogged," muttered Junior, who bolted out of the conference room without saying a word. Several of the men briefly followed as Junior jogged down the hallway toward the holding cell.

Alex sat defiantly in a dark corner of the cell, holding her knees up to her chest. Junior couldn't see her face because the auxiliary lighting from the hallway didn't shine into the corner where Alex was huddled.

"Stand up," ordered Junior.

Alex didn't move.

"Come over here, now!" he yelled as a crowd of curious deputies began to surround him.

Alex slid off the steel bench and walked over to Junior. She looked him directly in the eye. "What?" Alex was challenging him.

The two strong-willed, unyielding sets of eyes stared at each other as everyone grew silent.

"Well, lookie who we have here, boys," said Junior. "This is quite the prize, but she's only one out of the three on our most-wanted list. Git her out so I can find out what she knows."

CHAPTER 31

8:00 p.m., November 1
Harrison-McGarity Bridge
Crump

Stubby positioned his men. One of the biggest challenges he thought he'd face—besides getting shot at, something he hadn't experienced since Cambodia—was interference from the refugees. He was encouraged to find they were harmless. A few were desperate and had to be subdued. But overall, he didn't feel threatened by any of them. These were not the gangs of roving marauders that he expected out of the Memphis area. They were ordinary people looking for a way to survive.

He encouraged them to stay under the bridge and out of the line of fire. While the exchange with Junior's men would take place over the arch in the four-lane bridge, there was a possibility of a stray round as Stubby and a few of Javy's men beat a hasty retreat off the bridge at the end of the operation.

The bridge was only five hundred feet long, but with the pronounced hump in the middle allowing for an eighty-foot clearance above the river, they wouldn't come into view of Junior's men until they were a few hundred feet away. There would be several seconds as they positioned the truck to block the east span of the bridge where they'd be vulnerable. When it became time to back off the bridge, there would be several hair-raising moments.

Javy and a group of eight men would wait at the bridge's entrance to provide Stubby and the other shooters cover while hightailing it off the bridge. Another half dozen men would keep the onlookers at bay, hopefully encouraging them to take cover. Everybody had a role.

They awaited the flashlight signal from Jake. He struck up a conversation with several of the refugees and learned about the massacre in Adamsville. It saddened Stubby, as he had several longtime friends living there. It also reminded him of the evil that existed within Junior Durham. He was frightened more than ever for Alex's safety.

He never thought to obtain the type of gear he had been issued as an Army Ranger. His new AR-10 was the only reminder of the load-out he'd become accustomed to as a soldier. He'd provided Javy's top man with an AR-15 just like the one belonging to Alex. It was an excellent weapon, and it was symbolic that it would play a role in her rescue. The other two men would use their shotguns firing 00 buckshot. The effectiveness of the shotgun from roughly a hundred yards was a concern, but the deterrent effect of raining continuous rounds of double-aught buck on the heads of Junior's frightened men was what Stubby counted on. He would provide the high-powered accuracy of the NATO 7.62 rounds. Let the other men keep Junior's men on the defensive.

A flash of light below indicated to Stubby that it was time. He would drive the truck to the apex of the bridge span and then park it facing Savannah. He would then open fire on the checkpoint, at which time, hopefully, the high-pitched sound of the outboard motor would be masked.

Stubby wouldn't be able to see the small boat emerge from behind Wolf Island as it raced across the three-hundred-foot width of the Tennessee River. He only hoped they would get across while he pinned down Junior's men on the bridge. With any luck, he'd draw even more attention, effectively tying up a large part of Junior's forces.

He prayed that he could extract the men off the bridge without getting shot in the back. He had a surprise for the enemy that would buy them some time.

Stubby eased up the bridge with the headlights off and got to just past the center point, where the truck could easily be seen by the men behind the barriers. The standoff began. The interior dome lights

150

wcre disabled and the lack of ambient lighting gave Stubby plenty of cover. While he waited, he got to work on his surprise.

"Hey!" came a shout out of the darkness from the end of the bridge. "State your business!"

Stubby didn't respond. The men opened all four doors of the Wagoneer and then popped open the rear hatch. He shook his head and smiled before giving instructions.

"We'll just open fire," said Stubby. "Slow and steady at first. Be as accurate as you can, but most importantly, stay behind the car doors and be safe. We need to keep them occupied for at least ten minutes. Does everybody understand?"

"*Sí!*"

Stubby opened fire, sending round after round downhill toward the men. Shouts filled the air and a siren began to blare. Stubby hadn't anticipated their ability to warn others although the sound of gunfire probably woke the entire town. He faintly heard the outboard motor start near the riverbank.

Tink—tink—tink!

They began receiving return fire. Several rounds ricocheted off the hood of the Wagoneer. This old warhorse had seen plenty of action in the last month. Today would be its final mission.

All of Stubby's men fired back. Rounds were flying in both directions, but his men remained behind cover. In a firefight between civilians, most rounds were destined to miss their target. Because of the darkness and his lack of a night scope, he didn't expect to find the mark either. But he continued to rain bullets on their heads nonetheless. This barrage had a purpose.

Stubby checked his watch. It had been ten minutes and was time to put an exclamation point on this message to Ma and Junior. He started the truck and checked the rope tied to the door frame. It was secure. Before they left the ranch, Stubby had adjusted the carburetor so that the Wagoneer's big motor would idle at a high rate. When he put it into drive, the Wagoneer eased its way forward, picking up steam as it rolled downhill.

Junior's men focused their attention on the truck, so Stubby instructed his guys to retreat. It was up to him now. Just as the truck reached the bottom of the bridge, the tires were shot out with a *BOOM!*

But the sound of the tires exploding was muted in comparison to the explosion created by Stubby shooting out the small propane tanks and gas cans strapped to the rear of the truck. The massive explosion ignited the fuel tank, causing the rear end of the Wagoneer to lift into the air and stand the truck on its nose momentarily before flipping over onto the top of the concrete barriers protecting Savannah.

Stubby walked backward off the bridge, awaiting the inevitable response from Junior's men. It never came. It was out of his hands now.

CHAPTER 32

8:00 p.m., November 1
Tennessee River
Savannah

Chase rode point with his rifle, studying the east bank of the river. Jake, who was much heavier than Colton and Chase, rode in the last seat and steered the outboard motor. The underpowered fifteen-horsepower engine was not designed for nearly six hundred pounds of men, but it persevered.

Throughout the hail of gunfire on the bridge above them, Colton searched through the channels of the Midland two-way radio. As soon as the siren went off, chatter picked up on channel 1. To the uninformed listener, the gibberish about red and left and various numbers would mean nothing. Colton was able to discern what it meant, however. The words repeated periodically during their ride across the river.

Tiger Tails. Red right. Tiger Tails. Red right. Return. Red right return.

A listener might pick up on the red-right-return reference and associate it with boating parlance. However, Colton immediately took it to mean that the Tiger Resistance should rendezvous at the home on Pickwick Street where he'd first met Coach Joe Carey, his son Beau, and adopted sons Jimbo and Clay Bennett.

The three men arrived at the clearing near where Town Branch emptied into the river. This uninhabited stretch just south of the bridge was used for shore fishing and picnics. Tonight it was completely deserted. As Jake and Chase pulled the boat onto shore and covered it with tree limbs, a massive explosion caused them to hit the ground and scramble for cover.

153

Colton took a deep breath as the history of the Jeep Wagoneer and the Ryman family sped through his mind. Trading the shiny, but worthless Corvette to those good old boys in Arkansas had been one of his greatest deals. The Wagoneer had survived a lot, and now it served its purpose in trying to rescue Alex.

"Let's go," said Jake as he found his way over to the creek. "Stubby said to follow it towards town and take the left fork, which is Town Creek."

"Eventually, it will start to look familiar to me," said Colton.

They worked their way upstream, resisting the need to rest. Several cars sped past them from the south toward the main part of town. Stubby was correct in his prediction. Junior was reinforcing the west flank.

"We have to pick up the pace," said Colton, who was carrying Alex's AR-15 by the handle. They began to jog up a slight incline when they came upon a four-lane road. The three crouched below a stone bridge and listened. "We're near the jail. This is where I escaped before. We're on the right track."

Chase crawled to the end of the stone structure and looked up the road. There were several men gathered in a gravel parking lot. They seemed agitated and one began pounding the hood. Curse words were being thrown around. Chase rejoined the guys.

"Stubby's really pissed them off. They're distracted. We can make a run for it—one by one."

"I'll go first and cover you guys," said Colton.

The crossing was pulled off without a hitch. They ran through the woods with only an occasional barking dog breaking the silence of the night. The gunfire had stopped shortly after the Wagoneer exploded. It appeared Junior's men were regrouping.

The rumble of a loud muffler urged them to pick up the pace. Up ahead, through the sparsely leafed trees, he could see CR128. It was very familiar and he began to run toward the street at a full sprint. Chase stayed with him, but the heavier Jake lagged behind.

"C'mon, Dad," said Chase, who joined Colton behind some brush. "Where to from here?"

"There," said Colton, pointing across the way. "The third house is their meeting place, kinda like a headquarters."

"Isn't that downtown to our left?" asked Jake, who had regained his breath.

"Yeah, they're right under Junior's nose," replied Chase. "Should we run over to the house, or try to raise them on the radio?"

"Are they armed?" asked Jake, breathing heavily.

"Yes."

"Try the radio first," Jake suggested.

Colton thought for a moment. *How could he reach out to Coach Carey without giving away their position or his?* He needed to refresh Carey's memory so he knew it was safe to contact him back. He recounted their conversation and came up with a simple message. He hoped it would resonate with the Tiger Resistance.

"Tiger Tails. Tiger Tails. Ryman plus two. Ryman plus two. Young one sacked. I repeat, young one sacked."

Colton waited. There was no response. *Did I scare Coach Carey away? Did he suspect this was a trick by Junior?* Minutes passed. It was excruciating. Just as Colton was pressing the button on the Midland to give it another try, a cryptic message came across the radio.

Point of entry—where they first met.

Colton replied, "Red right return, point of entry."

He turned to Jake and Chase. "Follow me." They'd accomplished an important second step in the rescue of his daughter.

CHAPTER 33

10:00 p.m., November 1
Hardin County Detention Center
Savannah

Junior flung his hat across the room in a feeble attempt to hit the wall hook adjacent to the portrait of the forty-fourth president of the United States. He refused to hang the new guy's portrait.

The trash can full of beer cans was the next target of his rage. The kick sent it across the room and down the hallway at the feet of several sheepish deputies who were responsible for guarding the westernmost checkpoint entering Savannah.

Junior stood alone in his office, hands on his hips, where he had a clear line of sight to the smoldering mass of steel overturned on the concrete barriers.

"How did you let that truck get so close?" he bellowed at them. "Didn't any of you have the balls to come out from behind your comfy hiding place and take the fight to the enemy? I've been hunting these people day in and day out for a month, and you let 'em get away!"

Junior flung himself into the chair and spun around in a complete three-sixty. He pulled out his shiny, stainless steel .357 revolver and slammed it on the desk.

"Come in here, you cowards!" he shouted to the five men, who shuffled their feet amidst the beer cans in the hallway. "Now!"

Only one of the men had the bravery to speak up, despite the barrel of the .357 pointed at his crotch. "Sheriff, we were taking a barrage of gunfire and they had us pinned down. I'm guessing there

156

were at least seven or eight different attackers. Sheriff, we were easily outnumbered."

Junior leaned back in his chair and assessed the five men in front of him. He'd heard the details of what happened twice before. It was clear that this was a diversion of some kind and that the night was young. The parents of this young girl were coming for her, but they weren't gonna use the bridge. *They must've slipped across the river!*

Junior took a deep breath and mindlessly reached for his gun. The men inched backward and one even made a motion towards his own sidearm. Junior began to twirl it on his metal-top desk with a pencil. The pistol would rotate several times and then stop. Junior would repeat the process in an odd form of Russian roulette.

"Relax, boys. I ain't gonna shoot ya. It's just beyond me how you guys couldn't take out their tires or somethin'. Heck, when they shot up the Fairlane, that teenager in the cell hung out the window and placed a dozen rounds in my car and the tires. All of this while her momma blew past me with a big grin on her face."

"We're really sorry, Junior."

"Okay, listen up," said Junior, pointing to the four men who remained speechless. "I want you to grab some guys and fan out along the riverbank on both sides of the bridge. Put more guys on the south end. Look for boats heading our way or that may be stashed around. If you find anything, let me know immediately. That little trick on the bridge was just for starters. They're not finished yet, and neither are we."

"Yes, sir," one of the men replied as they left Junior's office.

"Pick up those beer cans on the way out!" Junior turned to the last man and tossed the jail cell keys to him. "Get the girl. She needs to spend a *little quality time* with the sheriff."

Junior continued to spin the powerful handgun. He was perfecting his technique as he got at least ten rotations out of each effort. Spin too hard, the weapon might fall off the table and accidentally discharge. Spin too soft, and the gun didn't provide enough entertainment for his unstable mind. Junior was learning to apply just enough pressure to get the desired result.

Alex was forced down the hallway and stumbled into the half-opened door due to the newly installed ankle cuffs around her legs. The Realtree Camo sweatshirt she wore had been loaned to her by Emily. Pieces of grass still hung to the embroidered stitching of the logo. Holes had been torn in the knees of her jeans as a result of the scuffle with Junior's men. Her face, however, was defiant. Junior admired that, although she might change her attitude soon.

"Sit down," he said to Alex.

Alex stood taller and jutted her chin out.

"Please, young lady. Don't make this difficult. Sit down or we'll make you sit."

Alex hesitated before sitting in the chair closest to the desk. Her eyes momentarily darted toward the gun and widened slightly.

Junior leaned over the desk and caught her gaze. "Do you want to go for it? With your hands tied behind your back? How're ya gonna shoot it, with that sharp tongue of yours?"

Alex slouched in the chair.

"Much better," said Junior. He then motioned for his man to leave the room. "Shut the door behind you. Nobody comes in until I say so, got it?"

"Yes, sir."

"You remember me, don't you?" asked Junior.

Alex remained silent.

"Well, I sure remember you. You try not to forget someone who tried to kill you."

Junior stood up and walked toward Alex. He ran his hands through her long hair. She winced and shied away from his touch.

"Yeah, I'll never forget seeing these goldilocks flying out the window of the truck right before you shot at me with that assault rifle. Nope, never forget that."

He continued to circle her, fiddling with her hair. Alex was stoic. She wasn't showing any signs of fear.

"Oh my goodness, did my boys mess up your sweatshirt?" he asked as he brushed the grass off the front of her chest. Alex scowled and slid the chair away from him with her feet.

"And look at this, you've torn holes in your jeans." Junior bent over and slid his fingers inside her pants at the knees. Alex was repulsed and shuddered at his touch.

Junior continued to torment her. "I'm thinkin' we should get you out of these raggedy clothes and into a comfy orange jumpsuit. Whadya think?"

Alex broke eye contact and looked toward the .357 again. Junior grabbed her chin and forced it upward to make eye contact with him.

"Whadya think?" he repeated. "Should we get you undressed and into something more comfortable, or should we talk about what's going on tonight? Your choice, missy. I personally hope that you don't cooperate. I'm feelin' it, you know?" Junior forced his crotch onto Alex's shoulder.

"Fine." She finally spoke, attempting to lean away from his body. "Let's talk."

"Dang it, I was really hopin' you'd stay stubborn." Junior laughed. "Listen, don't get me wrong. I have big plans for you and me. But I'm the romantic type. I believe we should have you appropriately dressed. We'll have a few drinks first, perhaps pop a couple of special pills I keep for, you know, *dates*. Wouldn't that be better?"

Alex barely nodded in response. "What do you want to know?"

"Names, for starters."

Alex hesitated as her eyes darted back and forth. *Thinking.*

"I'm Jennie Dalton, My parents are Josh and Carol."

Junior stared at her for nearly a minute. "You mean Rennie, don't you?"

Eyes darting. Sweat beads were forming on her forehead.

"No, sir, Jennie."

"Well your father, if he really is your father, said your name is Rennie. Rennie! Not Jennie!" Junior slammed his hand on the desk and started to get up.

"No, it's Jennie, I swear it! My dad lied because he was afraid your men might try to hurt me. He didn't want to say my real name."

Alex had regained her composure as she began to play a role. She continued. "I don't mind telling you the truth because I know you won't hurt me. You're the sheriff."

Junior nodded his head and sat down. "Where are your parents?"

"I believe that they're on their way to get me as we speak."

"What makes you think that?" he asked.

"I could hear the gunfire and the explosions. They're probably outside now. Wouldn't it be better to let me go?"

Junior laughed hard and deep from inside his belly. Her statement was genuinely funny. "Yeah, I don't think so. My guess is that they'll walk right in the front door and unselfishly offer themselves in exchange for your safety."

"That only happens on TV shows," said Alex dryly. "The good news is, they know exactly where to look for me. I mean, duh, I'm a prisoner. You're the sheriff. This is a jail, right?"

Junior stood and holstered his weapon. He opened the drawer to his desk and grabbed a set of car keys.

"You've got quite a mouth on you, Jennie, Rennie, or whatever your name is. You've also got a point. Plus, there's someone else that needs to see you live and in the flesh."

Alex stood as well. "Let me guess, you're taking me home to meet your mama. I can hardly wait."

Junior bristled at the girl's smart mouth, but he wanted to take her to Ma before he taught her a lesson or two. He flung the door open and instructed his man to get the cars ready. They were gonna take Alex across town to Cherry Mansion. Her parents would never go looking for her there.

CHAPTER 34

10:00 p.m., November 1
Coach Carey's Home
Savannah

Colton and Coach Carey spent several minutes catching up on the events since the Rymans and the Tiger Resistance parted ways that early morning at the Clifton Bridge over a month ago. There hadn't been any memorable events in Savannah. Junior and Ma continued to exercise dominion and control over the residents as well as the newcomers. Carey and his gang of *disdants*, as Junior referred to them, continued to be a source of aggravation for the Durhams.

When Colton reached out on the radio, Carey already knew what had happened. His boys were spread throughout the town, keeping a watch on Junior's primary locations such as the checkpoints, the Detention Center, and Cherry Mansion. When the Chevelle returned earlier in the day and a girl with long blonde hair was hauled into the jail, Clay Bennett happened to be on watch from the upper level of the abandoned hotel across the street. He had no doubt that the captive was Alex.

Since that time, Carey had positioned the Tigers strategically around the Detention Center to observe the manpower of the deputies posted there as well as devise a strategy for rescuing Alex.

Tap—tap. Pause. *Tap—tap—tap.* Pause. *Tap.*

The conversations stopped as the knock at the front door indicated one of the Tigers had returned. Carey stood to the side of the front door and pointed a handgun directly at the bolt lock. Jimbo Bennett took the other side and slowly eased the door open. A set of hands popped into the doorway first and then the rest of Clay Bennett quickly followed.

"Jeez, guys," he said under his breath. "Junior and them don't know the code."

"We're on high alert, bigger brother," chimed in Clay.

"I am bigger and smarter, doughboy," shot back Jimbo. "Coach, they've moved her. I didn't call it in 'cause we've been keeping chatter down on the radios."

"Which way did they go?" asked Carey.

"I was positioned at the top of the hotel and ran to the Main Street windows. I'm not a hundred percent, but I believe they left for Cherry Mansion."

"How many?" asked Carey.

"Three cars with a couple of men each. Junior took Alex in the back of the land-yacht Caddy with two other guys. Cherry Mansion is the only location north of the bridge and near the waterfront that makes sense."

"Good work, son," said Coach Carey. "Beau! Let's put out an APB on Alex. Try Cherry Mansion first."

Beau cued up his two-way radio. "Tiger Tails. Tiger Tails. Blue left. Blue left. I-formation. I-formation. On two-six-five. Hut-hut. Hut."

"Wow," said Jake. "What did all of that mean?"

Beau adjusted the squelch on his radio and then explained, "Blue left, of course, means the northwest quadrant of Savannah. I-formation refers to keeping watch over a particular location. Two-six-five is the street number and code for Cherry Mansion."

"What about the hut-hut-hut?" asked Chase.

"I'm the team quarterback," replied Beau. "That means the play is in motion and they need to get on it now. We should get a response quickly."

The group stood around the kitchen table, nervously waiting for a response. After several minutes a faint voice came across the radio.

The member of the Tiger Resistance whispered, "Tiger Tails. First down."

"She's there," said Coach Carey. "Apparently they've just arrived. Please, everybody grab a chair."

The three adults and four young men exchanged ideas on how to rescue Alex unharmed. The first debate revolved around why Junior would remove such a valuable asset from the most secure facility in town. Some voices in the group were of the opinion that he didn't know Alex's true identity, but Colton disagreed. The blown-up Wagoneer would give that away.

Others in the group thought they were laying a trap for Colton and Madison. Junior was smart enough to know that the jail was impenetrable. They needed to lead her to a location that appeared, at least on the surface, accessible. Cherry Mansion made sense.

There was a regular armed contingent protecting Ma and Bill Cherry. Plus, one of the girls that the Tiger Resistance had rescued from the forced brothels established by Junior told stories of girls being held in the basement of the mansion for the personal benefit of Junior and Cherry.

"You've got to be kidding me," said Jake. "What's wrong with these people?"

"They were power hungry before the collapse and were forced to restrain themselves because of the law," said Carey. "Now, they openly defy the laws of man and the laws of decency."

"This is why we have to save Alex, Dad," said Beau. "I mean, Junior will keep her there, you know, for himself."

Colton shuddered and buried his face in his hands. Jake, who still held Chase responsible for Alex's abduction, stared at his son until he looked away in regret. Colton took a deep breath and turned the conversation toward Cherry Mansion.

"What do you know about the place?" he asked.

"Well, the good news is that all of us have been there," replied Carey.

"Me too," added Jake. "It's been years, but I remember the layout."

"That's good," Coach continued. "She's likely being held in the basement, Junior's home on the property, or one of the outbuildings.

We have at least two Tigers watching the building at all times. They'll be able to bring us up to speed when we get there."

"Won't they be watching for us?" asked Jake.

"Probably," replied Coach Carey. "We'll set up several diversions. They'll assume that you folks are coming across the river, Colton. We'll give them what they want. We've been saving several old trolling boats for something like this."

"Plus, we've got a friend on the other side," said Beau. "He's a hunter with some kind of high-powered rifle. It's a fifty-caliber or something."

"That sounds more like a cannon," joked Colton. "Is he tapped into your network?"

"He is," replied Carey. "His place sits up on one of the mounds at the top of Lemert Road. We'll send him instructions. When this all goes down, calling plays and using code will be out the window. There can be no misunderstandings of the plan."

"That's a long way to fire a rifle," said Chase.

"He claims it will send a bullet a mile. I reckon we'll find out."

CHAPTER 35

11:40 p.m., November 1
Savannah

It would've been suicide to drive the old Chevy too close to Cherry Mansion. On a normal day, Junior's men closed off the perimeter access to the house, which included a roadblock where Riverside Drive intersected with Main Street near the mansion's grounds. Carey drove the group to a safe house several blocks away, where they met up with several members of the Tiger Resistance.

Over the two months following the collapse of the grid, the Tigers had become adept at moving on foot through both wooded and subdivision environments. Over time, they'd become comfortable with both types of surroundings as they learned to use their senses like animals do. Sounds, smells, and movement all impacted their ability to survive as they had been on the run, hiding from Junior's men from the moment they realized they'd be enslaved to work in the quarry.

The Tigers began living in the shadows of Savannah, where dogs became accustomed to their activities. Neighbors began to appreciate the resistance that these young men put up against Junior. Over time, the *disdants*—the mispronounced word for dissidents, as Junior referred to anyone who opposed him—became well known throughout the community.

The Tiger Resistance activities were never disclosed to civilians until they became widely known. The boys adopted a solemn oath to tell no one about their resistance operations. When questioned following the assistance given to the Rymans, the members of the resistance claimed ignorance. They would do the same after this night was done.

The boys had become masters of urban concealment and camouflage. They learned to dress according to their surroundings in both the daytime and night. They moved through the shadows and learned to hide their silhouettes. They effectively disguised their shapes by using foliage, rags, and color variations to break up their outlines.

Lastly, and most important for tonight's operation, they learned to move without drawing attention to themselves. The teams would remain spread apart. They avoided any source of light that would cast a shadow that increased the likelihood that their movement would be detected.

The Tiger Resistance moved like ghosts through a haunted cemetery, unafraid and undetected. These young men had learned that the evil of the living was far more menacing than the fear of the dead.

Coach Carey's team was in place. They remained a hundred yards away from Junior's men, who'd blocked the driveway entrance to Cherry Mansion with two of the cars from his earlier motorcade. Junior's car was parked in front of his separate, bungalow home located on the east side of the Cherry Mansion estate.

Candles were flickering in the upper windows of Cherry Mansion, but the first floor was dark. From recollection, the master suite in the nearly two-hundred-year-old home was located on the upper level as well as a butler's quarters. Downstairs, two guest rooms, one of which was occupied by the owner of the home, Bill Cherry, and the primary living quarters consisting of parlors, dining rooms, and the kitchen remained dark at this late hour.

"Our watchman tells me that Junior took Alex inside," started Coach Carey. "Moments later, candlelight appeared in the upper windows. There is a sitting area at the top of the stairs and Ma's bedroom. My guess is that Junior was anxious to show off his notorious prisoner."

Colton looked down and shook his head. His daughter was being paraded around like someone's prized heifer. Within minutes, she'd either become Junior's latest conquest, her childhood being ripped from her, or Colton would have her in his arms. Her life hinged upon the elaborate plan of these strangers who'd saved them once before and relished the opportunity to do it again.

"I see shadows moving behind the sheers," said Jake. "Look, the guard at the side door turned on his flashlight to light up the entrance. Someone is coming out."

Junior had a firm grip on Alex's arm as he dragged her through the door frame and onto the porch. He was being rough with her, which raised Colton's ire.

"I'm gonna kill that guy!" he whispered.

"Let's watch how this plays out," said Coach Carey. He was calm under pressure. They listened as Junior's voice carried across the lawn and into the neighboring yard where Carey, Colton, Jake and Chase crouched behind a one-hundred-and-fifty-year-old stone wall.

"You stupid child!" shouted Junior at Alex. "You insulted my mother. If you weren't valuable trade bait, I'd give you to the boys and let them pass you around."

Colton started to jump the fence, but Jake pulled him down. "Hold up, buddy."

The partly cloudy skies allowed enough moonlight for the men to be seen in their tan uniforms and white shirts. They clearly stood out against the graying clapboard walls of the mansion.

"Jessie," shouted Junior to one of the men guarding the entrance to his residence, "come get this girl for me. I need to talk to Ma about tomorrow."

A man darted across the lawn in between the hedgerows and centuries-old oak trees. He was dressed in darker clothes and was difficult to see.

He bounded up the porch steps of Cherry Mansion as Junior shoved Alex in his direction. She stumbled over her ankle cuffs and fell toward the deck, but one of the men caught her.

"Get your hands off me!" shouted Alex.

"Ah, sorry, ma'am. Did I grab too much? Would you rather I let you fall down?"

With that statement, he pushed her back towards the other guard. Alex screamed as the two men tossed her back and forth like a rag doll.

"Look here, don't damage the merchandise." Junior laughed. "Take her to my house. I'll be there in a minute. I gotta finish this conversation upstairs first."

Junior turned and moved back inside the dark first floor of the antebellum home. The two men each grabbed one of Alex's arms and began to drag her across the lawn.

"I can take them out," whispered Chase. "I've got 'em in my sights."

"No, son. It's too risky. You might hit Alex. We stick to the plan."

Coach Carey turned to Colton. "Last chance. We can try to negotiate, but I know these people. They are depraved human beings and they will not deal fairly. We have the element of surprise, and with Alex isolated, the odds just shifted in our favor."

Colton looked to Jake, who nodded once. Colton's love of Alex was like nothing else in the world. There were no laws or levels of pity that could protect those who would do her harm. He would destroy the Durhams and all that stood with them without remorse for the fear they'd placed in his daughter on this night. There would be no mercy.

"Let's roll," he said with conviction.

Coach Carey nodded. "Tiger Tails. Tiger Tails," he said before pausing. "KICKOFF!"

CHAPTER 36

Midnight, November 1
Cherry Mansion
Savannah

KICKOFF!

During an NFL football game, a fan watches a period of four to six seconds of quickly moving interactions between twenty-two men. There are violent collisions as the opponents dial in on their adversary. Every player has a specific, primary assignment in addition to multiple reactive duties based upon conditions on the field. If a defense is slow to react, the offense can move the ball for big gains. If the offense misses a key element of a play, like a block, or if the play is slow in developing, a defense will likely stop them or throw the ball carrier for a loss.

When interviewing NFL players, the one consistent comment they make is the difference in the speed of the game at their level of play compared to college football. The speed of the athletes is incredible and so much can happen in just four to six seconds.

A military-style assault on a defensive position is similar. The attacker, which is on offense, has a plan to circumvent the enemies' defenses to achieve an objective. Those defending a position must rely upon preplanning in order to anticipate an attacker's possible tactic. If the defender has planned well in advance, they can repel their attacker. However, like in football, if the defense is slow to react or fails to execute a key duty in performing their role, the attacker can make great gains.

Cherry Mansion was surrounded, but not by an overwhelming force. Coach Carey and the Tiger Resistance didn't have many weapons and they certainly were not as powerful as those carried by the Hardin County deputies within Junior's charge.

However, just like an onside kick could catch the receiving team off guard during a kickoff, a well-executed plan involving trickery and misdirection could confuse an overwhelming force into making mistakes.

"This way!" shouted a man on the porch of the mansion.

"No, this way!" responded one of the men in the yard.

The scene was reminiscent of a bunch of seven-year-olds chasing a tennis ball back and forth over the net during a match. The men within the protective gates of Cherry Mansion would race toward the lake only to turn around and run towards town. They'd dart south toward the bridge checkpoint and then run back toward the house.

The chaos was visible to Chase, who briefly allowed himself a chuckle while remaining keenly focused on the task at hand—getting Alex back safely. He followed the men dragging her towards Junior's house through his scope. It was dark, but the ambient light provided him a pretty good look at the enemy.

After *KICKOFF* was announced over the Tiger Resistance channel 1, which was designated by that day's player, Beau Carey, several events disrupted Savannah.

Two of the disabled police cruisers operated by the local police exploded near the entrance to the Sheriff's Department. This immediately drew a reaction from Junior's men, who assumed the rescue attempt was coming at the Detention Center.

Round after round from high-powered hunting rifles rained down upon the checkpoint at the bridge. More men were redirected to shore up the barrier's defense under the assumption that a frontal attack using vehicles was imminent.

On the other side of Cherry Mansion, the Hickory Pit Restaurant erupted into flames after several Molotov cocktails were hurled through its windows. A natural gas pipe feeding the restaurant's kitchen broke, creating an explosion that added to the bedlam.

The distraction that caused Junior's small contingent of protectors at Cherry Mansion the most consternation was the repeated barrage of fifty-caliber bullets that continuously slammed into the front of Cherry Mansion. From three-quarters of a mile away, a man sat at a table and quietly chambered round after round, took aim at the home he could barely see through his scope, and fired. Plate-glass windows shattered and the roof was pelted with the slugs.

It was the high-pitched sound of the approaching boats that cemented the diversion. Finally choosing a side of the property to defend, Junior's men raced down the hill to intercept the watercraft. The boats sped toward them as the deputies opened fire, but the trolling boats advanced forward undeterred. Bullets riddled the small aluminum flat-bottom boats, causing them to rock slightly on the water. They stayed on course—harmlessly puttering toward the eastern banks of the river in front of Cherry Mansion.

Like a football play, the havoc lasted four to six seconds. Also, like in a football game, there were occasions when an over exuberant player took one additional second or two after the whistle blew and delivered a late hit, earning his team a fifteen-yard penalty. On the field of battle, a mistake like this could be deadly.

Chase had never taken his eyes off the prize. His guilt was overwhelming. He realized he'd fallen for Alex and now his mission in life was to get her away from Junior and safely back to Shiloh Ranch. He wasn't going to let them take her away again.

Shouts came from his left as men raced from Riverside Drive toward the house. His job, along with his dad and Colton, were to pick off anyone who attempted to provide reinforcements. Jake and Colton opened fire on them. Chase remained focused on Alex and her captors.

The men dragged Alex through some landscaped beds and she fell to the ground. They brusquely hoisted her up and continued. Hedges continued to obstruct Chase's view, but he was sure he could get a clean shot.

Chase took a deep breath and moved his finger onto the trigger of his rifle. He steadied his aim and blocked out the shouts coming from all around him. He got Alex into this mess and he would get her out of it. *It was time.*

He squeezed the trigger.

CHAPTER 37

Midnight, November 1
Cherry Mansion
Savannah

Ma Durham stood defiantly in the upstairs parlor of Cherry Mansion. She loved this room, as it provided her views of the river and the town, which she proudly controlled with an iron fist. As the glass shattered at her feet and the plaster from the ceiling fell on her graying hair, anger built up inside her.

Once again, her life was disrupted by one of those young hussies. Junior had brought that girl into Cherry Mansion, her place of refuge, to parade the girl like she was some exotic animal captured on an African safari. She indulged him while he went on this hunt for the family of three that had embarrassed him and his men. Dragging her inside Cherry Mansion in the middle of the night was unforgivable.

"Ma, you need to take cover!" screamed Junior through the dark. He'd run into all of the upper level rooms and doused the candles. Only an eerie fog of candlelight smoke could be seen through the moonlight finding its way through the sheers.

CRASH!

A bullet found its way through a downstairs window and shattered the mirror in the dining room, which had hung there since its predecessor was broken during the Battle of Shiloh. Ma flinched. Loud noises had startled her since the days when her now deceased husband Leroy would come home drunk and break things— including her and the boys.

Ma ignored the motorboats as they approached from the river. She was mesmerized by the scene in her yard. The girl was struggling to get away. Ma admired her tenacity as she attempted to break free from a certain fate.

She contemplated why Junior chose this one to take back to his house. He could have locked her up in the basement cells of Cherry Mansion with the others. No, he considered her special. Perhaps because she had eluded him before, or maybe it was because she presented a challenge. This young woman was strong-willed, and it could be that she represented everything Junior sought in a mate, other than his typical testosterone-fueled intentions.

Junior reached for his mother's arm in an attempt to pull her to safety and it briefly broke Ma out of her trance. She relented and they turned toward the stairs. The effort might have saved her life.

CRACK! TING! HISS!

CRACK!

The entire sequence took a few seconds. The first shot missed its mark and punctured a hole in the five-hundred-gallon propane cylinder adjacent to Junior's house. The second also missed but struck two gas cans sitting near to the ruptured propane tank, spilling the flammable liquid underneath the tanks.

CRACK—CRACK—CRACK!

A staccato burst came from one of Junior's men.

Ma and Junior instinctively spun to view the shoot-out. In the darkness, a muzzle flash was seen to their left at the low-lying slave fence. It was the final shot, which illuminated the night sky with a fireball.

TING! BOOM!

The propane tank exploded and both ends were thrown hundreds of feet in opposite directions. The last gunshot had nicked metal, setting off a spark and a chain reaction between the propane-oxygen-gasoline mix.

Junior's home was doused in flames and the old wooden structure ignited. The centuries-old magnolia trees surrounding the home were incinerated. Flames and dark smoke danced a hundred feet into the sky.

The concussive effect of the explosion shattered the upper

windows of Cherry Mansion, and shards of glass pelted Ma as she curled up in a ball on the floor. Junior scrambled to help her and yelped as pieces of glass cut into his hands.

Ma gained her strength to view the carnage. As the sky was lit up in hues of orange and yellow, a figure emerged from the direction of the bridge—a man wearing a dark sweatshirt with the number 1 on the back. He ran past burning pieces of wood and dodged under collapsing tree branches. There was no hesitation. No fear. He was on a mission.

Burgundy. It was Hardin County Tigers burgundy. *Number 1.* Gunfire continued to fill the night air from all directions. The young man was undeterred. He'd reached his destination. Briefly, he crouched down and lifted up a lifeless body.

Number 1 began running towards the neighborhoods to Ma's left. He was fired upon but escaped unscathed with the blonde hair of the young woman flowing over his shoulder.

Ma stared into the fire. The roof of Junior's home collapsed to the ground, causing a rush of sparks and flames to gush out in all directions. Despite the intense heat created by the burning home and the surrounding vegetation, a chill came over her body. Ma unconsciously balled up her fists, unaware that a figure had joined her in the window. It wasn't Junior.

It was an aberration — a ghost who had been in a similar position one hundred fifty years before. The hissing sounds coming from the flames provided a voice for Union Major General William Wallace, who whispered in Ma's ear.

Fight fire with fire. Fight fire with fire.

Ma gritted her teeth and set her jaw. She mumbled the words but only loud enough for General Wallace to hear.

"When you poke the hornets' nest, ya better make dang sure you kill 'em all. If you don't, you're gonna suffer their wrath."

Thanks for reading!

The saga continues in …
HORNET'S NEST
Book five of The Blackout Series

SIGN UP to Bobby Akart's mailing list: eepurl.com/bYqq3L to receive special offers, bonus content, and you'll be the first to receive news about new releases in The Blackout Series, The Boston Brahmin Series and the Prepping for Tomorrow series—which includes nine Amazon #1 Bestsellers in 33 different genres. Visit Bobby Akart's website for informative blog entries on preparedness, writing, and his latest contribution to the American Preppers Network.

www.BobbyAkart.com

And before you go …

THANK YOU FOR READING SHILOH RANCH!

If you enjoyed it, I'd be grateful if you'd take a moment to write a short review (just a few words are needed) and post it on Amazon. Amazon uses complicated algorithms to determine what books are recommended to readers. Sales are, of course, a factor, but so are the number of reviews my books get. By taking a few seconds to leave a review, you help me out, and also help new readers learn about my work.

APPENDIX A

Please learn from, and enjoy, a sneak peek of Bobby Akart's best-selling analysis on the threats we face from an EMP: Electromagnetic Pulse, a part of **The Prepping for Tomorrow Series** by Bobby Akart.

  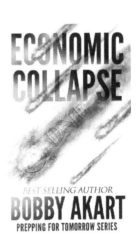

PART FIVE
WHO IS RINGING THE CLARION BELL?

COMMISSION TO ASSESS THE THREAT TO THE UNITED STATES
FROM ELECTROMAGNETIC PULSE (EMP) ATTACK

Chapter Ten
Respected Advocates

Former Speaker of the House Newt Gingrich

Newt Gingrich is well-known as the architect of the "Contract with America" that led the Republican Party to victory in 1994 by capturing the majority in the U.S. House of Representatives for the first time in forty years. After he was elected Speaker, he disrupted the status quo by moving power out of Washington and back to the American people. Under his leadership, Congress passed welfare reform, the first balanced budget in a generation, and the first tax cut in sixteen years. In addition, the Congress restored funding to strengthen defense and intelligence capabilities, an action later lauded by the bipartisan 9/11 Commission.

Speaker Gingrich has warned the world of his worst nightmare: an electromagnetic pulse. "This could be the kind of catastrophe that ends civilization — and that's not an exaggeration," Gingrich recently said, addressing members of the Electromagnetic Pulse Caucus. The prevailing theory of Speaker Gingrich is that a Russian-made medium-range nuke in the hands of terrorists out on a barge or freighter off the eastern seaboard or in the Gulf of Mexico could do this sort of damage.

Congressman Trent Franks

Congressman Trent Franks is a conservative, Reagan Republican, and is currently serving his seventh term in the United States Congress. Congressman Franks serves on the House Judiciary Committee and is a member of the House Armed Services Committee, serving as the Vice-Chair of the Subcommittee on Emerging Threats and Capabilities and a member of the Strategic Forces subcommittee.

In his capacity as co-chair of both the Missile Defense and the Electromagnetic Pulse Caucuses, he leads efforts to reduce national security vulnerabilities in our electric energy grids and to increase America's missile defense capability against all enemy missile threats including those potentially launched by jihadists seeking to bring nuclear terrorism to America. Congressman Franks firmly believes the foremost responsibility of our federal government is to provide for our nation's common defense.

Former Congressman Roscoe Bartlett

Former Congressman Roscoe Bartlett was a U.S. Representative from Maryland's 6th congressional district, serving from 1993 to 2013. He is a member of the Republican Party and was a member of the Tea Party Caucus. At the end of his tenure in Congress, Bartlett was the second-oldest serving member of the House of Representatives.

In 1995 Bartlett, who is a scientist, engineer, and inventor with 20 patents, was one of the few members of Congress who understood the threat from EMPs. Between 1995 and 1999, Bartlett held a series of congressional hearings on the EMP threat, including the first unclassified hearings ever held on this subject. The hearings proved that in the wake of the collapse of the Soviet Union, America's defense and intelligence communities stopped paying attention to EMP threats.

In the late '90s, during the U.S.-backed and NATO-led bombing campaign of Serbia, Russians leaders who were backing Serbia, threw an EMP threat in the face of the U.S. congressional delegation. Vladimir Lukin, the former ambassador to the United States, warned that if Russia wanted to hurt the U.S. in retaliation for NATO's bombing of Yugoslavia, Russia could fire a submarine-launched ballistic missile, and detonate a single nuclear warhead at high altitude over the Midwest. He added that if one missile wouldn't do the job, the Russians had more on hand.

Bartlett warned Congress that the resulting electromagnetic pulse would massively disrupt communications and computer systems, effectively shutting down the U.S economy. After hearing this EMP threat, then Congressman Bartlett introduced a bill signed into law by President George W. Bush that established the Congressional EMP Commission in 2001. When the Democrats gained control of Congress in 2006, they re-authorized the EMP Commission that continued its work until 2008. The Congressional EMP Commission report, an Executive Summary of which is found in Exhibit C, warned that terrorists, rogue states, and nations like China and Russia could make a catastrophic EMP attack on the United States.

James Woolsey, Former Director of the Central Intelligence Agency

Mr. Woolsey previously served in the U.S. Government on five different occasions, where he held Presidential appointments in two Republican and two Democratic administrations—most recently (1993-95) as Director of Central Intelligence. During his 12 years of government service, in addition to heading the CIA and the Intelligence Community, Mr. Woolsey was: Ambassador to the Negotiation on Conventional Armed Forces in Europe (CFE), Vienna, 1989–1991; Under Secretary of the Navy, 1977–1979; and General Counsel to the U.S. Senate Committee on Armed Services, 1970–1973. He was also appointed by the President to serve on a part-time basis in Geneva, Switzerland, 1983–1986, as Delegate at Large to the U.S.–Soviet Strategic Arms Reduction Talks (START) and Nuclear and Space Arms Talks (NST). As an officer in the U.S. Army, he was an adviser on the U.S. Delegation to the Strategic Arms Limitation Talks (SALT I), Helsinki and Vienna, 1969–1970.

Mr. Woolsey currently chairs the Strategic Advisory Group of the Washington, D.C. private equity fund, Paladin Capital Group, chairs the Advisory Board of the Opportunities Development Group, and he is Of Counsel to the Washington, D.C. office of the Boston-based law firm, Goodwin Procter. In the above capacities, he specializes in a range of alternative energy and security issues, focusing on the threat we face as a nation from an EMP.

Dr. Peter Vincent Pry

Perhaps there is no greater advocate of protecting our nation from the devastating impact of an EMP, than Dr. Peter Vincent Pry.

From the Task Force on National and Homeland Security website:

"Dr. Pry is Executive Director of the Task Force on National and Homeland Security and Director of the U.S. Nuclear Strategy Forum, both Congressional Advisory Boards, and served on the Congressional EMP Commission, the Congressional Strategic Posture Commission, the House Armed Services Committee, and the CIA.

The Task Force on National and Homeland Security is a privately-funded and operated body with a mandate to educate and help protect the United States from the existential threat posed by a natural or manmade electromagnetic pulse (EMP) catastrophe and other threats vital to U.S. national and homeland security that imperil the survival of the American people. A natural EMP from a great geomagnetic storm, a rare but inevitable threat that many scientists fear is overdue and may soon recur, perhaps as soon as the next solar maximum, could collapse electric grids worldwide and all the critical infrastructures – communications, transportation, banking and finance, food and water – that sustain modern civilization and the lives of millions. A nuclear EMP attack would inflict a similar catastrophe upon the U.S., slowly killing about two-thirds of the national population, 200 million Americans or more dead within one year, from starvation, disease, and societal collapse. Dr. Pry believes such an attack could be executed by both state and non-state actors, in the latter case through the launch of a nuclear-capable ballistic missile from a freighter or other platform off the coast of our country."

Frank Gaffney, Center for Security Policy

From the Center for Security Policy website:

"Frank Gaffney formerly acted as the Assistant Secretary of Defense for International Security Policy during the Reagan Administration, following four years of service as the Deputy Assistant Secretary of Defense for Nuclear Forces and Arms Control Policy. Previously, he was a professional staff member on the Senate Armed Services Committee under the chairmanship of the late Senator John Tower, and a national security legislative aide to the late Senator Henry M. Jackson.

For twenty-five years, the Center for Security Policy has pioneered the organization, management and direction of public policy coalitions to promote U.S. national security. Even more importantly, the Center's mission has been to secure the adoption of the products of such efforts by skillfully enlisting support from executive branch officials, key legislators, other public policy organizations, opinion-shapers in the media and the public at large.

The philosophy of "Peace through Strength" is not a slogan for military might but a belief that America's national power must be preserved and properly used for it holds a unique global role in maintaining peace and stability.

The process the Center has repeatedly demonstrated is the unique ability that makes the Center the "Special Forces in the War of Ideas": forging teams to get things done that would otherwise be impossible for a small and relatively low-budget organization. In this way, we are able to offer maximum "bang for the buck" for the donors who make our work possible. This approach has enabled the Center to have an outsized impact."

F. Michael Maloof, Author, and former senior security policy analyst to the Secretary of Defense

F. Michael Maloof, a former senior security policy analyst in the Office of the Secretary of Defense, has almost 30 years of federal service in the U.S. Defense Department and as a specialized trainer for border guards and Special Forces in select countries of the Caucasus and Central Asia.

While with the Department of Defense, Maloof was the Director of Technology Security Operations as head of a 10-person team involved in halting the diversion of militarily critical technologies to countries of national security and proliferation concern and those involved in sponsoring terrorism. His office was the liaison to the intelligence and enforcement community within the Office of the Secretary of Defense in halting diversions and using cases that developed from them as early warnings to decision-makers of potential policy issues.

Following the September 11, 2001, terrorist attack on the United States, Maloof was detailed back to report directly to the Under Secretary of Defense for Policy to prepare an analysis of worldwide terrorist networks, determine their linkages worldwide and their relationship to state sponsors. Before his career at the Defense Department, Maloof was a legislative assistant to various U.S. Senators specializing in national security and international affairs.

George Noory, media icon and advocate of EMP preparedness

George Noory, the host of the nationally syndicated program, Coast to Coast AM, says if he weren't a national radio talk show host, he'd be in politics. Heard by millions of listeners, Coast To Coast AM airs on I Heart Radio, SiriusXM Satellite, and over six hundred radio stations worldwide.

In 2014, Noory announced a campaign to protect and insulate the U.S. power grid against an EMP event or attack via nuclear weapons, ballistic missiles, and solar flares, all of which could endanger the lives of millions of Americans. The threat of an electromagnetic pulse event or attack on the U.S. has prompted Noory, host of "Coast to Coast AM," the most-listened-to overnight radio program in North America, to launch a campaign to prepare a defense.

"I implore all individual states, the President and members of Congress to immediately develop a plan to protect our power grid," said Noory. "The preservation of our great nation and the lives of its people are critical." The goal is to protect and insulate the U.S. power grid against an EMP event or attack from a solar flare, nuclear weapon or ballistic missile, all of which could endanger the lives of millions of Americans, according to Noory.

Chapter Eleven
The EMP Commission

The EMP Commission

Through the warnings of Representatives Franks and Bartlett, Congress finally began to recognize the potential threat of this powerful nuclear phenomenon. Congress established the EMP Commission under the National Defense Authorization Act of 2001 in order to provide an independent assessment of this threat against the United States. The authorizing provision directed that the EMP Commission investigate and report to Congress its findings and recommendations for the United States concerning four aspects of the EMP threat:

The duties of the EMP Commission, among other things, included assessing the following:

1. The nature and magnitude of potential high-altitude EMP threats to the United States from all potentially hostile states or non-state actors that have or could acquire nuclear weapons and ballistic missiles enabling them to perform a high-altitude EMP attack against the United States within the next 15 years

2. The vulnerability of United States military and especially civilian systems to an EMP attack, giving special attention to vulnerability of the civilian infrastructure as a matter of emergency preparedness

3. The capability of the United States to repair and recover from damage inflicted on United States military and civilian systems by an EMP attack

4. The feasibility and cost of hardening select military and civilian systems against EMP attack.

The Commission is charged with identifying any steps it believes should be taken by the United States, to better protect its military and civilian systems from EMP attack.

Multiple reports and briefings associated with this effort were produced by the EMP Commission including the often cited Critical National Infrastructures Report.

According to the Commission report, protecting the United States against the evolving EMP threat will require a mix of active defenses, passive defenses, and policy changes. Specifically, the United States should:

- Develop a clear policy about how it would respond to an EMP attack. An adversary may be emboldened to use EMP because the U.S. has no clear retaliation policy. As the commission's report makes clear, an EMP attack could devastate both civilian and military assets without harming humans--in the short term. An adversary could therefore, calculate that the United States would respond less severely to an EMP strike than it would to a more traditional attack that results in physical destruction and casualties. That makes EMP very attractive. It could carry decreased risk but promise great reward. By itself, a policy guaranteeing significant retaliation may not deter all hostile groups from using EMP, but it may deter some. Better yet, a policy to retaliate combined with other actions--such as installing active defenses, increased passive defenses, and assuring military survivability--would decrease the likelihood of an EMP attack against the United States because such measures would make a strike less likely to succeed. If it did succeed, the consequences for the United States would be minimal. Thus, the value of an

EMP strike would be significantly reduced, but the risk of launching an attack would be greatly increased because the U.S. would not only have a policy to retaliate, but also the capability.

- Protect the vital nodes of America's power grid and telecommunications systems. Much of America's power grid and telecommunications systems is vulnerable to EMP attack. In the near term, hardening America's entire critical infrastructure is not feasible. However, protecting those elements of U.S. infrastructure that would be essential to any post-EMP recovery (e.g., large turbines, generators, high-voltage transformers, and electronic telecommunications switching systems) is possible. These major nodes are not only critical to the nation's power-grid and telecommunications capability, but would be extremely difficult and timeconsuming to rebuild or repair. Protecting these critical infrastructure nodes may be expensive in the near term, but it could save the nation significantly in both money and lives in the future.

- Conduct a national vulnerability assessment and prepare a national recovery plan. Although protecting the nation's entire electronic and telecommunications systems against EMP strike is unreasonable, protecting some of those assets is possible. The Department of Homeland Security (DHS) should work with the private sector to identify which parts of the nation's power grid and telecommunications infrastructure are critical to preserving the nation's core capabilities. These assets would also be the most essential to recovery efforts in a post-EMP environment. By protecting these nodes, the United States could significantly reduce the time needed to recover from an attack. Additionally, DHS should develop a contingency plan for recovery from an EMP attack that would minimize confusion.

- Retrofit portions of the U.S. armed forces to ensure EMP survivability. The United States' military must end its nearly complete vulnerability to an EMP strike. This glaring hole in U.S. defenses is a liability that America's adversaries will surely exploit if it is not corrected. As with civilian infrastructure, hardening

America's entire military apparatus against EMP is prohibitively expensive. However, the nation should invest the resources to retrofit enough of the military's land, sea, and air assets to guarantee any potential adversary that the U.S. will be able to respond comprehensively to any kind of attack. Hardening military equipment against EMP costs approximately 10 percent of the original cost of the equipment. While this is high, it is a necessary expense given the risk.

- Begin building military systems that are engineered with EMP protections. Although retrofitting against EMP is extremely expensive, engineering EMP resistance into a system from the beginning adds only about 1 percent to the system cost. Given that so much of military equipment is already old and that force transformation will result in many new systems and platforms, now is an opportune time to begin dealing with this problem. In addition to saving money by incorporating EMP resistance into new systems instead of retrofitting existing equipment, America's transformed military will increasingly rely on many sophisticated electronic networks and systems. A successful EMP strike against U.S. forces that disrupted or destroyed these systems would effectively turn America's technological advantage into a distinct liability.

- Deploy ballistic missile defense. The surest way to protect the United States from a high-altitude EMP is by deploying a ballistic missile defense system that can intercept and destroy a warhead before it could be detonated above the U.S. This would prevent an EMP attack and eliminate any potential harm to U.S. systems, and it could even deter rogue leaders from considering the use of EMP. Deploying a missile defense architecture that can intercept a missile early in flight (during the ascent phase) would render rogue missiles ineffective, thereby undermining the rationale to use them. Moreover, because protecting America's entire civilian electronic infrastructure is not fiscally feasible and because a ballistic missile is the most likely delivery vehicle for an EMP attack, the most prudent method to protect America is a missile defense system that could destroy a ballistic missile before it reaches U.S. airspace.

As the EMP Commission reported, the threat of an EMP attack on America is real and one for which the United States is vulnerable. While the world focused on weapons of mass destruction and ballistic missiles, the scientists and policy analysts that made up the EMP Commission believed it was imperative that an EMP attack must be considered with equal weight. The profound impact that an EMP attack would have on America—a developed, modern, electronically oriented country, has forced other similarly situated nations to reassess their protection against such attack.

Looking toward the future, America should consider its options for protecting its infrastructure against such a debilitating attack. Those options are limited but include deploying an effective missile defense system and hardening electronic systems against EMP. As the commission indicated, the implications of an EMP attack need to be assessed further with greater severity and inevitability as America considers possible protective actions against this threat.

The EMP Commission was reestablished via the National Defense Authorization Act for Fiscal Year 2016, to continue its efforts to monitor, investigate, make recommendations, and report to Congress on the evolving threat to the United States from a high-altitude electromagnetic pulse attack.

Chapter Twelve
United States Policy Stance

Protecting the homeland means more than our borders

The Congressional EMP Commission spent eight years developing a plan to protect all infrastructures from EMP – a plan that would also mitigate threats from cyber-attack, sabotage, and natural disasters. The Commission estimated in 2008 it would cost $2 billion to harden the grid's critical nodes (i.e., roughly 2,000 large and medium-sized transformers and their associated SCADA systems, etc.) The remainder of the proposed plan could have been implemented within five years, at a cost of $20 billion.

Those sums are modest when compared with the unimaginably high costs associated with trying to recover from a HEMP attack. To put this in perspective had Washington adopted the Commission's plan, it would have been completed at the time of this book's release. By comparison, $20 billion, the high estimate of the Commission's suggested plan, is equal to seventeen days of interest on our national debt. The cost, however, has been an excuse for inaction.

In 2008, the bipartisan Electromagnetic Pulse Commission testified before Congress that U.S. society is not structured, nor does it have the means, to provide for the needs of three hundred million Americans without electricity.

- The current strategy for recovery from a failure of the electric grid leaves us ill-prepared to respond effectively to a manmade or naturally occurring EMP event that would potentially result in damage to vast numbers of components nearly simultaneously on an unprecedented geographic scale;

- Should the electrical power system be lost for any substantial period, the consequences are likely to be catastrophic to society, including potential casualties of more than ninety percent of the population, according to the Chairman of the EMP Commission;

- Adverse impacts on the electric infrastructure are potentially catastrophic in an EMP event, unless practical steps are taken to provide protection for critical elements of the electric system.

Finally, most experts predict that the occurrence of severe geomagnetic storms is inevitable; it is only a matter of when.

In 2015, the Senate Homeland Security and Governmental Affairs Committee debated a bill to protect our critical infrastructure as the power industry urged lawmakers to keep the complexity of the electric grid in mind as part of the legislation. The bill, introduced by Sen. Ron Johnson, R-Wis., the committee Chairman, called for the federal government to develop a strategy to protect critical infrastructure from geomagnetic disturbances caused by solar storms, and electromagnetic pulses, which are generated by nuclear and non-nuclear devices.

The bill included an amendment by Johnson, acting under lobbyist pressure, which addressed electric cooperative industry concerns. Lobbyists argued that combining electromagnetic pulse and geomagnetic disturbance threats in planning, preparing or mitigating efforts were improper. They suggested pulling the threats apart and addressing them separately.

The current legislation in the House combines the two types of threats. According to industry representatives, they should be treated separately because they require distinctly different planning, preparation, mitigation, and recovery efforts.

The power sector claims it practices *defense in depth* to balance preparation, prevention, response, and recovery for various hazards to electric grid operations. The industry's priorities are to protect the most critical grid components against the most likely threats, build in system resiliency, and to develop contingency plans for response and recovery.

One industry representative, Bridgette Bourge, said, "When considered as part of the broader spectrum of potential threats to the electric grid, a nuclear-induced electromagnetic pulse is considered an extremely low likelihood, high-consequence event. That doesn't mean the electric industry disregards or ignores its significance, but that it is considered appropriately as part of a broader risk management strategy."

"These events, and threats of these events, are very different and should be treated that way," said Bourge. "They are unique in how and what they impact. It is true that a geomagnetic storm is significantly less damaging than a nuclear EMP."

In other words, we don't think there is a likelihood that a high-altitude electromagnetic pulse attack will take place in the U.S., and therefore we don't want to go through the expense of hardening the power grid against it.

Chapter Thirteen
Recent Legislative History

U.S. Congress

In 2005, the Final Report of the Congressional Commission on the Strategic Posture of the United States was released and provided in part:

"The United States should take steps to reduce the vulnerability of the nation and the military to attacks with weapons designed to produce electromagnetic pulse (EMP) effects. We make this recommendation although the Commission is divided over how imminent a threat this is. Some commissioners believe it to be a high priority threat, given foreign activities and terrorist intentions.

"Others see it as a serious potential threat, given the high level of vulnerability. Those vulnerabilities are of many kinds. U.S. power projection forces might be subjected to an EMP attack by an enemy calculating – mistakenly – that such an attack would not involve risks of U.S. nuclear retaliation. The homeland might be attacked by terrorists or even state actors with an eye to crippling the U.S. economy and American society. From a technical perspective, it is possible that such attacks could have catastrophic consequences. For example, successful attacks could shut down the electrical system, disable the internet and computers—and the economic activity on which they depend—incapacitate transportation systems (and thus the delivery of food and other goods), etc.

"Prior commissions have investigated U.S. vulnerabilities and found little activity under way to address them. Some limited defensive measures have been ordered by the Department of Defense to give some protection to important operational communications. But EMP/IEMI vulnerabilities have not yet been addressed effectively by the Department of Homeland Security. Doing so could take several years. The Congressional EMP Commission has recommended numerous measures that would mitigate the damage that might be wrought by an EMP attack."

In response to the report, it took the Stimulus Bill of February

2009 to allocate $11 billion to the Department of Energy for "smart grid activities, including modernizing the electric grid. Unless such improvements in the electric grid are focused in part on reducing EMP vulnerabilities, vulnerability might well increase."

GRID ACT 2010 -The Grid Reliability and Infrastructure Defense Act

In 2010, the House passed the GRID Act, which would have protected 300 of the country's biggest transformers. The measure died in the Senate later that year.

In a surprising election-year gambit, Alaska Sen. Lisa Murkowski gutted the legislation despite strong bipartisan support that would have protected the U.S. power grid from solar flares and Electromagnetic Pulse weapons. Her staff claimed she preferred a "clean" energy bill backed by Senate Democrats.

The original bill, known as the GRID Act, authorized the federal government to take emergency measures to protect some 300 giant power transformers around the country. It passed the House of Representatives by a unanimous voice vote in August, an unusual show of bipartisan support in this Congress.

But when it went to the Senate, the bill was gutted of the measures to protect the power grid from EMP attack by Murkowski and committee chairman Jeff Bingamon, D-N.M., while other portions of the bill were added to her energy bill, S. 1462, the American Clean Energy Act of 2009.

"Sen. Murkowski stripped H.R. 5026 of the main elements designed to protect our infrastructure and did not add them to her bill," said Andrea Lafferty, executive director of the Traditional Values Coalition. An aide to Murkowski said that Murkowski voted for stripping out the EMP provisions of the bill on practical, not political, grounds.

"The bill was going nowhere. The administration opposed it, and favored a government-wide effort, not a piecemeal approach." The aide added that blaming Murkowski, the ranking Republican on the Energy Committee, for altering legislation being managed by the majority Democrats was "an election-year gambit by far right wing groups. Murkowski did not place a hold on the House bill."

The SHIELD Act – Secure High-voltage Infrastructure for Electricity from Lethal Damage Act

The SHIELD Act is the first legitimate attempt Congress has taken to protect the power grid from an EMP attack or solar flare. Reps. Trent Franks and Yvette Clarke introduced the bipartisan SHIELD Act, which mandates many of the same safeguards as outlined in the GRID Act of 2010.

Here is what the SHIELD ACT would do:

- The SHIELD Act, which amends section 215 of the Federal Power Act, encourages cooperation between industry and government in the development, promulgation, and implementation of standards and processes that are necessary to address the current shortcomings and vulnerabilities of the electric grid from a major EMP event

- The SHIELD Act incorporates most of the EMP-related language of HR 5026 from the 111th Congress, which passed overwhelmingly through the House, but was stalled in the Senate during the Lame Duck due mostly to additional language regarding cyber-security threats

- The SHIELD Act also requires that standards be developed within six months, as opposed to one year, of enactment, to ensure a faster timeline of protection.

When the bill was introduced, former Speaker Gingrich voiced his support, but the House Energy and Commerce Committee blocked the legislation.

GRID ACT 2014

The Grid Reliability and Infrastructure Defense (GRID) Act would allow the Federal Energy Regulatory Committee—*FERC*— to issue emergency orders to protect the electricity infrastructure from threats, said Rep. Henry Waxman (D-Calif.) and Sen. Ed Markey (D-Mass.), the bill's sponsors. FERC would also attain regulatory power to protect against grid vulnerabilities.

"Unless we act now, the United States will continue to remain vulnerable to the 21st century cyber armies preparing to wage war on our banking, health care, and defense systems by knocking out America's electricity grid," Markey said in a statement. "The GRID Act will help secure our nation's electrical grid against devastating damage from physical or cyber terrorist attacks, and from natural disasters."

Markey previously sponsored the GRID Act in 2010 when he was in the House. It passed there, but not in the Senate.

"We will remain vulnerable to attacks that could cause devastating blackouts until security is increased and regulatory gaps are closed," Waxman said. "The GRID Act provides regulators the authority they need to ensure that the grid is adequately protected."

The bill's provisions, and the rules FERC would be authorized to establish are designed to protect against "physical, cyber, electromagnetic pulse and other threats" to the electric grid.

Electric utilities opposed the GRID Act the last time it was proposed. The National Rural Electric Cooperative Association said the bill would give FERC too much power over utilities.

CRITICAL INFRASTRUCTURE PROTECTION ACT (CIPA) 2015

In the summer of 2015, the House of Representatives approved unanimously H.R. 3410, the Critical Infrastructure Protection Act (CIPA). This legislation marks a breakthrough. For the first time in four years, Congress has acted to begin to protect the nation's most critical of critical infrastructures; the U.S. electrical grid. It now falls to the Senate and to President Obama to ensure that the House-passed bill becomes the law of the land.

CIPA's lead sponsors were Reps. Trent Franks (R-AZ), a senior member of the House Armed Services Committee and co-chairman of the Electromagnetic Pulse (EMP) Caucus, and Pete Sessions (R-TX), the chairman of the powerful House Rules Committee. The measure enjoyed strong bipartisan support, including from the House Homeland Security Committee's Chairman Michael McCaul (R-TX), and the Chairman and Ranking Member of the Committee's Subcommittee on Cybersecurity, Infrastructure Protection, and Security Technologies, Reps. Patrick Meehan (R-PA) and Yvette

Clark (D-NY).

The CIPA legislation requires the Department of Homeland Security to:

- Include in national planning scenarios the threat of electromagnetic pulse (EMP) which would entail the education of the owners and operators of critical infrastructure, as well as emergency planners and emergency responders at all levels of government of the threat of EMP events

- Engage in research and development aimed at mitigating the consequences of naturally occurring or man-caused EMP events; and

- Produce a comprehensive plan to protect and prepare the critical infrastructure of the American homeland against EMP events.

TRANSPORTATION BILL AMENDMENT – November 2015

The transportation bill that President Obama signed in November of 2015 includes provisions intended to protect the grid from terrorist attacks and natural disasters, giving the Secretary of Energy emergency powers and creating a Strategic Transformer Reserve.

The legislation, which will provide $305 billion in highway funding over five years, cleared the Senate 83-16, following a 359-65 vote in the House. The bill represents both a vindication and a rebuke of former FERC Chairman Jon Wellinghoff's controversial campaign to raise awareness of the grid's vulnerability to sabotage.

It also checked off an item on current FERC Chairman Norman Bay's wish list. Testifying before the House Energy and Power Subcommittee, Bay said it was essential that the government have emergency powers to respond to both an EMP attack and cyber attack. "That emergency authority does not need to reside with FERC. It could reside elsewhere in the federal government," Bay said. "But someone needs to have it."

Title 55 of the bill includes five "Energy Security" sections, including Section 61003, which authorizes the President to declare a grid security emergency in response to a geomagnetic storm, electromagnetic pulse, or cyber attack. Such a declaration would authorize the Energy Secretary to issue emergency orders to protect or restore electric infrastructure critical to *national security, economic security, public health or safety.*

Section 61004 requires the Secretary to submit a plan to Congress within a year for the development of a Strategic Transformer Reserve, including enough large transformers (100 MVA or higher) and trailer-mounted emergency mobile substations *to temporarily replace critically damaged large power transformers and substations that are critical electric infrastructure or serve defense and military installations.*

These provisions are a response to the April 2013 attack on Pacific Gas and Electric's substation in Metcalf, California. At least two gunmen were believed involved in the attack on the 500/230-kV substation near San Jose, causing more than $15 million in damage that shut down the substation for nearly a month. The gunmen targeted transformer radiators, firing an estimated 150 rounds and hitting 10 of 11 banks. The Metcalf attack was the most significant incident of domestic terrorism involving the grid to date.

Former Chairman Wellinghoff found himself under fire after The Wall Street Journal quoted him in an article about a confidential FERC analysis that concluded the country's entire grid could be shut down for months by disabling only nine critical substations. Transformers are typically custom designed and can take over eighteen months to replace. The WSJ article did not identify the locations of those substations or its source for the study, but it quoted Wellinghoff as saying, "there are probably less than 100 critical high voltage substations on our grid in this country that need to be protected from a physical attack."

NERC, members of Congress and Wellinghoff's former FERC colleagues complained that the disclosures had jeopardized, not improved, security. The Department of Energy Inspector General Gregory Friedman warned that FERC's protection of information on the vulnerability of the grid is "severely lacking" and suggested that Wellinghoff had offered too much information when questioned about the disclosures.

As a result of Wellinghoff's disclosures, Section 61003 requires

FERC to develop regulations governing how it classifies information as critical electric infrastructure information (CEII), including "appropriate sanctions for commissioners, officers, employees or agents of the commission who knowingly and willfully disclose critical electric infrastructure information in a manner that is not authorized." The section also exempts CEII from disclosure under federal, state or local public records laws.

In testimony before the House subcommittee, current Commissioner Cheryl LaFleur suggested policymakers have more work to do.

"I think the reliability standards that we've put in place, which require every transmission owner to identify the most critical facilities and protect them, are an important step," she said. "But I think beyond that, a lot of the protection has to come from how we build the grid — building more redundancy so we kind of 'de-criticalize' those places so that a physical attack won't cause as much damage, and building in more standardization. If something goes wrong we can share transformers more, rather than having to build a custom one in every place."

GAO REPORT: CRITICAL INFRASTRUCTURE PROTECTION: Preliminary Observations on DHS Efforts to Address Electromagnetic Threats to the Electric Grid

What the GAO Found

As of July 2015, the Department of Homeland Security (DHS) reported taking several actions that could help address the electromagnetic threats to the electric grid. GAO's preliminary analysis of DHS's actions indicated they fell into four categories: (1) developing reports, (2) identifying mitigation efforts, (3) strategy development and planning, and (4) conducting exercises.

In other words, they did what our government does best—talk about it.

The GAO's Report was of the DHS when it wrote: "Preliminary findings indicate that DHS Actions to Address Electromagnetic Threats were Conducted Independently of the EMP Commission Recommendations." In other words, they did their own thing.

The DHS reported its actions were not taken in response to the 2008 recommendations of the Commission to Assess the Threat to the United States from Electromagnetic Pulse Attack (EMP Commission). The GAO also recognized that DHS does not have a statutory obligation to specifically address the recommendations, but the implementation of them could help mitigate electromagnetic impacts to the electric grid, such as helping to assure the protection of high-value transmission assets. Moreover, the GAO's preliminary work suggested that DHS, in conjunction with the Department of Energy (DOE), has not adequately addressed an essential critical infrastructure protection responsibility—identification of precise internal agency roles and responsibilities related to addressing electromagnetic threats. For example, although DHS recognized one component as the lead for assessing solar weather risks, the component has not yet identified any specific roles related to collecting or analyzing risk information.

DHS has also coordinated with federal and industry stakeholders to address some, but not all risks to the electrical grid, since the EMP Commission issued its recommendations. The GAO preliminarily identified eight projects in which the DHS coordinated efforts to help protect the power grid, including developing plans to address long-term power outages, participation in exercises, and research and development activities. Although these are positive steps, the GAO's preliminary work indicated that the DHS has not effectively coordinated with utilities to identify critical assets or collect necessary risk information, among other responsibilities. The GAO announced it will continue to assess the issues in this statement as it completes its work and will publish a report with the final results in late 2015.

NDAA 2016, Section 1089: EMP Commission revived

Section 1089 of the bill restores the EMP Commission, which previously had a run from 2001 to 2008. Also, the EMP Commission's charter will expand to make clear its charge also covers non-nuclear EMP weapons, EMP-like effects from natural forces, and the study of how potential adversaries might propose to use EMP in their military doctrine.

The Commission was directed to assess the following:

(1) The vulnerability of electric-dependent military systems in the United States to a manmade or natural EMP event, giving special attention to the progress made by the Department of Defense, other Government departments and agencies of the United States, and entities of the private sector in taking steps to protect such systems from such an event

(2) The evolving current and future threat from state and non-state actors of a manmade EMP attack employing nuclear or non-nuclear weapons

(3) New technologies, operational procedures, and contingency planning that can protect electronics and military systems from the effects a manmade or natural EMP event

(4) Among the States, if State grids are protected against manmade or natural EMP, which States should receive highest priority for protecting critical defense assets

(5) The degree to which vulnerabilities of critical infrastructure systems create cascading vulnerabilities for military systems

STATE LEGISLATION

Policy makers on a local level have already begun to get smart and challenge the electrical industry to higher standards. At the National Council of State Legislatures in 2015, several lawmakers said they're preparing legislation similar to a 2013 bill introduced in Maine. Here are a few of the more significant state legislative actions:

- On June 11, 2013, the State of Maine passed the first legislation in the nation to protect the electric grid against electromagnetic pulse (EMP) and geomagnetic disturbance (GMD). EMPs, such as high-altitude nuclear explosions, and GMDs, such as major solar flares and storms, have the potential to critically disrupt or destroy the electric grid.

- On March 10, 2015, Virginia Governor, Terry McAuliffe signed a bill requiring the commonwealth's Department of Emergency Management (DEM) to plan for responses to disasters caused by electromagnetic pulses (EMPs). This requirement is part of the DEM's overall mission of disaster preparedness.

- Arizona implemented a requirement in 2014 for its emergency management agency to incorporate EMP preparedness into its disaster planning. Louisiana's preparedness office is examining the possible effects of an EMP event. In 2013, Kentucky set up an interagency working group to examine EMP preparedness efforts.

- In Texas, there are currently two bills that address the protection of the electrical grid. Specifically, they relate to a study by the Electric Reliability Council of Texas on securing critical infrastructure from electromagnetic, geomagnetic, terrorist, and cyber attack threats. They are House Bill 2289, and Senate Bill 1398.

The FAST ACT—Fixing America's Surface Transportation Act

There is good news. On December 4, 2015, President Obama signed into law the "FAST Act"—an acronym for Fixing America's Surface Transportation Act. Part of a massive highway and transportation bill, the FAST Act also includes energy security amendments to the Federal Power Act ("FPA"), several of which affect utilities and others in the electric industry. These changes potentially impact owners, operators, and users of electric infrastructure; even relatively small, intrastate utilities not ordinarily subject to control by the Federal Energy Regulatory Commission ("FERC").

The FAST Act creates a new Section 215A in the FPA, much of which revolves around the newly-defined terms *critical electric infrastructure* and critical electric infrastructure information. *Critical electric infrastructure* ("CEI") is broadly defined to include both physical and virtual systems and assets of the bulk-power system, whose destruction or incapacity would have a negative impact on national or economic security, public health, or safety. *Critical electric infrastructure information* ("CEII") could mean potentially any information related to CEI, and generated by or submitted to FERC or any other federal agency, other than classified national security information.

The primary purpose of the act is to encourage information

sharing between the public sector and the private sector. The FAST Act reduces the restrictions of disclosures of CEII, and also promotes information sharing among government and industry participants. As suggested in the definition of CEII, the full impact of these provisions will depend on rules FERC must promulgate within the next year, which will determine both procedures and substantive criteria for designating CEII and preventing its unauthorized disclosure. The Act itself does specify, however, that no federal, state, local, or tribal entity is required to disclose CEII on the basis of any public disclosure law at any level, including the federal Freedom of Information Act (FOIA). Our government seems intent on protecting on our grid, and not letting our adversaries know how we're doing it.

Depending on the rules regarding implementation, these provisions could prevent disclosure of a wide swath of industry information submitted to the federal government, including FERC filings. By definition, CEII might include, any "information related to critical electric infrastructure, or proposed critical electrical infrastructure, generated by or provided to [FERC] or other Federal agency, other than classified national security information," and designated according to the rules to be established. Significantly, the new federal protection preempts state and local laws, preventing CEII disclosure even by a state or local agency pursuant to a state or local public disclosure law. However, to be designated as CEII, the information must have been generated by or submitted to a federal agency.

The new Section 215A gives the Department of Energy ("DOE") increased authority in case of a "grid security emergency," including malicious physical or electronic acts, magnetic disturbances due to the sun, direct physical attacks, and related threats and reliability disruptions. When the President identifies such an emergency, DOE can order emergency measures the Secretary of Energy ("Secretary") deems necessary to protect or restore CEI reliability. FAST requires little administrative process prior to issuance of these emergency orders. Though the DOE must adopt procedures for such cases, the

Secretary may issue emergency orders "with or without notice, hearing, or report." The President must notify, but does not require the consent of Congress in making the emergency determination. It will be incumbent upon the DOE to consult with affected governments and CEI owners and operators.

An emergency order under the new FPA section 215A could affect "any owner, user, or operator" of CEI in the U.S., even entities not ordinarily subject to FERC jurisdiction (for example, municipally owned utilities, rural electric cooperatives, and federal power marketing agencies like the Tennessee Valley Authority and Bonneville Power Administration). The DOE's new authority also explicitly extends to the North American Electric Reliability Corporation ("NERC") and other regional power suppliers.

To overcome industry objections regarding the costs of implementing the law, if CEI owners, operators, or users incur expenses in complying with an emergency order, but cannot recover those costs through their existing rate structures, the new law directs FERC to establish mechanisms for recovery of those costs.

The issue of backup transformers has finally been addressed. The new law requires DOE's Office of Electricity Delivery and Energy Reliability, in consultation with FERC, NERC, and the Electricity Subsector Coordinating Council, to submit a plan to Congress evaluating the feasibility of establishing a Strategic Transformer Reserve for storage in strategic locations of spare large power transformers and emergency mobile substations. The plan would determine adequate amounts and locations to temporarily replace critically damaged large power transformers and substations. The reserve would reduce the vulnerability of U.S. critical infrastructure to physical or cyber attack, electromagnetic pulse, solar disturbance of the earth's magnetic field, severe weather, and earthquake.

The DOE's plan must include the funding options available to establish and maintain the Strategic Transformer Reserve, including imposing fees on owners and operators of bulk-power system facilities and CEI. Additionally, the plan must assess the possibility of imposing fees on the large power transformer owner/operators and substations that constitute CEI, to pay for Strategic Transformer Reserve operating costs.

Electric cooperatives have been concerned about the conflicts between the state laws and regulations imposed by the federal government. FAST amends Section 202(c) of the FPA (FERC's existing emergency authority) to clarify that FERC emergency orders override federal, state, and local environmental laws. Congress intended to resolve the perceived conflict facing power plant operators, who feared violating either an emergency order from FERC or environmental regulations if an emergency arose.

Consistent with this administration's concern for the environment, any emergency order must still minimize environmental impacts and must be consistent with all applicable environmental laws, "to the maximum extent practicable." FERC must also consult with federal environmental regulators, before an order can remain in effect longer than ninety days. Further, FERC must incorporate any condition submitted by the environmental agency, or explain its determination of why that submitted condition would impede an adequate emergency response.

These specific provisions regarding the environment, ensure that utilities and other operators of electric generation and transmission facilities can now comply with FERC emergency orders with the enhanced assurance that they will not incur environmental liability, whether civil (including citizen suits) or criminal. The exemptions afforded under FAST provides that such acts or omissions, even when taken to "voluntarily comply" with an emergency order, will not be considered violations of any federal, state, or local environmental law. This protection continues, even if courts later alter or strike down the underlying FERC order. The existing language of Section 202(c) does not appear to limit FERC's emergency authority to utilities otherwise under its jurisdiction, so it appears that the new exemption could benefit virtually any operator of electric infrastructure, should an emergency arise.

The FAST Act offers the electric power sector several benefits, most notably, the exemption from environmental regulations to the extent that they conflict with FERC emergency orders, improved cost recovery for compliance with such orders, and also some degree of added protection of sensitive information from public disclosure. On the other hand, system participants will now be subject to broader federal control, especially in emergency situations. The Strategic Transformer Reserve planning also foreshadows potentially significant costs that Congress could impose on owners, operators, and users of generation and grid assets in the future. Conclusively, most of the new agency powers and responsibilities just enacted apply not only to utilities and grid operators accustomed to dealing with FERC, but also to entities not ordinarily subject to FERC jurisdiction.

SUGGESTIONS TO U.S. POLICYMAKERS

At Heritage.org, Senior Policy Analyst, Michaela Dodge and Policy Analyst, Jessica Zuckerman provided this list of what Congress and the Administration should do:

- Mandate additional research into mitigating EMP threats. Similar to what Maine is doing, the U.S. should undertake additional research into how an EMP would affect electronics and electrical systems and how these vulnerabilities can be removed or lessened.

- Determine which countries could undertake EMP attacks. The U.S. should understand where potential EMP attacks could come from and produce intelligence estimates on nations that are pursuing or already have weapons capable of producing an EMP. This information can then be used to better inform policymakers on how best to respond to potential threats and prevent EMP attacks from occurring.

- Improve and fully fund U.S. missile defense. Ballistic missiles are one of the most effective means of delivering an EMP. U.S. missile defense should be advanced to address the threat, especially as the East Coast remains less protected than the West Coast. Improved command-and-control features and interceptors tied to forward-deployed radar would give the Standard Missile-3 (SM-3) interceptor the ability to counter long-range ballistic missiles in the late midcourse stage of flight. The government should improve the SM-3's ability to intercept short-range ballistic missiles in the ascent phase of flight. Ultimately, the U.S. should develop and deploy space-based missile defense, the best way to protect the U.S. and its allies from ballistic missiles.

- Develop a National Recovery Plan and National Planning Scenario for EMP. The catastrophic cost of an EMP event means that it deserves careful preparation and planning. Such plans should take the advice of the EMP commission and employ a risk-based approach that recognizes that certain infrastructure—particularly electrical and telecommunication systems upon which all other sectors depend—is most important in preparing for and recovering from an EMP event. Additionally, DHS should have a National Planning Scenario dedicated to EMP so that local, state, and federal authorities understand what would happen in an EMP event and what their respective responsibilities are in terms of both response and recovery.

- Prepare and protect critical cyber infrastructure. Cyber infrastructure is completely and uniquely dependent on the power grid, which makes it particularly vulnerable to an EMP. The U.S. should explore ways to protect and shield the circuit boards of critical networks. Additionally, the U.S. should consider the interdependency between the nation's cyber infrastructure and the other critical infrastructures and take actions to prevent cascading failures.

Chapter Fourteen
U. S. Department of Defense Preparations

Military moves NORAD to Cheyenne Mountain

New concerns are being raised that the nation's electrical grid and critical infrastructure are increasingly vulnerable to a catastrophic foreign attack -- amid speculation over whether officials are eyeing a former Cold War bunker, inside a Colorado mountain, as a *shield* against such a strike.

The North American Aerospace Defense Command is looking for ways to protect itself in the event of a massive EMP. A $700 million contract with Raytheon to upgrade electronics inside Colorado's Cheyenne Mountain facility may provide a clue about just how worried the military is about the threat.

The Cheyenne Mountain bunker is a half-acre cavern carved into a mountain in the 1960s that was designed to withstand a Soviet nuclear attack. From inside the massive complex, airmen were poised to send warnings that could trigger the launch of nuclear missiles.

The Air Force moved out of Cheyenne Mountain, which was built to survive a nuclear attack, in 2006, establishing its NORAD headquarters at Peterson Air Force Base in Colorado. But that facility, inside the mountain, could offer protection against a so-called EMP attack.

The head of NORAD recently suggested, at an April 2015 Pentagon press conference, that Cheyenne may still be needed. "My primary concern was, are we going to have the space inside the mountain for everybody who wants to move in there?" Admiral William Gortney told reporters, "I'm not at liberty to discuss who's moving in there, but we do have that capability to be there. And so, there's a lot of movement to put capability into Cheyenne Mountain and to be able to communicate in there."

NORAD spokesman Capt. Jeff Davis, told Fox News, "The mountain's ability to provide a shield against an EMP is certainly a valuable feature, and that is one reason we maintain the ability to return there quickly, if needed."

Now, officials say that the Pentagon is looking at shifting communications gear to the Cheyenne bunker.

"A lot of the back office communications is being moved there," said one defense official.

Officials agree that the military's dependence on computer networks and digital communications makes it much more vulnerable to an electromagnetic pulse, which can occur naturally or result from a high-altitude nuclear explosion.

Under the 10-year contract, Raytheon is supposed to deliver "sustainment" services to help the military perform "accurate, timely, and unambiguous warning and attack assessment of air, missile, and space threats" at the Cheyenne and Peterson bases.

Raytheon's contract also involves unspecified work at Vandenberg Air Force Base in California and Offutt Air Force Base in Nebraska.

Pentagon constructs $44 million EMP-proof bunker in Alaska

Fort Greely, Alaska is home to one of America's two domestic missile defense bases. Now, it's getting armored against high-altitude electromagnetic energy attacks—like the kind emitted from nuclear blasts. The Pentagon is spending millions on a bunker designed to protect against exactly that. According to contract documents from the Army Corps of Engineers, the military plans to spend $44 million on an "HEMP-protected" bunker housing the base's missile launch control systems. The base at Fort Greely houses anti-ballistic missile interceptors stored in silos, and can also control and direct interceptors fired from a similar site at Vandenberg Air Force Base in California.

The sum allocated to the Fort Greely project is small in comparison to the $41 billion the Pentagon is spending on its ground-based defense program through FY2017. The plan calls for the installation of dozens of missile interceptors in Alaska and California. These interceptors will carry kinetic kill weapons, designed to impact and destroy ballistic missiles during their mid-course phase. Mid-course defense refers to the flight pattern of ballistic missiles as they travel through space—and before they reenter the atmosphere moving at extremely high speeds.

But a missile defense site wouldn't count for much if it could be knocked out by an EMP. The Pentagon is concerned enough with that scenario to protect its missile defense site. "The EMP and blast-proof building design also will provide a blueprint for subsequent launch-control buildings at Fort Greely," reported the trade journal, Military and Aerospace Electronics. Naturally, EMP-shielding also protects against lightning strikes, so it's a good insurance policy to shield the base's critical launch systems, in any case.

The contract points out that when the military first constructed the silos, the building housing the key launch components, "was not blast protected, HEMP shielded, and did not provide the utility redundancy to support a deployed weapons system." By protecting the base from EMP blasts, the Pentagon means the ability, "to resist the effects of a surface blast due to the accidental explosion of a missile as it exits a silo."

What are the United States government and the military preparing for? Why are they finally taking the threat seriously?

APPENDIX B

PREPPER'S CHECKLIST

From www.FreedomPreppers.com

PREPPERS CHECKLIST

Preppers who are not adequately prepared place added risks on the people who rely upon them. A well-organized Prepper Checklist with assigned responsibilities will maximize your odds of survival. Your Prepper Checklist is a list of functions, or capabilities that you need to provide for in each of the survival categories. A comprehensive prepper checklist acts as both a shopping list of items that you need to get or put into a kit and a to-do list. This Prepper Checklist accomplishes both.

A Preppers Checklist is always evolving. Your Preparedness Plan will change as your knowledge and skills advance. This Preppers Checklist allows for the individual needs of each Prepper while still accomplishing common goals.

The list is broken up into general categories to help keep things organized. You can learn more on FreedomPreppers.com

Prepper Basics are the minimum requirements of preparedness that you should strive to accomplish as fast as possible. They are the basic levels of preparedness that a new prepper starting out should achieve as soon as possible. Advanced Preppers levels allow for surviving longer durations and/or increases the capacity of your prepper group.

Remember the Prepper Rule of Threes and buy backups to everything!

Three is two, two is one, one is none.

Off Grid Energy Options

• Ability to recharge NiMH or NiCd batteries from an indefinite power source , in the sizes you use (AAA, AA, C, D, 9V)

• Minimum 4,000 Watt Generator, preferably tri-fuel (gas, propane, natural gas or solar)

• Fuel storage to power generator for four hours per day, ninety days total

• Put Uninterruptible Power Supplies on all computers and other sensitive critical electronic equipment in a Faraday Cage

• Spare extension cords

• Battery maintenance items

• Solar-power, or other renewable/long-term power, setup capable of running all mission critical devices for indefinite period, working eventually to powering entire household

• Deep Cycle Batteries

• 1000 Watt Inverter

• Stored Gasoline

• Sta-Bil for stored Gasoline

• Stored Diesel

• Spare parts for Alternate Energy generations, (fuses, wire, connectors, inverter parts, etc.)

• Candles

• Propane Lanterns

• Oil Lamps

• Headlamps for everyone

Clothing

• Three complete changes of rugged clothes for all members

• Three complete changes of sleep clothes for all members

• Seven changes of underclothes for each member

• One pair of rugged, waterproof boots for each member

• Socks – Socks - Socks

- One pair of comfortable shoes (sneakers, sandals, etc.) for each member
- Outer gear (boots, gloves, mittens, scarves, hats, etc) for all climates (cold weather, rain, etc.)
- Spare shoe & boot laces
- Fourteen changes of underclothes for each member
- Spare boots (rugged and waterproof)
- Spare comfort shoes
- Ability to make/repair clothes
- Ability to make/repair boots and shoes
- Quantity of various materials for repairs and creation of clothing
- Second (spare) set of outer gear for all climates

Communications
- World Band Radio
- Hand Crank Weather Band, AM/FM Radio
- Base Station Short Wave Radio
- Ham Radio, Bao-Feng or equivalent
- CB Radio
- Two-Radios
- Bullhorns
- Tactical Communications (0 – 5 miles), generally a hand-held radio unit (FRS, GMRS, Ham, CB, etc.), to transmit and receive, with extra batteries (see also alternate energy)
- Shortwave radio with SSB capability, for general listening of world events
- Basic computer to access the Internet and review files (.doc. .pdf. .html. etc.) {it should be obvious that an Internet connection goes along with this}
- AM/FM radio, battery operated (TV sound optional, but might be worthwhile if you are close to a TV broadcast tower that can run on emergency power)
- Plans and equipment for making expedient antennas (see Information and Plans)
- Radio and computer manuals and backup discs (see

Information and Plans)
If you have a cell phone, have a 12VDC charging cord for it, and a spare battery for it

• Pocket list of contact numbers for family, friends, team members (see also Information and Plans)

• Long distance phone calling card that doesn't expire

• Pocket list of frequencies (see also Information and Plans)

• USB drive containing pocket computer system (OS, files, programs, PGP, etc.)

• USB drive containing your data files

• Door Intercom for communicating with people outside your door, while staying safe inside

• Short-distance Communications (up to 50 miles) (generally, a mobile ham VHF/UHF radio and a vehicle or yagi antenna), transmit and receive

• Pocket radio for short-distance digital communications (can be particularly useful for local Groups/Teams/Family Units)

• Long-distance communications (greater than 50 miles), generally ham HF, transmit and receive

• Ham Radio Email, like Wavemail or Winlink/Netlink over HF and possibly VHF (Packet)

• Satellite phone

• Always store your electronics in Faraday Cages when not in use.

• Defense (Safety and Security)

• Each member of the household should have the following weapons:

• Full size handgun and a concealed carry weapon (same caiber)

• Shotgun

• Hunting rifle (for sniping and hunting)

• Battle rifle (AR15, AR10, or AK47)

• .22 Caliber rifle and handgun for training

• A "throwaway weapon" that your willing to give up in the event of gun confiscation. It's better to give up a "throwaway" to divert attention from your real weapons cache.

- One thousand rounds per weapon.
- Every handgun has a holster, every rifle and shotgun has a sling; cases for all firearms
- Several magazines for every firearm that uses one
- Cleaning gear for all firearms
- Spare parts for every firearm, and detailed manuals
- Reloading equipment and supplies for each of your main calibers
- Security system that monitors home inside perimeter
- Knives
- Machete
- Compound Bow
- Extra Arrows
- Slingshot
- Snare Wire
- Monitoring system so that you know when someone has breached key areas of your property
- Outside floodlights on motion sensors covering the outside perimeter of home and any other key areas on property
- Put out small fires (a fire extinguisher for kitchen, garage and every level of the home)
- Smoke & carbon monoxide detectors on all floors
- Camera surveillance around home, complete 360 degrees
- Motion and seismic sensors monitoring perimeter and other key areas of property
- External fire suppression system
- Add laminate to exterior windows (resists break-ins, etc.)
- Hardened Safe room, from physical assaults (weather, crime, etc.)
- Night Vision (mono- or binocular)
- You can't have too many fire extinguishers. You need to be able to put out a fire quickly, especially if there is no fire department available.

Financial Preparedness
- Cash on hand
- Supply of hard currency (silver, gold, etc.)
- Supply of barter goods (We suggest heirloom seeds)
- Ability to capitalize on opportunities (like, group buys or cheap land after a crisis/pandemic)
- Know the silver content of junk silver and the gold content of various coins and how to convert that into current market value
- Know how to calculate and determine specific gravity for various metals (how to spot fake silver and gold)
- Use gold to store larger amounts of wealth and silver for smaller amounts. Silver is also better in a barter environment.

Cooking Off The Grid
- Gas Grill
- Camp Stove
- Rocket Stove
- Solar Dehydrator
- Meat Grinder
- Grain Grinder
- Non-electric Can Opener
- Fire Pit
- Solar Oven
- Spare Propane
- Matches and Lighters
- Butane Stove
- Cast Iron Cookware
- Food Storage
- Stored food for as long as you plan on living
- Wheat
- Rice
- Pasta
- Beans
- Oatmeal
- Dry Milk

- Honey
- Sugar
- Vinegar
- Lemon Juice
- Cooking Oil
- Coffee/Tea
- Canned Goods
- Spices
- Condiments
- Water Enhancers
- Baking Essentials (Yeast, Salt, etc.)
- Sprouting Seeds
- Non-hybrid, Heirloom Garden Seeds
- Portable capability for minimum-prepared foods for 14 days (for traveling, short-term missions, etc.)
- Gather more food: hunt, fish, trap/snare, gather wild plants
- Dress and prepare gathered food
- Keep perishable food cold using alternative energy methods for 30 days (see Alternative Energy)
- Disposable flatware for 30 days
- Open cans and other packaging
- Cook food 3 times a day with alternate methods for 30 days (minimum, work up to 90 days)
- Have cookware that can be used over an open fire (pots, pans, kettles, etc.)
- Durable cooking utensils (including pots, pans, etc.)
- Equipment to cook over fire pit (grates, tripods, hooks, etc.)
- Recipes for making a variety of dishes from the food you store
- Spices to make food more palatable, enjoyable, varied
- One year's worth of food, in any combination of every day, minimum-prepared, and long-term storage foods, with the experience and equipment to prepare it
- Portable capability for minimum-prepared foods for 30 days or more (for traveling)

- Grow food and harvest the seeds for the next planting
- Grow and tend livestock
- Preserve food on indefinite basis (canning, smoking, jerking, etc)
- Keep perishable food cold using alternative energy methods
- Minimum-prepared foods are those that require little or no cooking before eating.
- Disposable Flatware—plates, bowls, cups, spoons, forks, knives, napkins, etc. The idea of disposable flatware is to reduce consumption of water and is typically for shorter-term events.
- Cooking Oils

Preparedness Plan

- Acquire the proper insurance (home, renter, auto, health, life etc.) and safeguard the insurance plan and contact information
- Document with pictures and/or video all possessions for insurance purposes, including writing down the serial numbers for guns and electronics.
- Post in a quick-access location the numbers for all emergency services (police, fire, ambulance, poison control, utility services), and include non-emergency numbers for the same services as well as family, friends, neighbors, etc.
- Post a list of important websites next to (or along with) the important phone numbers.
- Copies of personal information like birth certificates, SS cards, driver licenses, with current pictures, kept in fire safe.
- A list of "last-minute purchase items" – in case you have time to "top off"

Current inventory

- Resource materials (books, CDs, etc.) covering a wide range of topics
- Instruction and repair manuals for everything
- Backups of all important computer files
- Hard copies (printouts) of all critical information contained in computer files

- Backup copies of your computer data on discs, USB flash drives, portable HDDs
- An evacuation plan and prioritized grab list
- Plans and equipment for making expedient antennas (see Communications and Computing)
- Pocket list of contact numbers for family, friends, team members (see Communications and Computing)
- Pocket list of radio frequencies used (see Communications and Computing)
- Forms of entertainment (games, books, music, DVDs, CDs, MP3 players drawing, coloring, cards, football, frisbee, baseball/throwing ball, soccer ball, etc.)
- Maps of surrounding area with extensive notes on routes and areas, including conditions at different times of the year (see Navigation and Signaling)
- "Range cards" for your entire property

Personal Items
- Purse
- Wallet
- ID
- Watch
- Money
- A "last-minute checklist" is generally a bad thing to implement. It's better to have all the equipment and supplies on hand before an event occurs.
- A Grab List is a list of items that you want to take with you in case you need to evacuate your home. The grab list should include everything that you would want to take, in priority order, so that you don't have to try and remember while you're scrambling to evacuate.
- Additional Entertainment considerations include games for kids, books (or reading material) for both education and learning resources, and books that show how to play more games (adult and children) using cards and other materials.

- It's a good idea to keep important documents in a fire-resistant safe
- Lighting
- Flashlights
- Lanterns, Battery and Oil
- Light Sticks
- Solar Lights
- Candles
- Area light (prefer safe LED or fluorescent instead of flame-based light)
- Spotlight, handheld, battery powered (see Alternate Energy)
- Provide power to all normal light for home with Alternative Energy.
- Spare parts for all lights (bulbs, etc.)
- LED lights are preferred due to their lower consumption of battery power.
- Navigation & Signaling
- Maps of surrounding area, including topo, road atlas, etc. (see also Information and Plans)
- Compass, several quality instruments
- Protractor, rulers, grid squares, alcohol-erase markers, pencils, grease pencils etc. for map use
- Waterproof map cases, waterproofed maps, or maps covered in clear acetate
- GPS with built-in mapping software and direct-entry of information (coordinates, descriptions, etc), preloaded with the appropriate maps
- Power support for GPS (see Alternative Energy)
- Prepping for Pandemics, Nuclear + BioTerror Attacks
- N100 or P100 masks/filters
- Tyvek suits, including hood and over-boots
- Nitrile gloves
- Air filtration system capable of providing positive pressure in a saferoom area, with spare filters
- EMP surge protectors on all sensitive equipment

- Decontamination gear and supplies
- 6 mil plastic in rolls and metal tape for safe rooms plus back up materials
- Potassium Iodine/Iodate (KI) tablets, enough for a minimum of 14 days for each person
- Log book for noting exposures and readings, pencils, pens, calculator, ruler, log-log paper
- Radiological Instruction manual (like "Fallout Survival" by Druce D. Clayton; FEMA)
- Air filtration system capable of providing positive pressure to whole house, with spare filters
- EMP surge protectors on all house outlets
- Radiation meters (survey and dosimeters)
- Fallout shelter
- Hygiene & Sanitation
- Toilet Paper
- Two pairs of eyeglasses, both with current prescription
- Eyeglass retaining straps
- Toiletries: Make sure you can do everything in the bathroom that you do on a daily basis, including:
- Bath / wash (soap)
- Dental care
- Denture care
- Hand Wash
- Clean eye contacts
- Nail trimmers
- Hair comb/brush
- Makeup
- Shave cream and disposable razors
- deodorant/antiperspirant
- Keep skin from drying (lotion)
- Tweezers
- Clean ears
- Nose tissue
- Dry self (towels)

- Feminine hygiene items
- Garbage disposal and recycle/reuse
- Plastic trash bags for waste both human and other to keep buckets clean
- Deodorizers (Lysol, baking soda and vinegar, liquid porta-potty enzymes, etc.)
- Lice/Nit comb
- Camp showers
- Body Bags

Cleaning Supplies
- Bleach/Pool Shock
- Comet
- Baking Soda
- Washing Soda
- Borax
- Bar Soap
- Vinegar
- Mop and Bucket
- Broom and Dust Pan
- Scrub Brushes
- Dish Pan
- Trash Bags
- Trash Cans
- Burn Barrel
- Compost garbage and waste
- Spare buckets

Pets & Animals
- 30 days of stored food and water for each pet
- Ability to handle pet waste if pet cannot go outside for 30 days
- Pet care needs, special medications, toys, etc for 30 days
- Leashes and kennels for each animal
- Tie-down stake
- Pest control for pets
- Shot / Vet record

- Up-to-date shots
- 90 or more days of stored food and water for each pet, eventually working towards an indefinite supply for all pets
- Ability to handle pet waste if pet cannot go outside for 90+ days
- Pet care needs, special medications, toys, etc for 90+ days
- Pet first-Aid kit
- Tested recipes for pet food from stored and/or gathered food sources, food scraps, etc.
- Shelter, Fire & Warmth
- Tents, enough tent space to contain all members and gear
- Tarps, decent selection for general and miscellaneous use
- Sleeping bag or other bedding of choice for each member, capable of keeping person warm in sub-freezing temperatures
- Ability to make fire in, at least, 3 different ways
- Spare sheets and blankets
- Pillows
- Alternate heating source for home
- Land Mobile – more durable and mobile sheltering system (e.g., camping trailer)
- Shelter building tools (see Tools, Repair and Utility)
- Shelter repair supplies: plywood, wood strips, plastic sheeting, screws, nails, etc. (see also Tools, Repair and Utility below)
- Pre-cut plywood for covering windows if you are in a Hurricane area
- Ability to repair and maintain your home: Plumbing, Electrical, Carpentry, Roofing, Fencing, Concrete, Welding, etc.
- Tools, Repair & Utility
- Buckets, with and without lids
- Basic socket set
- Basic screwdriver set
- Basic wrench set
- Basic set of saws (wood, metal, etc.)
- Basic set of files

- Basic wrench set
- Multi-meter
- Tarp and plastic sheeting for temporary repair of roof, windows, and siding from storm damage. Large-head nails and wood strips to attach them
- Multi-tool, quality construction
- Hammers
- Shovels
- Pickaxe
- Axe
- Hatchet
- Rope
- Wire (bailing and electrical)
- Twine
- Fuses
- Crimp connectors
- Scissors (need several pair for different tasks; a good set of scissors is indispensable)
- Soldering iron
- Solder
- Drill and drill bits
- Measuring tool (tape measure, carpenter's rule, etc.)
- Repair/Mend clothing
- Sewing kit
- Clothes pins, wooden
- Eyeglass repair kit
- Gather & prepare firewood (axes, saws, splitter, etc.)
- Chainsaws
- Supply of nails, screws, and some lumber for structural repair of house
- Parts & tools to repair critical plumbing items
- Spare buckets, with and without lids
- Welding setup
- Transportation
- Keep all vehicles in good repair

- Four wheel drive on main vehicle, or traction-enhanced (locking differentials, etc.)
- Main vehicle needs to be able to carry everyone in family, including a minimum of gear and supplies for 1 week
- Main vehicle needs to run on standardized fuel (gasoline, diesel), not specialized fuel (high octane, bio-mix, propane,etc.)
- Stored fuel for one full tank (e.g., if your vehicle's tank holds 20 gallons, store 20 gallons) in man-portable containers
- 'Fix a flat' or Slime
- Self-vulcanizing plug kit
- Air compressor (12 VDC)
- Hose clamps, various sizes (or hose wrap or duct tape)
- Siphon hose
- Funnels
- Full-sized spare tire
- Emergency road equipment (flares, warning reflectors, etc.)
- Navigation (maps, GPS, etc.), stored in vehicle
- Basic spare parts (hoses, belts, sparks plugs, fasteners, etc.)
- Extra fluids (oil, coolant, transmission fluid, washer fluid, etc.)
- Tool kit, stored in vehicle
- Fire extinguisher
- Jumper cables
- Recovery strap/tow rope
- Extended fuel storage
- Additional spare parts for vehicle

Water
- Bottled Water
- Canteen/Camelback
- Rain Barrel
- Water Bottle with Filter
- Water Purification Tablets
- Pool Shock/Bleach
- Kettle w/ Lid for Boiling Water
- Charcoal and Sand

- Mosquito Netting
- Coffee Filters
- Purify / disinfect water with Bleach or Calcium Hypochlorite
- Pre-filter / purify / disinfect water with coffee filters or panty hose
- Berkey Water Filter, a Life Straw, or similar devices for home and bugging out
- Dedicated "dirty water " containers* equal to about 30 gallons, plus additional containers to catch rain water
- Spigot-controlled water (on / off valve) – Sillcock Key
- Have 5-day supply stored in containers that are easy to move when full
- Portable capability to pre-filter / purify / disinfect water for additional 30 days or more
- Gather large quantities of water, in excess of 100 gallons at a time
- Rain Catchment System

Weather Information

- NOAA weather radio
- Basic understanding of clouds, weather systems and storms typical in your area
- Weather reference book or poster
- Thorough understanding of weather related alerts, watches and warnings
- Handheld weather measurement instruments
- Powered Weather monitoring station
- Attend Weather Spotter class/participate in area SKYWARN activities/training

Medical Supplies

- Nitrile Gloves (hypoallergenic), in various sizes for larger group supplies
- Cold packs/Hot packs, instant and/or reusable
- Scalpels and/or Field Knife
- Ace Wraps

- Israeli Bandage or other compression bandages
- Celox or Quikclot hemostatic clotting agents (stops moderate to severe bleeding in wounds)
- Tourniquets (CAT, SOF-T, SWAT, EMT are examples)
- Compressed Gauze (H and H brand is an example)
- Steri-strips or Butterfly Closures and Tincture of Benzoin (to help the strips stick to skin)
- Nail Scissors or Clippers
- Hemostat Clamp 5", Straight or Curved
- 3-0 Nylon or Silk Suture
- Super Glue or Medical Glue
- Tweezers (in various sizes and tips for larger group supplies)
- Penlight and Headlamp
- Bandage Scissors 7.25" Stainless steel (better) or EMT scissors
- Adhesive Bandages, various sizes (non-latex if possible)
- ABD Dressings, in small and large sizes
- Gauze Dressings Sterile and Non-sterile, various sizes
- Non-Stick Sterile Dressings (Telfa type), various sizes
- Roller Gauze Sterile Dressings (Kerlix), various sizes
- Moleskin or Molepad
- Mylar, Solar, or Survival blanket
- Cloth Medical Tape
- Duct Tape
- Triangular Bandage with safety pins, and bandannas
- Ammonia Inhalants
- Antibiotic Ointment or Creams, like Triple, Bacitracin, Neomycin and Bactroban (Rx)
- Alcohol Wipes, Povidone-iodine (Betadine) Wipes, BZK wipes (Benzalkonium Chloride)
- Burn Gel and Hydrocortisone Cream
- Sting Relief Wipes
- Hand Sanitizer
- Lip balm, and Sunscreen

- Ibuprofen Tablets, Benadryl Tablets and Rehydration Packets
- Waterproof Paper and Pencil
- First Aid Reference Book
- Headlamps, with extra batteries (for night or poor lighting conditions)
- Instant Glucose and/or Raw Unprocessed Honey
- Chest Seals, Vented, 2 per pack (entry and exit wound coverage)
- Oral Airways (to keep airway open)
- Nasal airways- NPAs (keeps airways open) and Surgical lube
- Soap and/or Dr. Bronner's Castile liquid soap
- CPR Shields
- Safety Pins (large), Rubber Bands and Paper Clips
- Scalpel and disposable blades (lots)
- Neck Collars, various sizes
- Extra Large Absorbent Pads (ABD or other brand)
- Petrolatum/Xeroform dressings in various sizes
- Burn Dressings and Burn Blankets
- Coban or Self-Adhering Wraps
- Liquid Bandage (Like New Skin)
- Medical Tapes, various types (Elastoplast, Silk, and Paper) and sizes (1 inch, 2 inch etc.)
- Skin Tac Liquid Adhesive Barrier (prepares skin for application of tapes, dressings and protects the skin with a hypo-allergenic sticky film) or equivalent Skin Prep Wipes
- Moleskin or Spenco Second Skin Blister kit
- Styptic Pencils
- Eye Cups, Eye Pads, Patches and Eye wash
- SAM splints and Slings
- Blood Pressure Cuff, various sizes (sphygmomanometer)
- Stethoscopes
- Bio Glo Strips (Fluorescein sodium Rx only)- used to stain the eye

• Cobalt Blue light bulb to shine on the injured eye - visualization of cuts or foreign objects
• Cotton Swabs (Q-tips), Cotton Balls, Cotton-tipped applicators, Cotton Rounds
• Face Masks (surgical and N95)
• Chest Decompression Needles
• Tongue Depressors
• Magnifying Glasses
• Extra Batteries
• Glow Sticks
• Multi Tools
• Safety Pins and Rubber bands
• Paracord 550
• Ring Cutter
• Kelly Clamps, straight and curved in various sizes
• Needle Holders
• Half Circle sewing needles and Silk Thread
• Sutures in many variations, such as:
• Silk, Nylon and Prolene 0, 2-0, 3-0, 4-0(non-absorbable)
• Sharps Disposal Box
• Suture Removal Tray
• Surgical Staplers and Staple Removers
• Iodoform Sterile Packing Gauze
• Micropore Tape
• Styptic Pencil (stops bleeding from superficial cuts)
• Silver Nitrate Sticks and Cautery Pens
• Saline Solution (several liter bottles), or DIY with recipe in this book
• Irrigation Syringes (60-100 ml is good) and Irrigation Cups (like Zerowet)
• Hair Combs and Brushes (hygiene)
• Nail Files, Foot Files and Heel Creams
• Thermometers (rectal and ear)
• Hot Water Bottles and Ice Bags (both reusable)
• Ziploc Bags, Plastic Wrap

- Aluminum Foil (use to sharpen scissors, by cutting the foil several times)
- Cotton Sheets (100% in white)
- Eye Droppers and Bulb Syringes
- Measuring Spoons and Cups
- Antiseptic Solutions in large and medium quantities (Betadine, Hibiclens, etc.)
- Hydrogen Peroxide 3% and 6-7%
- Rubbing Alcohol
- Enema Bags
- Nutritional Supplements (Boost, Ensure)
- Vitamins, multi, and Pregnancy Vitamins
- Sunblock
- Lip Balms
- Insect Repellants
- Bactine or equivalent (for cuts and bug bites)
- Fels-Naptha/Zanfel Soap (poison ivy, oak and sumac)
- Poison Ivy Wipes (like Zanfel)
- Hydrocortisone Cream 1%
- Lidocaine Cream or jelly 2.5% (topical anesthetic)
- Dermoplast Spray and Solarcaine Cool Aloe Burn
- Medi-First Burn Spray (analgesic, antiseptic and liquid bandaid all in one)
- Biofreeze Gel or Cold Freeze Spray for intact skin only
- Acetaminophen/Ibuprofen/Aspirin
- Benadryl (Diphenhydramine)
- Epinephrine (Epi-pen, prescription injection for severe allergic reactions)
- Claritin (Loratadine)
- Anti-Nausea Medication (Meclizine hydrochloride 2.5mg tablets)
- Zofran (Rx for nausea and vomiting)
- Ear and Eye Drops
- Cough Syrup and Lozenges/Drops
- Expectorants (to loosen up thick mucus)

- Decongestants (to move mucus out of the respiratory system)
- Vicks Vapor Rub
- Nebulizer, saline, tubing, mask or mouth piece (plus Rx Albuterol single dose liquid)
- Sleep Aids (like Alteril, Tylenol PM, Melatonin, Chamomile or Valerian Tea etc.)
- Fiber Supplements (Metamucil)
- Stool Softeners and Laxatives
- Suppositories and Finger Cots
- Beano or equivalent (to reduce gas formation with certain foods)
- Anti-Diarrheal, Imodium (Loperamide)
- Pepto-Bismol (Bismuth Subsalicylate)
- Heartburn Medications and natural treatments
- Rid Shampoo/Nix Lotion or Creme Rinse and Nix Electric Lice Comb (for lice)
- Oral Rehydration Packs and Gatorade Packets (or make it from scratch)
- Water Purification Tablets
- Emergency Water Bag
- Water Filters, portable and large family size
- Waterproof Matches, lighters and other methods to start fires
- Gold Bond Foot Powder
- Calamine lotion
- Burn Cream (Rx Silvadene), Burn Gel or burn treatments (sprays) with anesthetic
- Colloidal Silver (for external treatments)
- Anti-fungal Cream (Terconazole)
- Anti-fungal Powder (Tinactin)
- Fluconazole 100 or 150mg tablets (Rx antifungal)
- Urinary Pain Reliever (Uristat or AZO tablets)
- Wart Removal cream/ointment/solution/freeze
- Hemorrhoid Cream or Ointment (Preparation H)

- Zinc Oxide cream or ointment
- A & D ointment
- Vaseline
- Muscle Rub (like Icy Hot, Blue Emu, or Arnica salve)
- Tens Unit or equivalent (Muscle Stimulation pain reliever machine)
- Oral Antibiotics (discussed later)
- Radiation Pills, Thyrosafe or equivalent, one box per person (if your area may be exposed to radiation)
- PMS Medication, like Pamprin (which acts as a mild diuretic also), and natural remedies
- Caffeine Pills
- Natural Equivalents of any the above; see natural medicine chapters
- Birth Control Accessories (condoms, birth control pills, cervical caps, etc.)
- Emergency Obstetric Kit (comes as a pack) and Nitrazine strips (pH strips)
- Midwifery Reference Books
- Fetal Electronic Doppler or Fetoscope
- Maxi Pads and Tampons (female use, and tampons for nose bleeds)
- Measuring Tapes
- Paper, pencils, pens and permanent markers

Dental Kit
- Cotton Pellets and Rolls
- Dental mirror
- Tongue Blades
- Toothpaste and Toothbrushes
- Baking Soda and Peppermint Oil
- Hydrogen Peroxide 3% (oral rinse to treat or prevent gum issues)
- Syringes 12cc Curved tip
- Dental Scraper
- Dental Pick and Toothpicks

- Dental Floss and Dental Wax
- Oral Analgesics
- Canker Sore Tx (like Orajel or Hurricane Gel and Kank-A, and Orabase)
- Clove Bud Oil (anesthetic for toothache)
- Zinc Oxide (make a paste with oil of cloves and you get temporary dental cement), or...
- Commercial dental kits (Den-Temp, Cavit)
- Hank's Solution (used to preserve viability in knocked-out teeth)
- Pill Cups
- Scalpels, disposable
- 4-0 Chromic sutures (absorbable)
- Needle Holder
- Gauze 2 x 2 inches
- Actcel Hemostatic agent (stops dental bleeding, and dissolves naturally)
- Extraction Equipment (several different extractors and elevators)
- Spoon Excavator
- Generic or brand name Ibuprofen
- Gloves, Masks, and Eye protection

Natural Medicine: Supplies and Equipment
- Witch Hazel and Extract
- Bag Balm ointment
- Drawing Salve
- Raw Unprocessed Honey (local is best)
- Cayenne Pepper Powder (see medicinal garden chapter)
- Aloe Vera
- Herbal Teas, Tinctures, Salves, and Essential Oils (see Natural Remedies)
- Neti Pot (use only with sterile solutions) and Diffusers
- Medicinal Herb and Plant seeds (in long-term storage packaging)
- Herbal Medicine Reference Books

- Gardening Reference Books
- Mortar and Pestle
- Graters, Stainless Steel
- Clear and Brown Glass Jars with Lids
- Glass Bottles (various sizes) Green, Brown and Clear with Cork Tops
- Metal Tins, ½ ounce to 4 ounce sizes
- Sealing Wax
- Funnels, Kitchen Mesh Strainers and Cotton Muslin Bags
- Clocks and Kitchen Timers
- Kitchen Scale
- Grain Alcohol and Vodkas (for making tinctures), other spirits as needed
- Copper Distiller (to distill essential oils, etc.)
- Cheesecloth
- Coffee Filters
- Tea Ball Infuser
- Coconut, Olive, Neem, Sesame, Shea Nut, Wheat Germ, Castor, Grapeseed, Soybean Oils
- Vegetable Glycerin, Vitamin E Oil, Steric Acid, Grapefruit Seed Extract, Citric Acid
- White cosmetic clay (Kaolin), makes an excellent poultice base
- Beeswax and pastilles, Cocoa Butter wax and wafers, Shea Butter
- Gelatin or Vegetable Capsules, Capsule Making Machine
- Teapots, Coffee Pots
- Coal Tar Shampoo
- Selenium Shampoo
- Baking Soda and Corn Starch
- Apple Cider Vinegar and White Vinegar
- Epsom Salts
- Sugar, Salt, and Salt Substitutes (part of rehydration formula)

- Cayenne Pepper Powder (for sore throat gargle and to help stop mild-mod bleeding)
- Saline Nasal Spray (or sterile homemade solution)

The Armageddon Field Trauma Center

- Extensive medical library
- Pandemic Protective Gear: Face Shields, Tyvek Coveralls, Hoodies, Aprons, Boots, Gloves
- Goggles, indirect vented
- Treatment Table and Stretches
- Cots or Beds and Chairs
- Bedside Table and Mayo Stands
- Portable Lights and Stands
- Lanterns, Candlesticks and Holders
- Waste Bins and Biohazard bags, trash bags
- Foldable Stretchers
- Heavy Plastic Sheeting, Large Rolls
- Duct Tape, Large Rolls
- Mosquito Netting
- Portable Large Capacity Tent or Shelter
- White 100% Cotton Sheets and Pillow Cases
- Pillows, with waterproof cases
- Blankets, Towels, Patient Gowns
- Basins, Bowls and Washcloths
- Portable Shower or Curtain for privacy and Portable Sinks
- Shampoo and Conditioner
- Hair Clips and Rubber Bands
- Nail Brushes, Emory Boards and Nail Clippers
- Large Capacity Water Filtration Systems
- Water Pitcher and Cups
- Lemon Glycerin Swabs or equivalent
- Disposable Razors
- Waterproof Pads
- Bedpans and Portable Male Urinals
- Laundry Soap, Bleach, buckets, mop handle, dedicated laundry scrub brushes

- Clothesline
- Scrub Suits
- Fire Extinguishers
- Extra Reading Glasses in various strengths
- Charting Materials and Forms
- Clip Boards, Pencils and Pens (don't forget the sharpeners)
- Watch with a Second Hand and Stopwatch
- Scales, newborn and adult sizes
- Resuscitation Facemask with one-way valve
- Resuscitation Bag (Ambu-bag)
- Endotracheal Tube/ Laryngoscope (allows you to breathe for patient)
- Portable Defibrillator/ AED (expensive)
- Pulse Oximeter
- O2 Concentrator, tubing, and face mask or nasal cannulas, with portable power source
- Portable EKG monitor (battery operated is preferred)
- Blood Pressure monitors (battery operated, wrist sizes are handy)
- Otoscope and Ophthalmoscope – (instruments to look into ears and eyes)
- Microscope
- Glucose Monitor
- Urine test strips and Hemacult Test Strips
- Pregnancy test kits
- Sterile Drapes (lots)
- Portable Refrigerator A/C and D/C capacity
- Air Splints (arm/long-leg/short-leg)
- Plaster of Paris Cast Kits (to make casts for fractures) Adult and Pediatric
- Cast Removal Tools
- Crutches, Walking Canes, Wheelchair
- Drain and IV Sponges (dressings with a slit cutout) and Tegaderm film dressing
- IV Equipment, such as:

- Normal Saline (longest shelf life), Ringer's Lactate IV solutions
- IV Tubing sets - maxi-sets + standard sets
- Blood collection bags + filter transfusion sets
- Syringes 2/5/10/20 mL
- Needles 20/22/24 gauge
- IV Start Kits with Tegraderm Dressings
- Angiocath IV Needles: 16/18/20/24 gauge
- Paper Tape (1/2 or 1 inch) for IV lines
- IV Stands (to hang fluid bottles)
- Paracord (various uses)
- Assorted Clamps (curved and straight, small and large)
- Scalpel Handle with Blades (sizes 10, 11, 15) and/or disposable scalpels
- Triage tags (for mass casualty incidents)
- Saline Solution for irrigation (can be made at home as well)
- Foley Catheters, Sterile Lubricant, Foley Insertion Trays and Urine Bags
- Nasogastric Tubes (to pump a stomach)
- Autoclave or Pressure Cooker (to sterilize instruments, etc.)
- Stainless Steel Tongs (to place inside sterilizer and use to pick out sterilized instruments)
- Self Sealing Sterilization Pouches with indicator strips
- Ultraviolet Sterilization Wand or Unit
- Vacuum Bags and Food Saver
- Cidex Solution or equivalent (for cleaning instruments)
- Dedicated Scrub Brushes for Cleaning Instruments only
- Surgical Trays and Bowls, stainless steel only
- Heavy Trash Bags and Biohazard Bags, various sizes
- Human Remains Pouch (HRP) with ID cards or tags
- Shovels and Hatchets
- Bucket, Scrub Brushes and Mop (to clean hospital surfaces and floors)
- Bleach and/or Pool Shock (to DIY bleach)
- Quick Lime Powder (sanitation of human waste)

- Toilet Paper, Tissues and Paper Towels
- Pill Bottles and Labels
- Books, Deck of Cards, Games, Music, Paper, pens, colored pencils/crayons and Activity books
- Poster Board, Permanent Markers and Red Duct Tape, for signage outside the Hospital

COMMON SURGERY TOOLS and EQUIPMENT
- Sterile Towels and Sterile Gloves
- Scrub Brushes in sterile single packages
- Hibiclens Antiseptic Surgical Scrub (to clean skin before invasive procedures)
- Mayo Scissors and Metzenbaum scissors
- Needle Holders, Sterile in various sizes
- Surgical Marking Pens
- Suction Pump with Internal 12V Rechargeable Battery
- Bulb and Large Syringes, Sterile (for irrigating wounds during procedures)
- Lap Sponges and large quantity of dressings and gauze
- Obstetric forceps (for difficult deliveries)
- Speculums, small to ex-large sizes
- Uterine Curettes (for miscarriages, various sizes)
- Uterine "Sound" (checks depth of uterine canal)
- Uterine Dilators (to open cervix; allows removal of dead tissue)
- Bone Saw Kit (for amputations)
- 1% or 2% Lidocaine (local anesthetic in injectable form- prescription medication)
- Chest Tube Set-up (connected to bedside suction)
- Penrose and Jackson Pratt Drains (to allow blood and pus to drain from wounds)

Prescription Medications to Stockpile
- Medrol Dose packs, oral steroids
- Epi Pens and Inhalers (Ventolin)
- Metformin 500mg, 1000mg or 750mg ER tablets
- Salbutamol Inhalers (for asthma/severe allergic reactions)

- Antibiotic and Anesthetic, Eye ointment/drops and Ear drops
- Oral Contraceptive Pills
- Metronidazole, oral antibiotic and anti-protozoal
- Amoxicillin, oral antibiotic
- Cephalexin, oral antibiotic
- Ciprofloxacin, oral antibiotic
- Doxycycline, oral antibiotic
- Clindamycin, oral antibiotic
- Trimethoprin/Sulfamethoxazole, oral antibiotic
- Ceftriaxone, IV antibiotic
- Diazepam IV sedative to treat seizures
- Diazepam in oral form, sedative
- Alprazolam, oral anti-anxiety agent
- Tramadol (pain medicine which is also available from a veterinarian)

Made in the USA
Lexington, KY
02 June 2017